HEART
QUEST™

HeartQuest brings you romantic fiction
with a foundation of biblical truth.
Adventure, mystery, intrigue, and suspense
mingle in these heartwarming stories of
men and women of faith striving to build
a love that will last a lifetime.

May HeartQuest books sweep you
into the arms of God, who longs for you
and pursues you always.

Finders Keepers

CATHERINE PALMER

HEART
QUESTᴛᴍ
Romance fiction from
Tyndale House Publishers, Inc.
WHEATON, ILLINOIS

Visit Tyndale's exciting Web site at www.tyndale.com

Check out the latest about HeartQuest Books at www.heartquest-romances.com

HeartQuest is a trademark of Tyndale House Publishers, Inc.

Edited by Kathryn S. Olson
Designed by Melinda Schumacher

Scripture quotations are taken from the *Holy Bible,* New Living Translation, copyright © 1996. Used by permission of Tyndale House Publishers, Inc., Wheaton, Illinois 60189. All rights reserved.

Library of Congress Cataloging-in-Publication Data

Palmer, Catherine, date
  Finders keepers / Catherine Palmer.
    p. cm. — (HeartQuest)
  ISBN 0-8423-1164-5
  I. Title. II. Series.
PS3566.A495F56 1999
813′.54—dc21   99-29831

Printed in the United States of America

05   04   03   02   01   00   99
 9   8   7   6   5   4   3   2

This book is for Andrei Joseph Palmer.
Your joy, determination, and devotion to Jesus Christ
are my constant inspiration.

I love you, my precious son.

The Chalmers House

Dandy Donuts & Bake Shop

the Public Library

Amb

Walnut Street

PARK

Mansion Street

DAILY HERALD

TASTE HUT

Everyone who seeks, finds.
MATTHEW 7:8

ACKNOWLEDGMENTS

Without the devoted help of so many people, this book would not exist. I want to thank my beloved husband, Tim, for your faithfulness in reading and editing each of my manuscripts before it goes out. Thanks to Geoffrey for your enthusiasm over your mom's writing. Kathy Olson's professional, loving, and judicious in-house editing is invaluable. I praise God for allowing me to work with this wonderful woman. My deepest appreciation also goes to the HeartQuest team, whose dedication to our mission can be seen in every novel. Becky Nesbitt, Kathy Olson, Anne Goldsmith, Diane Eble, Danielle Crilly, and Jan Pigott—I love you, fellow gardeners! The vision and encouragement of Ron Beers and Ken Petersen have paved the path for everything I do. May God bless you both. I thank Dr. Kenneth Taylor and Mark Taylor for supporting my ministry and for being such beacons in the world of Christian publishing. And Travis Thrasher, of course, you are my rock. Thanks for making Tyndale so much fun to write for!

I also want to express my deepest appreciation to those who have had such profound, life-changing effects on Andrei: Sue Hogue, Marcia Heberle, and Glenda Briggs. The classroom teachers who have brought the light of learning into Andrei's life are Mrs. Tyson, Mrs. Cox, Mrs. Chapman, Mrs. Eisinger, and Mrs. Williamson. Others who have shaped and molded our little fellow are Mrs. Stegman, Mr. Nolke, Mrs. Hanson, Mrs. Wolf, Mrs. Winkler, Mrs. D., Mrs. Steenbergen, all the cafeteria workers, and Mr. Love. Thanks to Marsha for teaching Andrei how to make pottery. May God richly bless each and every one of you.

ONE

"I am like the rose that came out of the gravy," Nikolai Hayes announced as he walked down the steps of Ambleside Chapel following the Easter morning service. "You know, Mommy? That rose?"

"A rose came out of gravy?" Elizabeth Hayes took her son's hand to cross the street. "I'm not sure I understand, sweetheart."

"Like in the song at church," Nick said. "Up from the gravy, a rose."

Elizabeth pursed her lips to stifle a laugh. "Up from the grave he arose," she corrected.

"That's what I said. When you got me from the orphanage in Romania, it was like I came out of the gravy." He spread his arms and launched himself into a spin across the sidewalk. "And now I am a rose!"

With a gasp, she caught his thin arms just in time to prevent him from twirling out into the street. Not that the eight-year-old would have been in much danger. Traffic crawled through Ambleside, Missouri, even on this Easter Sunday morning. Most folks had chosen to walk to church beneath the pink haze of redbud trees that lined the town square. A gust of fresh air from the direction of the nearby Missouri River scattered white dogwood blossoms across the pale green grass as families strolled home for dinner.

"Good morning, Miss Hayes!" A stooped gentleman lifted his hat, his face a wreath of soft wrinkles. "And young Master Nikolai. Good morning to you, too."

"It's Boompah!" Nick cried, pulling away from his mother and racing across the grass. "Didn't you go to church, Boompah? Today's Easter! Jesus died and came alive again, did you hear?"

Jacob Jungemeyer chuckled as the child danced around him. Nick had always called the old man Boompah, though no one knew why. Now everyone close to him used the nickname. "I heard that good news, Nick," Boompah said. "And I went to church this morning, just like you. But my church is that way—down Main Street past Zimmerman's Sundries."

"Guess what, Boompah—I'm like the rose that came out of the gravy," Nick declared.

"Oh? And how is that?"

"Hey look, Nick, there's Montgomery," Elizabeth cut in, hoping to avert a detailed explanation. Mr. Jungemeyer had come to America during the Second World War, and his own English could be a little garbled at times. She felt sure their similar backgrounds played a part in the bond of friendship between the old man and the child she had adopted three years before.

"How are you feeling today, Boompah?" she asked as Nick raced off to greet his best friend. No doubt Montgomery would understand perfectly about the rose and the gravy.

"Ach, I am down in the back, as they say it." Boompah rubbed his spine. "Maybe Cleo Mueller will be able to find a pill for me at his drugstore on Monday. I call him."

"Good idea." She slipped her arm through his and allowed him to lean against her as they walked across the square past a bronze statue of Harry Truman. "Would you like to have dinner with Nick and me today, Boompah? I've got a ham in the oven, and I whipped up a batch of fresh yeast rolls this morning."

"Thank you, but I go to Al Huff's house this Sunday, like

always. They expect me, you know. Oh, Elizabeth, I am sure you will miss eating the Easter dinner with Grace. I think your church must seem very empty without her this morning."

Elizabeth nodded, recalling the jaunty rose-strewn hat she had always spotted three pews ahead of her. Grace Chalmers had never missed a Sunday service in her life. She was deeply missed by everyone in Ambleside, but Elizabeth was sure she felt the old woman's absence more than most. The huge brick Chalmers House with its arched windows and lacy gingerbread porch sat right next to the antiques shop she owned.

The day Elizabeth had hung the sign for Finders Keepers, Grace had dropped by the shop bearing a gift of twenty-five embroidered handkerchiefs to add to the inventory. In addition, she had purchased a small china tea set, delighted because she had owned one just like it as a child. Grace and Elizabeth had become fast friends, and the old woman's death the month before had been an unexpected blow.

"The auction is tomorrow," Elizabeth said as she and Boompah reached the corner of the square on which a replica of the Liberty Bell sat on display. "I can't believe everything's going to be sold. It seems a shame. The china her mother hand painted. The pillows Grace embroidered. Her books."

"The books. Ach, it will be impossible to think of Chalmers House without the books. And what is to become of the mansion itself?"

"Pearlene told me Grace willed the place to her nephew—lock, stock, and barrel. He's the one who scheduled the auction."

Elizabeth stopped and gazed across the street at the ivy-draped house. To the best of her knowledge, this so-called nephew had never visited his aunt a single time during her long life. He would have no idea that Grace had planted the lilac bushes that were in full bloom near the long front porch. He'd never seen his elderly relative on her knees weeding the dianthus that filled the central circle in the walkway leading to the ornate double doors. Grace had been so pleased that the steady breeze off the river wafted the sweet scent of her flowers across the whole town.

"You know, if Grace were alive," Elizabeth mused, "that vase in her foyer would be filled with lilacs and forsythia branches."

"The blue Chinese vase? Yes, I see it so many times when I go to deliver her groceries." Boompah nodded. "In the summer she puts in lavender and purple coneflowers. In the autumn, it is maple and pyracantha branches. In winter, cedar and . . ." He paused and peered at the house. "Who is inside there, Elizabeth?"

"In the mansion? Nobody. It's been empty for a month."

"Ja, but somebody is walking up the stairs. I see it just now, one minute ago."

Elizabeth frowned. "Boompah, the place is locked up tight. Maybe you saw a shadow from the maple tree."

"Mom, Mom!" Nick ran up and grabbed her hand. "Can Magunnery come to our house to play after lunch? Please, Mom? It's OK with her parents if it's OK with you. We want to swing."

"That's fine, Nick, but . . ."

"Yesss!" He pumped a fist in the air and raced away. "You can come, Magunnery!"

Montgomery, her bright red hair caught up in a pink bow, jumped up and down with joy. Normally clad in a pair of jeans, a T-shirt, and some well-worn sneakers, on this day the little girl was a pink confection of lacy petticoats and organdy skirts. Elizabeth waved at Montgomery's parents, confirming the coming visit. It was hardly news. Their child practically lived at the little apartment behind Finders Keepers.

"Look, I see it again," Boompah said, squeezing Elizabeth's hand. "There on the second floor. It is a person, maybe two."

Elizabeth let out a breath. "I hope it's not the kids."

The Ambleside High School students known as "the kids" had lately taken to piercing their ears, noses, and eyebrows, sporting fake tattoos, and looking for hideaways where they could smoke cigarettes and drink beer. Mick and Ben, Ambleside's dauntless police force, had been compelled to clear out Chalmers Park more than once. Twice they had locked the gates at 8 P.M. just to keep the kids dispersed.

"I try to hire them to work at the market," Boompah said, "but they steal the beef jerky and empty all pennies from the gumball machine. If those kids get into Grace's house, they will break something, of that I am sure. We better take a look right now."

He started across the street, giving Elizabeth barely enough time to grab Nick's hand. "Boompah, why don't you stay outside with Nick? I'll go check the mansion."

"You?" His sparse white eyebrows lifted. "Look at you, Elizabeth, very skinny and wearing those high-heel shoes."

"And you're down in the back. Besides, we don't know who—"

"Ach, who is nothing to me," he scoffed. "Did I not escape from Adolph Hitler himself? He tries to kill my family because we are of the Roma—the Gypsies. He tries to capture us and put us into his camps. But I escape!"

"Who's trying to kill you, Boompah?" Nick demanded, his green eyes flashing. "Where is he?"

"Adolph Hitler!" Boompah spat. "He is putting everybody into cars on the railroad. Like we are cattle."

Elizabeth left the old man wandering down the paths of memory, a curious little boy tagging along. Germany was a bit like Romania, she would tell her son later. Two evil rulers who cared nothing for tradition, faith, or humanity had tried to tear down the old and build new worlds of their own imaginings, destroying millions of lives in the process.

Elizabeth unlatched the iron gate and followed the brick path to the porch of Chalmers House. She knew her son could not fully comprehend the situation that had led him into an orphanage. But she would assure Nick, as she had so many times before, that God had a wonderful plan for his life. Hadn't Jesus brought them together—a lonely woman and an abandoned child? And wouldn't he continue the joy in their lives?

She slid a loose brick from the wall and drew out the key Grace had always kept hidden there. Doors were rarely locked in Ambleside, "but you never know," Grace had said.

No, you couldn't always know, Elizabeth thought as she turned the key in the door. It didn't pay to be careless.

"Hey, up there!" she called at the foot of the dusty staircase. "This house belongs to the Chalmers family. It's not open to the public."

She heard footsteps creak across the oak floorboards. "I mean it," she said, stepping onto the first stair. "You don't have permission to be up there. Now, get your backside out of here this minute, or I'll call Mick and Ben."

"Mick and Ben?" A pair of well-shined cordovan loafers began to descend; next came crisply pressed khaki slacks, a brown leather belt, a starched white oxford shirt, and a striped silk tie. "Are they in charge of backside removal?"

Elizabeth reached for the banister as a pair of deep-set gray-green eyes focused on her. "Uh . . . I thought . . . I thought you were one of the kids."

The corner of the man's mouth turned up. "No," he said. The hazel eyes surveyed her up and down for a moment. "And neither are you."

Elizabeth could feel herself flushing as he advanced. The man was good looking with his dark hair and deeply tanned skin, and she breathed a prayer of thanks that she wasn't wearing her usual Sunday-afternoon shorts and T-shirt. A quick inventory of her appearance assured her that she wore an ivory sheath that was the essence of elegance, a pair of matching heels, and her grandmother's pearls. And she'd painted her nails.

She touched the pearls at her neck with one hand as she extended the other. "I'm Elizabeth Hayes. I own the shop next door."

"Aha," he said, taking her hand in a firm grip. "Zachary Chalmers. Pleased to meet you."

"Oh, you're the nephew." Elizabeth let out a breath. "I should have guessed. You're here to look over Grace's things before the auction tomorrow."

"Does everyone in Ambleside know the details of my personal business, Miss Hayes?"

"Grace and I were close friends. And, yes, everyone knows everyone's business in Ambleside." She stepped back onto the marble floor. Now that she knew who she was dealing with, she could tackle her concerns head-on. "Listen, Mr. Chalmers, I realize you had little or no contact with your aunt during her lifetime. But I think you should be aware that the furnishings in this house were precious to Grace. Many of them are quite valuable. I hope you don't intend to just get rid of all these items without finding out exactly what your aunt had here. That vase, for example, is museum quality. You ought to ascertain its worth so it isn't just sold off like some knickknack from a curio store."

Without waiting for his response, she walked across the hall and lifted the vase in which Grace had always kept the season's bounty. "These things not only have monetary value," she said, "but they have great sentimental value. Grace was a wonderful woman. She was gentle and kind, and the furnishings in her home reflect that. This is her legacy."

Zachary Chalmers had remained at the foot of the staircase, but his eyes were locked on her. "As you mentioned,
I wasn't close to my aunt. I appreciate that you were her
friend, but her legacy has no sentimental value to me."

"It's more than just my feelings, Mr. Chalmers. Grace's
legacy means a lot to this whole town. Everyone in
Ambleside loved her. Her house was in the Chalmers family
for generations—"

"Not *my* side of the Chalmers family, ma'am." He hooked
his hands in his pockets and took a step toward her. "I
grew up in a trailer park at the edge of Jefferson City, and
my folks never even told me I had an Aunt Grace. She
never invited us here for a visit. Her name was never mentioned. So, while I appreciate your fondness for the woman,
I can tell you that I have no intention—"

"Boompah nearly got killed by the nachos!" Nick burst
into the house and ran to his mother. "They tried to catch
him and put him into a train. They were bad, evil nachos!"

"Nazis," Elizabeth clarified. She knelt on one knee and
took her son's shoulders. Clearly Boompah's story had
upset the child, and she knew it would be hours before she
could help Nick sort through the confusing information.
"Sweetheart, the trouble between Boompah and the Nazis
happened a long time ago. Boompah is fine."

"Yes, I am fine now," the old man announced as he
entered the room, "but where are the kids who have come
to steal from Chalmers House? I will speak to them. I am
not afraid!"

Elizabeth held out her hand to calm the old man.
"Boompah, there were no kids. You saw Grace's nephew
through the window. Mr. Chalmers is here to look things
over before the auction."

Like a trio of territorial cardinals, the three males inside
the mansion assessed one another. Clearly, each felt that he
was being intruded upon. Boompah sniffed as he observed

Zachary Chalmers's tailored appearance. Chalmers lifted one brow at the sight of Boompah's rumpled brown cardigan and sweat-stained hat. Nick frowned up at the newcomer, his own tie spotted with water from the drinking fountain at church.

"Are you a nacho?" he asked Zachary Chalmers, his green eyes wary.

"No, but I was a Tootsie Roll one Halloween." The man smiled. "What's your name, young man?"

"Nikolai Hayes. I was born in Romania, but my mommy came and adopted me three years ago. I'm eight years old. It's Easter today because Jesus died and came to life again. Did you know that?"

"I did."

"I have a swing in my backyard that Magunnery plays on with me. Do you want to see it? You could come to our house for lunch. We have extra, because Mommy invited Boompah, but he can't come."

"Nick!" Elizabeth grabbed her son's hand.

"We're having ham," Nick added. "And fresh rolls."

"Ham, huh?" Zachary Chalmers pondered a moment. "Well, I guess I could make room in my schedule—"

"Just a minute now," Elizabeth cut in. "Nick, please take Boompah outside and make sure he gets down the stairs all right. His back is sore."

"Boompah's going to Al Huff's house for lunch," Nick informed Zachary Chalmers. "Al owns the gas station, and he sells barbecue ribs and beans and cold slaw, too. He has a sign that says Eat, Get Gas and everybody laughs, but Al won't change it. Al and Thelma always have Boompah over for Sunday lunch. That's how they do it. It's called a tradition."

"Aha." Chalmers watched the little boy lead the old man out onto the front porch. "Bye, Nick. Bye, Boompah."

"My mom is the best cooker in the whole world," Nick

called over his shoulder. "You better come try her ham. You'll like it."

"My son is . . . enthusiastic," Elizabeth explained.

"I liked his comment about the nachos."

She smiled. "Nick still trips over words sometimes. You have to listen carefully to understand what he's trying to tell you."

"I'll do that." He took a step toward her. "So, is the lunch invitation good? I haven't eaten."

Elizabeth glanced out the door as Nick assisted Boompah down the stairs. "Look, Mr. Chalmers, we've just met, and I'm afraid I'm . . ." She tried to think of a good reason not to let him come. She wasn't too busy. She had no plans for the afternoon. There was plenty of food. But the man was a total stranger—and not a particularly pleasant one, at that.

"I'm sorry, but I'm not comfortable having you in my home." She shifted from one foot to the other. "I, uh, I hardly know you."

"Zachary Chalmers. Grew up in Jeff City. Trailer park. Aunt Grace's nephew. You already know me better than most people do."

And I don't like you, she wanted to add. The man was far too self-assured to be appealing, and his attitude toward Grace was cavalier. Clearly, he intended to sell off every stick of furniture in the mansion without the least compunction. He'd make his money and then drive away, leaving the old house stripped bare.

"Mr. Chalmers," she said, "I'm not in the habit of inviting men to my house for any reason. So if you'll excuse me, I need to get that ham out of the oven."

"I take it you're not married," he called as she headed for the door. "Neither am I."

"Good-bye, Mr. Chalmers."

"Zachary."

"Just don't forget what I told you about Grace's things," she said, turning in the open doorway. "You shouldn't let go of the past. This house is filled with traditions, memories, and heirlooms. Don't sell off your heritage, Mr. Chalmers."

"Out with the old, in with the new," he said. "I'm an architect, Miss Hayes, not a museum curator."

Elizabeth had to force herself to keep from slamming the door behind her. Of all the gall. *Out with the old, in with the new*. The man was clearly a nacho!

❦

"You'd better not go to that auction this morning, Liz," Pearlene Fox said as she swept the sidewalk in front of Très Chic, the ladies' apparel shop she owned. "You know good and well that man is going to sell every last thing right out of there. Phil said he wouldn't be a bit surprised if Zachary Chalmers tore down the whole mansion."

Elizabeth paused and leaned on her own broom. "Tore it down?"

"That's what Phil said. We were eating leftover ham sandwiches last night, you know how you do after a big meal, and I said to him, 'Do you reckon that nephew of Grace's is going to strip that mansion bare at the auction tomorrow?' And Phil said, 'Strip it bare and tear it down.' That's what he said, and you know Phil is always good for the latest news, him being on the city council and all. He said there was likely to be a wrecking ball over there by the middle of the week."

"Zachary Chalmers can't tear down the mansion!"

"I guess he can, too. It's his, you know."

"It belongs to Ambleside as much as to anybody."

"Make a good parking lot, Phil says. I've got to tell you, I agree with him, Liz. Our business would just about double if we had better parking around the square. As it is, folks are liable to get themselves killed trying to cross the street over there by the pavilion."

"I don't want a parking lot beside Finders Keepers. I want Chalmers House." Elizabeth could hardly believe what she was hearing. "Pearlene, what would Ambleside be without the mansion? It'd be like a smile with a front tooth missing."

"You're just attached to that old house because you loved Grace so much." Pearlene swept a pile of leaves off the curb. "Most folks think the mansion is an eyesore. Why, it's like something out of the Addams family. Besides, who'd ever want to buy it? There's no central air, the heating system must go back a hundred years, the plumbing's from the Dark Ages. And take a look at that ivy, would you? You can tell it's eaten clean through the mortar. I bet if you gave those vines a jerk, the whole house would fall right down."

Elizabeth propped her broom against the wall of her antiques shop and studied the old mansion next door. Movers had been carrying Grace's furniture onto the expansive lawn since just after dawn. Already the crowd that had gathered for the auction threatened to overflow onto the street.

"Are you going over?" Pearlene asked. "There's probably some good antiques you could snap up for resale in your shop. Phil was in the mansion a time or two, and he told me the place was loaded. Last night he said, 'Who'd want that old junk, anyhow?' and I said, 'Liz Hayes would, that's who.' And he said, 'That furniture's probably full of termites. They ought to put the whole mess in a bonfire and be done with it.' But that's Phil, you know. He doesn't understand antiques."

Out with the old, in with the new, Elizabeth thought, recalling her conversation with Zachary Chalmers. She'd never had much in common with Pearlene's husband, and she had a feeling he and Grace's nephew were two of a kind.

"Look at old Jacob Jungemeyer over there," Pearlene exclaimed. "He just up and leaves the market anytime he feels like it. And then he blames the kids when his gumball money turns up missing. I'll swan."

"I'm going to take a look," Elizabeth blurted out. She opened her front door and flipped the sign from Open to Closed. As she turned the key in the lock, she could hear Pearlene grumbling. Bad enough the Corner Market stood abandoned at nine in the morning, she was probably saying. Now Finders Keepers was shut down, and who knew which other store owners would lock their doors just to take a gander at the auction?

"Might as well shut down the whole town," she muttered as Elizabeth crossed the crowded lawn.

"Morning, Boompah," Elizabeth greeted the old man. He took off his hat and gave her a little bow. "Are you here to buy some of Grace's books?"

"Where can I put more books in my little house, Elizabeth? No, I am here to say good-bye to Grace. Ach, it is a sad day for Ambleside."

"There's her blue vase."

"Her hats thrown into a basket like so much dirty laundry."

"Her crystal."

"The painting of the horses."

"Her favorite chair. Oh, Boompah, I think Pearlene was right. I shouldn't have come."

The old man took her hand and patted it. "You want to come with me to Dandy Donuts? We have a cup of hot tea together, Elizabeth. Maybe we feel better."

"Good idea." They started across the grass, but as they passed the books, Elizabeth couldn't resist running her fingers over their familiar leather spines. Gilt-edged pages ruffled in the breeze. Classics that Grace had loved to read in the evenings lay scattered across card tables. *Moby Dick. Jane Eyre. Pride and Prejudice.*

"Her Bible!" Elizabeth picked up the old black leather

book and hugged it close. "How can Zachary Chalmers sell Grace's Bible? Where is he? I'm going to give that man a piece of my mind."

She scanned the crowd. Oblivious to the intricate wooden fretwork overhead, Zachary Chalmers stood on the porch and conferred with the auctioneers. His shirtsleeves were rolled to his elbows, and his dark hair ruffled in the river breeze. A pair of sunglasses concealed his eyes. Grateful she wouldn't have to actually look at him, Elizabeth tucked the Bible under her arm, left Boompah's side, and started for the house.

"Ma'am," a man called, catching up to her. "You can't separate the merchandise. I'm sorry, but that Bible belongs with the other books on the table. It's Lot 39. You can bid on the whole batch when the number comes up, but we can't let you carry off one book."

She glared at the man. "I'll have you know this is Grace Chalmers's Bible."

"I don't care if it's the Declaration of Independence. You can't cart it off. It belongs to Lot 39."

"You don't seem to understand." She flipped open the book, its pages underlined in inks of blue, black, red, and green. Notes in Grace's trembling hand filled the margins. "This Bible is a record of a woman's faith journey. It was a part of her daily life for years and years. She treasured every word."

"Maybe so, but you still can't take it from the table."

"But this Bible is not like the other books. This was personal."

"That's the nature of an auction, ma'am. Its purpose is to sell off personal goods. And we sell things in lots."

"Fine." She set the Bible back on the table. "Come on, Boompah, let's go get some tea."

"You're not staying for the auction, Miss Hayes?" Zachary Chalmers inserted himself between her and the old man.

"I'm not too crazy about hanging around here myself. Mind if I join you two for a cup of coffee?"

Elizabeth looked at her reflection in the man's sunglasses. "I'm afraid Mr. Jungemeyer and I would bore you," she said, unable to keep the flint from her voice. "We're part of the old guard, you know. We value the heritage a person leaves. We consider old tables, old vases, and old books worth preserving. We would never tear down an old house and put in a parking lot, Mr. Chalmers. So you'll just have to excuse us."

She took Boompah's arm and stepped off the curb. If the new was so eager to send out the old, he could find someone else to have a cup of coffee with. Maybe Phil Fox would join him.

"A parking lot?" Zachary Chalmers said behind her. "Where'd you get that idea?"

Elizabeth swung around, her heart suddenly lifting. "You're not planning to tear down the mansion and put in a parking lot?"

"No," he said, "I'm going to tear it down and build a new office complex."

Two

What was *her* problem?

Zachary studied Elizabeth Hayes as she walked away from him. Her blue eyes had flashed fire a moment before, and the way she tossed that thick mane of chestnut hair spoke volumes. She clearly thought he was some kind of brute.

Nacho.

He chuckled. Funny little kid she had adopted. Cute, too, with his big green eyes and mop of black hair. Zachary wondered what would possess an attractive, young, single woman to take on the responsibility of mothering an orphaned child. He had grown up with a raft of little brothers and sisters, and though he occasionally pondered the idea of marriage and family, he was in no hurry. He hadn't climbed the ladder of success this far to weigh himself down with such responsibilities.

Picking up the Bible that had provoked such emotion in the pretty Miss Hayes, he studied the worn black leather. Stamped in an intricate gold design of grapes and braided vines, the cover bore the words: *I am the vine, ye are the branches: He that abideth in me, and I in him, the same bringeth forth much fruit.*

Much fruit. Zachary doubted he'd brought forth much of anything that God would consider worthy fruit. Unless you could count the church he'd designed in Jefferson City. Maybe he'd get a star in his crown for that one.

Reflecting on his childhood salvation experience, Zachary

recalled the evangelical Christian church where he had been taught the tenets of his faith. His commitment to Christ had been real enough, but somewhere along the way he had gotten too busy for the rigmarole of church attendance. He hadn't picked up a Bible in years. Wasn't even sure he could find one at his apartment in Jefferson City.

"Your aunt was a real churchgoer," someone said at his elbow. Zachary looked up into a round, doughy face framed with a thatch of salt-and-pepper hair and a beard that was trying hard to conceal a second chin. "Name's Phil Fox, Mr. Chalmers. I own the barbershop catty-corner to the mansion. I run the bus stop, too. As a member of the Ambleside City Council, I'm happy to welcome you to our little town."

"You're a busy man." Zachary shook his hand. "Looks like quite a crowd here today."

"You ought to earn yourself some nice pocket change off this old stuff."

"Miss Hayes seems to think I'm making a mistake to sell."

"Liz owns the antiques store next door. She thinks everything ten or more years old ought to be worth a fortune." Fox laughed and shook his head. "I went into her place the other day, and I'm telling you, I never saw so much ratty-looking junk. She showed me this old white kitchen cabinet with peeling paint and dinged-up shelves. It looked like it came straight out of somebody's barn. Still had some hay stuck to the back and cobwebs all over the thing. When she told me the price, I like to had a heart attack. I'd have given maybe a buck to chop it up for firewood!"

Zachary smiled. "You never can tell what someone will find valuable."

"Now, that's the truth." He pointed a beefy finger. "You, sir, are an intelligent man."

Unsure of a response to this comment, Zachary set the Bible back on the table, excused himself, and started toward the porch where the auctioneer had begun the bidding. He'd never been to an auction, and he thought he'd like to watch the process for a few minutes before driving back to his office in the city.

"I guess a man like you wouldn't have much use for this old house," the town barber said, matching him stride for stride. "You probably noticed the condition it's in. You planning to sell?"

So that's what he was after. "I have plans for the property, but I'm not going to sell it."

"You're not going to try to live in it, are you? I mean, the heating system could blow any day now."

"I won't be living here." He stopped and faced the man. "I've rented an office above John Sawyer's law practice, and I've rented an apartment near the river."

"So you're moving to Ambleside?"

"Looks that way." He nodded and made to leave again. Was this whole town full of busybodies snooping into each other's business? He had no desire to share his plans with this man or anyone else.

"They say you're an architect," Fox said. "I don't know what you're going to find to design around here. These old buildings have been here more than a hundred years, and nobody's got any plans to tear them down. Unless you're planning to get rid of the mansion and put in a new building. We've got a new subdivision going up—lot of new houses. Or maybe you've heard that talk about a mall going in on the edge of town. I think that'd be a real dandy deal."

"Most of my clients are in Jefferson City. I'll be commuting."

"That's not a bad drive. You know, you could do a lot to help this town, Mr. Chalmers. Mind if I call you Zachary? Ambleside's in sad shape, I'm telling you. If I had my druthers, we'd bulldoze the whole square and start over with brand-new offices and stores, good air-conditioning, new sewer lines, sidewalks that nobody'd trip over. This could be a real nice place. Real nice."

Zachary thought Ambleside was real nice already, which was why he had decided to move here. He was tired of the city, tired of the competition, tired of the traffic, tired of the bureaucracy and politics. A person couldn't find a prettier, more congenial town than Missouri's capital, but Zachary had worn himself out in his struggle to rise to the top of his field. He was ready for a rest.

Detaching himself from the barber once again, he wandered over to one of his aunt's gold brocade settees. When he sat down, the metal springs prodded him through the seat cushion. A mouse must have nibbled a hole in one corner, he noted, because the matted horsehair was showing through. Why anyone would want such a piece of furniture when they could have a solid wood, foam-upholstered recliner was more than he could understand.

Here came Elizabeth Hayes now, escorting her elderly friend back across the street after their trip to the donut shop. They stopped again by the table of books and sorted through the pile, intent in discussion. The auctioneer's rapid-fire calls drifted over the heads of the milling crowd, and Zachary wondered how anyone could keep track of the price.

Though he knew Elizabeth considered his decision to sell the mansion's furnishings despicable, he realized he found the woman more than a little attractive. It wasn't just her glossy brown hair and bright blue eyes that drew him. Zachary realized he hadn't met anyone with such fire in a very long time. She'd been downright passionate about protecting the mansion from vandals the day before. And she certainly would have run Zachary through with a sword if she'd had one handy. *Treachery,* her eyes seemed to flash as she glared at him. *Villainy! Treason!*

He stood and ambled through the crowd toward the

table. If she spotted him, he'd get another tongue-lashing. Oddly, he looked forward to a lively interchange.

"She would have wanted you to have this," the old man was saying in his thick European accent. "I am sure this Bible Grace would give to you, Elizabeth. You were her friend. You loved her."

"I'd like to have it, Boompah, but I really ought to open my shop. Some of this crowd is bound to wander over to Finders Keepers, and if I'm closed, I could miss sales."

"Listen, the auctioneer is almost ready to call the lot. You make a bid, Elizabeth. You keep Grace's Bible safe."

She squared her shoulders and faced the porch. "All right, I will."

In a moment, an auctioneer's assistant gathered the contents of the lot and carried it to the front of the crowd. Curious, Zachary took a spot slightly behind Elizabeth. What would she pay for an old, marked-up Bible? What had been so special about his aunt? And if Grace Chalmers had been such a terrific lady, how come Zachary's father never once spoke the name of his eldest sister?

"We've got fifteen books here, folks," the auctioneer announced. "Maybe a first edition or two, you never know. Looks like _Moby Dick_. An old family Bible. _Withering Heights._"

As the bidding began, Zachary stifled a chuckle at the auctioneer's butchering of the classic title. Elizabeth offered ten dollars. The price quickly rose to twelve, fifteen, twenty.

"Twenty-five," Zachary said loudly when the auctioneer was ready to call a sale.

"All right, I've got twenty-five. Do I hear thirty?"

Elizabeth lifted her hand. Zachary raised the price to thirty-five. She turned and scanned the crowd for her rival as she bid forty dollars on the lot of old books.

"Fifty," Zachary called.

At the sight of him, her cheeks flushed in fury. Eyes fairly spitting blue fire, she raised it to fifty-five. Enjoying the battle, he upped it to sixty. Sixty-five. Seventy. Nostrils flaring, she set her hands on her hips and called out seventy-five.

Zachary acknowledged her victory with a slight nod. Fuming, she stalked over to the cashier and paid for her purchase as the old man began gathering up the books.

"Let me help you with that," Zachary said. "I understand you've got a bad back."

Boompah's sparse eyebrows lifted. "Ach, you better not to tangle with Elizabeth. She is a fighter, that one. You will lose the battle."

"Will I, now?" He picked up a stack of books that included the old Bible. "I'm a pretty tough competitor myself."

"But you are not yet fighting Elizabeth."

"I believe I am." He faced his opponent as she pushed between two bystanders. "Good morning again, Miss Hayes. I thought I'd help you get your purchases home."

"I don't need your help," she said through clenched teeth.

"It's no problem." He started toward the two-story brick shop. "I'm not busy anyway. Might as well do what I can."

"You've done enough. If you wanted the books, why didn't you just take them yesterday when you had the whole house to yourself?"

Her breathing sounded labored as she crossed the grass behind him. "This was more fun," he replied. "I've never bid on anything except design jobs. Perhaps if you had let me join you for coffee—"

"We had tea."

Balancing the stack of books against her hip, she fumbled her keys from the pocket of her skirt and opened the shop door. A sweet musty scent, mingled with the fragrance of wax candles, filled the large front room. As Zachary's eyes adjusted to the dim light, he made out the shapes of cupboards, tables, and rocking chairs. He set her books on a glass-topped counter and studied the room while Elizabeth worked her way around, switching on old lamps with fringed shades or painted glass globes. His first impression echoed Phil Fox's sentiment. Ratty-looking junk. Who would pay good money for this?

"Excuse me, but I'm going to put on some tea," she said, clearly dismissing him. "Thanks for your help."

"I go now too, Elizabeth," Boompah called after her. "Better open the market before Mrs. McCann comes to do her shopping."

"See you later, Boompah!" Her voice held a light, friendly note.

"Mrs. McCann is the librarian," the older man confided to Zachary as he settled his hat on his head. "With Mrs. McCann, you don't want to be late for nothing. If you think an overdue book makes her mad, you ought to see her when she can't buy her groceries!"

The door closed with the ring of little brass bells, and Zachary leaned against the counter, his arms crossed. So this was the town where he'd cast his lot. A musty antiques shop. A corner market. A library. Not bad. Maybe he'd even feel like part of the neighborhood one day. The idea appealed to him.

Now that he could see a little better in the dim light, he realized Elizabeth had arranged the shop into casual groupings of related items. One corner held a huge wooden cabinet filled with matched sets of old china. A table nearby had been laid out as if for dinner, with a creamy white cloth, heavy silverware, and dishes printed in a deep red pattern. Another area resembled a kitchen, with colorful tin cans stacked on white cabinets, fruit-printed dish towels hung up for display, and collections of green-handled implements. A bedroom area featured a large carved headboard, more linens, stacks of lamp shades, baskets filled with sachets, and piles of pillows.

"I like this place," he said as Elizabeth entered from the back.

"Holy moly, you nearly scared me to death." She set a teapot on the nearest table and let out a deep breath. "What are you still doing here?"

"I'm shopping."

She rolled her eyes. "See anything you can't live without?"

He looked into her appealing face and almost gave an answer he knew he'd regret. Of course he could live without a woman. This woman, in particular, had no use for him whatsoever. So why *was* he hanging around?

"Perhaps some books?" she said. "I've expanded my inventory, but they won't be cheap."

"Tea." He straightened and lifted a thin porcelain cup from the counter. "I'm not a man who likes to miss his morning tea."

"Oh, please." She picked up the teapot and carried it to a small table set with a bowl of sugar cubes, silver tongs, a warming plate, and a collection of flowered cups. "The cup you're holding is for sale. Twenty-five dollars, Mr. Chalmers. If you'd prefer, you can use one of these that I keep for my customers."

"No, I'm attached to this particular cup. I simply must have it." He held it against his cheek. "It's me, don't you think?"

She fought a grin. "Then get over here and let me dust it before I pour your tea." He obeyed, enjoying the sight of her slender fingers on the soft white cloth. "Why aren't you at the auction? Or are you just interested in your bottom line?"

"I'm more interested in why you find me so unpleasant."

She looked up. "You don't care a bit about Grace."

"I didn't know Grace."

"You're selling off all her things."

"I don't need her things. I have an apartment full of things."

"And you're going to tear down her home."

"I'll be lucky to get a bulldozer here before it falls down."

"That is bunk! Grace kept the house in the best shape she could manage." She poured, splashing hot droplets of tea on his hand. "I know Bud Huff went over there and fixed the roof for her two or three times. He and his father, Al, were always ready to help when she had a plumbing problem. There's no air-conditioning, but Grace grew up in a time when a lady relied on her fans. Besides, there's a nice breeze from the river almost every day."

"And there are termites in the first-floor woodwork."

"So exterminate them."

"Cracked windowpanes."

"Replace them."

"A leaky basement."

"Seal it."

"Do you think I'm made of money?"

"You will be after your little auction today." She crossed her arms and eyed him evenly. "You said you're an architect. Preserve the house."

"What for? I don't need a drafty old house. I need new offices. I want a place to settle down and make my living. When I heard I'd been left this estate, I realized this was my answer."

"Sell me the house, Mr. Chalmers."

"What?"

"Sell the mansion to me. I'll fix it up." She turned and began rearranging a display of cut glass, but he had heard the telltale tremor in her voice. "I'll set up my shop downstairs. Nick and I can live upstairs. Name your price."

"You couldn't afford it, and I'm not selling."

"How do you know what I can and can't afford?" She whirled on him. "You know nothing about me. You know nothing about this town. You think you can just come in here and tear down the cornerstone of Ambleside. Well,

I've got news for you, buster. Around here we don't destroy the old just to make way for the new. We value our heritage."

"Chalmers House is *my* heritage."

"This *was* your heritage." She picked up the old Bible and thrust it at him. "These pages are a record of Grace Chalmers's life. The words meant something to her. If you'd cared at all, you could have saved this Bible. You could have read her notes and learned about who she was and how she was a part of you. Grace gave you her house. She gave you every piece of furniture, every picture, every doily she'd ever crocheted. And you put it all on the auction block. So don't talk to me about heritage. Your heritage is heading off to antique shops and garage sales all over the United States right now. If you tear down Chalmers House, you might as well be bulldozing Grace's whole life."

She slammed the Bible on the counter, grabbed a wad of tissues, and headed for the back room. Zachary stared after her. All he'd ever intended was to make his personal dreams come true—and he was grateful to this unknown aunt for making that happen. Now it appeared he was publicly destroying the very foundation of a town.

Or maybe Elizabeth Hayes had a screw loose. She certainly was passionate about the whole thing. He set his cup on the counter—the tea untasted. So much for a little harmless flirtation. This was obviously not the time or the place.

And Elizabeth Hayes was not the woman for him.

❧

"What color are my eyes, Mommy?" Nick asked as he sat with his mother on the porch swing, watching the sunset pinken the bluffs that lined the Missouri River. "Magunnery says they're green."

"Montgomery is right." Elizabeth leaned her cheek against

her son's warm head. "You have green eyes and shiny black hair."

"But you have blue eyes and brown hair. Mrs. Henderson said we get our eyes and our hair color from our parents, so I think we're going to have to find us a daddy."

This leap of logic was so typical of Nick that Liz merely sighed and stroked his arm. She never fully understood the way his brain worked, and clearly his orphanage years had left the child with some interesting mental wiring. She'd found that if she listened hard, she could usually make sense of his thought processes.

"I need a daddy with green eyes and black hair," Nick explained, "so I'll look like my parent."

"Well, sweetheart, the color of your eyes and hair came from the woman in Romania who carried you in her tummy until you were born. And you were shaped by God into my very special son. Most of you is just like me."

He pondered, swinging his skinny legs that didn't quite reach the floor. "I think that man who was at Grace's house on Easter would make a good daddy for me. He has green eyes and black hair."

Elizabeth reflected on Zachary Chalmers, whose auction had cleaned out the mansion a week before and who hadn't been seen in Ambleside since. "That man was a stranger," she declared, hoping this would brand him an undesirable.

"It doesn't matter, Mommy. You see, I have to get a paper and draw a tree on it for my teacher. And then I'm supposed to write down my mommy and daddy, and then my grandma and grandpa, and then write the color of everybody's eyes and hair. So if we could get that man to be our daddy, I could draw my tree the right way."

Second-grade genetics studies. *Great,* Elizabeth thought, *just great.*

"I'll help you draw your family tree, Nick," she said. "We'll make it so it shows how special you are."

Nick was still swinging his legs. "I liked that man we saw at Grace's house. He was tall, and he talked really nice. He would be a good daddy for me."

"Because he has green eyes? Nick, it takes much more than that to be a good parent. I'm your mommy because I love you, and I take care of you every day. God gave you to me."

"But you could share me with a daddy. Magunnery has a daddy."

"Montgomery's mommy is married."

"You could get married."

"I could, but I haven't found the right man."

"What about the man at Grace's house?"

Elizabeth let out a breath. Nick had a tendency to get stuck on an idea and not let it go. He would turn it one way and then another until he had worked it out in his mind. In the process, he could just about drive his mother up a wall.

"Elizabeth?" Boompah ambled around the corner of the house and waved at the pair on the porch swing. "Here are some little cakes for you to serve with your tea at the shop tomorrow. I put them in the cart where I keep the bent cans and the old bread for two days. Nobody bought. So, I was thinking of Elizabeth. Maybe my little Nikolai would like to eat some, too."

Elizabeth and Nick got up and went to meet Boompah as he presented the bag of stale cakes with a little bow. In a personal quest to make up for Nick's years of malnourishment, the old man regularly donated odds and ends from his grocery store—torn boxes of cereal, dented cans, day-old bread, slightly wilted vegetables.

"Thank you, Boompah," she said, giving the old man's leathery cheek a kiss. "You're so sweet to think of us."

"I better to tell you something," he murmured, speaking low. "That man came back to town today. The nephew of Grace Chalmers. He rented an apartment here, do you know? Go down Walnut Street, turn right, left, right again, and there it is. Looking over the river. He bought a lot of groceries, let me tell you. I think he likes to cook on the barbecue grill—you know, steaks, chicken, hamburgers. He bought charcoal, that's why I think I'm right about the barbecue." Boompah winked and tapped his forehead.

"I understand he's a bachelor. He probably does grill a lot."

"He rented an office with Sawyer-the-lawyer," he went on, referring to the local attorney. "He's an architect, do you know? I think he's a nice man, but he told me he's going to tear down Grace's house in a month or maybe two. Can you believe it?"

"Oh, Boompah!" Elizabeth pressed her hand to her lips. This was awful. Bad enough to lose the mansion, but the constant presence of workmen and heavy machinery would affect her business. And the noise would be horrendous.

"I think," Boompah said, "that you better go right over to Sawyer-the-lawyer and talk to the Chalmers boy, Elizabeth. You better tell him you don't want him to tear down the mansion."

"I already told him. He won't listen."

"You better fight him, Elizabeth."

"But I don't want to fight anybody. I just want peace and quiet. I want things to stay the way they are."

"Guess what, Boompah, we're going to get a daddy," Nick announced, taking the bag of stale cakes from his mother and peering inside. "We have to find a daddy with green eyes and black hair so I can draw my tree."

"Nick, go sit on the swing. I'll be with you in a minute."

"Oh, bother!" The child, whose favorite character was Winnie the Pooh, stomped away. "Bother, bother, bother."

"In this town, Elizabeth, you are the one to fight,"
Boompah said firmly. "You are young and brave, and you
love Ambleside. It's not only this man who wants to tear
down Chalmers House. There are others. I hear them in the
market. They talk about building a mall on the edge of
town. They talk about parking lots. They talk about big
offices and new subdivisions to attract the people from cit-
ies to move here. That Chalmers boy is only the first. If you
don't stop him from tearing down Grace's house, more will
come. More old houses will fall. Ambleside will soon be just
like a big city, and our town will be no more."

Elizabeth knew what Boompah was talking about. Lately
a wave of enthusiasm for revitalizing the town had swept
through Ambleside. Phil Fox, who was up for reelection in
November, was behind the talk of malls and parking lots.
But how could one woman stand up against such a tidal
wave of public opinion?

"You better go talk to that Chalmers boy," Boompah
repeated. "Go see him at Sawyer-the-lawyer's office tomorrow. He'll listen to you. He likes you."

"He likes to irritate me. And I can't see him tomorrow.
I'm going to an estate sale in Russellville."

Boompah shook his head as he bid his farewells and
ambled away. Clearly he considered Elizabeth a coward of
the first order for her unwillingness to do battle with
Zachary Chalmers. But why should this be up to her? Why?

"Boompah could be my grandfather," Nick said as his
mother settled into the swing. "I could put him on the tree
near my daddy."

"Sweetheart, you can't put just anybody you want on
your family tree. You write down the names of people who
are related to you. Look at Grace's old Bible." She picked
up the worn book from the table nearby. She had intended
to spend some time reading it, but a shipment of sachets
had come in. And then there had been a box of candles to

price. And then . . . there was always something, wasn't there?

Opening the book, she turned through the crinkly, gold-edged pages, hoping the family tree could help her explain the concept to Nick. Near the middle, she located the slick paper on which marriage records and family milestones had been recorded. Though the writing on the chart was too small to read easily, a glance told her that most of it had been left blank.

"You dropped the letter." Drawing his mother's attention from the chart, the child hopped down from the swing and scooped up a note that had fallen from the Bible. He handed it to Elizabeth. "What does it say?"

A ripple ran down her spine as she studied Grace Chalmers's spidery handwriting. "To the finder of my Bible" the note read on the outside. She unfolded the single sheet and read her friend's message:

> You are holding my Bible, and by that I know I must have died some time ago, for I never let this precious book out of my sight. I write this late in the night when I cannot sleep. My thoughts are restless as I ponder the future. Please give this Bible to my dear friend Elizabeth Hayes. I want her to have it.

Elizabeth's eyes misted over as Nick elbowed her. "What does it say, Mommy? Is it a letter from Grace? I thought she was dead."

"She is dead, honey. She wrote this before she died." Elizabeth returned to the letter.

> I think of my home and the many years I have lived within these walls. Oh, it is only an earthly treasure. But I do hope it will live on to bless others as it has blessed me. I pray that Zachary

The letter stopped. Elizabeth turned it over, searching for more. Then she flipped through the pages of the Bible again. A pressed rose fell out. A crocheted bookmark. Nothing more.

"'I pray that Zachary,'" she whispered. "'I pray that Zachary' . . . what?"

"Who's Zachary?" Nick asked, leaning against her shoulder to peer at the letter.

"He's the man with the green eyes."

"My new daddy." Nick nodded. "You better take him that letter. Grace wanted to give it to him."

"Zachary Chalmers is *not* your new daddy, Nick."

"Not yet, but you better take him that letter because Grace loved him a lot."

"Why do you say that, sweetheart?"

"Because," Nick said, jumping down from the swing. "She must have loved him, because she was praying for him."

THREE

"Heading over to the Nifty Cafe?" Pearlene asked as Elizabeth passed the ladies' dress shop next door to Finders Keepers. "They've got strawberry pie on the menu today. Phil says Alma makes strawberry pie better than his mama did, and that's saying something."

Elizabeth tucked Grace's Bible more firmly in her arms and waited for the River Street light to change. For two days she had prayed about the situation with Chalmers House. Grace's letter had been filled with such longing. Clearly, Elizabeth's dear friend had loved the home and had hoped to make it a lasting gift to her nephew. What choice was there but to take the matter into her own hands? But the last person she wanted to know her business was Pearlene Fox. One word to her nosy husband, and the news would be all over town. *Elizabeth Hayes paid a visit to that new fellow in town, Zachary Chalmers. Now what do you suppose that was all about?*

"I like the Nifty's chicken salad," she told Pearlene. "Ez and Alma have the perfect recipe."

"But full of fat, let me tell you. I never saw so much mayonnaise, and Alma uses the high cholesterol kind. Phil says he won't touch the stuff. Says Ez leaves the mayonnaise jar out on the counter three or four hours at a time. You never know what kind of disease you're going to pick up from warm mayonnaise. You could flat die."

The light changed, and Elizabeth breathed a prayer of thanksgiving. Ambleside had only a few restaurants—five or

six, depending on the time of year—and she couldn't bear
the thought of striking Nifty Cafe chicken salad from her list
of favorite foods. Giving Pearlene a wave, she crossed to
the Corner Market. Through the plate-glass windows, she
could see Boompah at the cash register, busy with his
lunchtime traffic. Ruby McCann the librarian was apparently
displeased with a cantaloupe, and a line had formed behind
her.

Crossing Walnut Street, Elizabeth passed the hardware
store, the Nifty, and the drugstore. The old men who passed
each morning smoking pipes and chatting over the local
news on a bench outside Redee-Quick Drugs had already
gone on their way. Their beloved bench was empty now,
but the minute school let out, it would be filled by "the
kids," who never failed to leave their soda cans and gum
wrappers on the sidewalk.

The sign for John Sawyer & Sons, Attorneys swung gently
beneath the green-striped awning that shaded the sidewalk.
Sawyer-the-lawyer, as he was known, had had his sign
painted before his sons informed him they intended to
become a doctor and an insurance salesman. Nevertheless,
the wording remained, and Elizabeth liked to imagine old
Mr. Sawyer pretending one of his sons sat in the office
above his.

Of course, it wasn't a Sawyer who sat there, she thought
as she pushed open the tall glass front door. It was a
Chalmers.

Elizabeth gripped the Bible, as if it might somehow give
her strength.

"May I help you, Liz?" John Sawyer's secretary had moved
to Ambleside from Jefferson City after a divorce. Joanne's
eyes wore a sadness Elizabeth never failed to note. "Mr.
Sawyer just left to go to lunch. You can wait, but it might
be a while."

"No, actually, I, uh, I came to visit with Mr. Chalmers.

The, uh, the new architect?" She gestured vaguely at the
stairwell. "Isn't he renting some space upstairs?"

"Oh, sure, but you can't get to his office this way. You
have to go through that outside door, then down the hall,
turn left, up a flight, and then—shall I just take you there?"

"No, it's OK. I'll find my way."

"Good luck. You're going to need it."

With that fateful pronouncement, she went back to her
dictation as Elizabeth left the office and started through the
mazelike back of the building. Finders Keepers was a war-
ren of little rooms and narrow hallways, too. In the old
days, she supposed, the buildings around Ambleside's main
square had housed not only shops but storage rooms and
the homes of the families who owned them . . . just as her
antiques shop did today. It pleased her that she and Nick
had found the conveniently located building and had been
able to afford the rent.

Darkness shrouded the interior as she climbed the narrow
stairs and worked her way through the honeycomb of hallways. Cobwebs hung from door frames. Dust coated wood-
paneled walls. Floorboards creaked under threadbare
brown carpet. At the end of a long hall she spotted a thin
line of light under a closed door. Her heart in her throat,
she approached and knocked.

Inside she could hear papers shuffling, a chair rolling
across the floor, the squeak of metal springs, footsteps. The
door swung open.

"Hello, Mr. Chalmers, I—"

"Elizabeth Hayes!" A broad smile lit up eyes that were
most definitely green. "Hey, welcome to my office. This is a
nice surprise."

Disarmed, she took in a large room, a tilted drafting table,
walls hung with blueprints, and a tall case filled with books.
"I didn't mean to disturb you."

"Nah, I was just winding up the sketch for a little alcove

area in a state government building I'm designing in Jeff
City. If you'll give me a second . . ."

"Sure. Don't hurry." Feeling out of place and wishing she
were anywhere but here, Elizabeth stepped into the office
and sat down on a cardboard box near the door. She studied her adversary's broad shoulders bent over his drafting
table. The last time they had spoken, she all but threw him
out of her shop. And yet the sight of her had brought a daz-
zling smile to his face and a sparkle to his eyes.

Nick had been stuck on the man's dark hair and green
eyes ever since he decided he needed a daddy. The aware-
ness of loss in her son's short life always twisted Elizabeth's
heartstrings. His birth mother had placed him in an orphanage the day he was born. His birth father was unknown,
and no record existed of siblings or other relatives in
Romania.

Elizabeth's own family was limited. Her parents had been
killed in a car accident when she was a child. She had been
raised by her widowed grandmother, who had died some
years ago. In reality, there was almost no one for Nick to
put on his family tree. She had moved mountains to give
her son a good life, and she would do anything to ensure
that he felt fulfilled. Anything but marry just to give Nick a
father.

"There," Zachary announced, straightening. "Now they
can take their coffee breaks away from the bustle of the
office area." He swung around on his rolling metal chair
and gave her another of those heart-stopping smiles. "So,
what can I do for you today?"

"You can listen to me. I have some things I need to tell
you."

"Great." He stood. "But I listen a lot better on a full stomach. How about lunch? I hear the Nifty Cafe is the place to
eat."

"Well . . ." She glanced out the single window in the

office. Its view was a brick wall. "Really, I won't keep you long."

"But I'd like to take you to lunch. Come on."

Before she could think up another reason to turn him down, he was heading out the door. Mortified, Elizabeth tucked the Bible under her arm and followed. She didn't want the whole town of Ambleside to see her eating with this man. What would they think? The last thing she needed was to put the local gossips in high gear.

"Mr. Chalmers . . ."

"Zachary," he called over his shoulder.

"Please listen to me. I really just need to tell you about a note I found in your aunt's Bible. Actually, it's a letter, and she mentions you and me and the mansion."

"You and me?" He paused at the top of the stairs. Elizabeth barely stopped in time to keep from bumping into him. In the dim light, she could just make out his profile and the silhouette of his shoulders. "Why would my aunt write about us?"

"Not us *together,*" she clarified. "She wrote that she wanted me to have the Bible, and she said she hoped Chalmers House would be your legacy. She mentioned you by name . . ."

"Let me see that." He took the Bible and flipped through the pages until he found the folded note. "Is this it?"

"Yes, but you'll need better light to read it."

"I'll read it at lunch."

"I'm not going to lunch with you, Mr. Chalmers." She lifted her chin. "I came here to tell you again how important it is that Chalmers House remain standing. You can't tear it down. It's not just this town that needs the mansion. It's you. Grace wanted you to have her house, not an empty lot."

"Does the letter say that?"

"Sort of. It talks about how much she loves the house."

"Is it a will?"

"No, of course not. It's just a note she wrote one night when she couldn't sleep. But it expresses her feelings."

"If it's not a legal will, it won't stand up in court."

"I'm not taking it to court. Give me that!" She grabbed the note, but he refused to turn it loose. "Give me Grace's letter. I found it."

"You're going to use it against me."

"I just hoped to make you understand what Grace really wanted."

"What she wanted was for me to have the property and for everybody else to keep their nose out of my business."

"You? Why you? You never came to see her. You never knew her or loved her. Why would she leave you her house?" She tugged on the note, but he wouldn't let go. "I'll tell you why. Because she thought you would save it. She knew you were an architect, and she trusted you to see the value in the building for its architectural merits."

"She wrote that in the note?"

"No, but . . ."

"Elizabeth, what happens to the mansion is not your affair. It's not your responsibility, either. You rent a store next door to Chalmers House, that's all. If I want to put my offices on that lot—"

"It's not a lot. It's a house. A home!"

"A pile of bricks." He jerked the note from her fingers and stuffed it into his pocket. "Look, I made a decision to move to this town for reasons you don't need to know. Now that I'm here, I'm going to follow through on my goals. I can't entertain clients in this maze of dusty old hallways and force them to look out on my view of a brick wall. Whether you like it or not, I'm going to take down Chalmers House and build my office complex."

"Take down? Tear down, you mean."

"And I'll do my best not to interfere with your customers in the process."

"This isn't about my customers. This is about Ambleside!"

"I think this is about you and my aunt. I'm touched that you loved her. And I'm trying to understand your obsession with her house . . ."

"Obsession?"

"Fascination. Whatever."

"Do one thing for me, would you? Get a plat of this town, study the layout, and try to imagine the square without the mansion. Then take a walk through the old house and try to see it for what it is. It's a gem of nineteenth-century architecture. It's a tribute to an age gone by. Then walk through the grounds . . ."

"You asked me to do one thing, and you listed at least three. Look, Elizabeth, I'm taking a vacation in a couple of weeks, and I'll use some of that time to think over what you've been saying. In the meantime, you'd better start getting used to the idea of a sign next door that reads Zachary Chalmers: American Institute of Architects, because that's who's going to be your neighbor."

"Let me buy the mansion then. I can make a large enough down payment that you could buy a lot on the edge of town and build whatever you want."

"Have you always been this persistent?"

She leaned against the wall and let out a breath. "Yes."

"Good. I like that. Now, let's go to lunch."

"You're the one who's stubborn," she said as he headed down the stairs. "And I'm not having lunch with you. I'm going back to my shop and open up for the afternoon."

"Fine, be that way." He gave her yet another of those grins as he pushed open the door and stepped out into the sunlight. "You'll regret it."

"I regret everything about you. And I want Grace's letter back!"

"See ya around, Elizabeth," he called as the door banged
shut behind him.

❧

Too bad about Elizabeth Hayes, Zachary thought as he
detailed the brickwork on the front view of his design for
the state office complex. She was a pretty woman, obviously intelligent, and certainly passionate. But she was
about to drive him straight up the wall. Her visit to his
office the other day had thrown him for a loop.

In moving to Ambleside, he had expected all kinds of
obstacles—zoning laws, client confusion, and all the in-
conveniences of small-town living. But he hadn't anticipated
a blue-eyed spitfire who was bound and determined to
keep him from his objectives.

He couldn't leave that mansion standing. It would cost a
small fortune to rehab it. And then what? He'd have an
expensive old house that nobody would want. Who'd buy
the thing from him? Maybe someone could use it for a
bed-and-breakfast. But Ambleside wasn't exactly a tourist
resort. The building itself was too cumbersome for a modern family's home. No doubt anyone who could afford the
place would prefer a large wooded lot and a top-of-the-line
executive home to a downtown Victorian mansion.

As for Elizabeth's request to purchase the property herself, he questioned whether she could even come close to
the price he would need to ask for the place. Even if she
could buy it, she could hardly rehab it on the income she
made from Finders Keepers. The image of a single woman
running an antiques shop didn't exactly shout extravagant
wealth. Unless she had a trust fund or something.

"Knock, knock, knock!" someone called outside his door.
"Is anybody inside there?"

Zachary wheeled around, listening to the sounds of

furtive conversation and muffled giggling. "Uh . . . I'm in here. Would you like to come in?"

"Yes," the voice called. "Is it OK?"

"Just go in!" someone else said. "Go in, go in!"

The door flew open to reveal two small children—a girl with bright red hair done up in two pigtails, and a boy Zachary recognized as Elizabeth Hayes's adopted son. As one, they stepped into his office, glanced shyly at each other, and began to giggle again.

"Well, this is an unexpected pleasure," he said, coming to his feet. "May I help you, sir and madam?"

As the girl dissolved into uncontrolled laughter, the boy squared his little shoulders and marched forward.

"Magunnery and I, Nick Hayes, have come to visit you," he announced.

"I can see that. Is Magunnery going to be all right?"

Nick looked over his shoulder and then rolled his eyes. "Her mommy doesn't know where she is. We're not supposed to leave the backyard, and we might get into trouble. When Magunnery does something naughty, she always laughs."

"I see." He fought a grin. "I'd hate for the two of you to get into trouble, so maybe you'd better tell me why you came, and then you can head back home."

"I came because I want you to be my daddy."

Zachary blinked. "Your *daddy?*"

"Yes."

"Aha. Well."

"Would that be OK?"

"Umm, what does your mom think about the idea?"

"She says you're a stranger. But I met you already once, and besides, you have green eyes and black hair."

Zachary tried to make sense of the trend of the conversation, but he wasn't having a lot of luck. "Look, maybe you

should start by telling me *why* you want me to be your
daddy."

"Because I need one." Nick nodded. "That's the reason. I
need a daddy."

"I have a daddy," the little redhead piped in. She seemed
to be regaining control of herself. "His name is Luke Easton.
My daddy loves me."

"And so, because you have a daddy, Magunnery, that
means Nick wants a daddy."

"No," the boy said. "I want a daddy because I need one.
You would be a good daddy for me."

"Well, that's very interesting." Zachary stuck his hands in
his pockets and tried to think of a way out of this. "Why
don't you two sit down on that box there while I think
about it. I'll, uh, get you some paper to draw on. You could
draw me a picture, how about that?"

"I didn't come to drawl."

"Drawl?"

"Drawl pictures. I came to ask you to be my daddy."

The boy was as persistent as his mother. "Why did you
pick me?" Zachary asked.

"I like you."

"I like you too, Nick, but being a dad is a big job. For
one thing, I'm not married to your mom."

"You could get married to her."

He'd walked right into that one. "I don't think your mom
wants to marry me."

"You could ask her." The solemn green eyes gazed at
him. "She would be a nice wife for you. She cooks really
good food, and she hardly ever yells. I think you would like
her a lot."

"She's pretty, too," the little girl piped in.

"That's very true," Zachary said, his heart softening at the
child's earnest request. "I'll tell you what. This is clearly a
serious mission you two have come on, and I'm going to

give it a lot of thought. In fact, I'd like you both to sit down here and draw me a picture of Nick's mom so I can put it on my desk while I think about it. And in the meantime, I'll give her a phone call, so she can come over and walk you guys safely home."

The two stared at one another, stricken. "If my mom finds out we came here," Nick said, "she'll get really mad."

"But you said she hardly ever yells."

"This would make her yell."

"Mmm. We wouldn't want that." He was having a hard time keeping a straight face. "Looks like I'm going to have to walk you two home myself."

The boy's face lit up. "Really? Maybe you could ask my mom on a date and then you could kiss her and get married."

"I think we'll need to take our time on that plan—"

A sharp knocking drew the attention of everyone in the room. Well, it appeared they were going to get to see Elizabeth Hayes yell. Not that Zachary hadn't seen her mad before. In fact, he was beginning to think he had a knack for bringing out her worst.

"Come on in," he called.

The door opened, and in stepped Phil Fox, the town's barber, bus station attendant, and city councilman rolled into one stocky little package. He was all grins. "Looks like you already got company here!"

"I'm pretty busy," Zachary said.

"This won't take but a minute. I've got something real important to discuss with you."

❧

"They were headed thataway," Pearlene Fox told Elizabeth, gesturing toward the Corner Market. "I tell you what, if they were mine, I'd tan their hides for running off like that."

Her heart in her throat, Elizabeth raced down the sidewalk and across River Street without waiting for the light to change. Boompah met her on the sidewalk as he was rolling up his awnings for the day. "That way," he said, pointing toward the hardware store.

Why hadn't he stopped Nick and Montgomery? Elizabeth could have wrung these people's necks. Didn't they know that two children shouldn't be roaming the streets alone? OK, so Ambleside wasn't exactly a mecca for crime, but anything could happen.

"That way," Ez pointed as he was removing pies from the window of the Nifty Cafe.

Elizabeth increased her pace. How could Montgomery's mother have taken her eyes off the children? She'd been resting! So, who didn't need a rest? You never turn your back on children at play.

"Next door," Cleo Mueller said. The pharmacist at Redee-Quick Drugs was locking up for the evening. "I saw the two of them run by when I was leaving to make a delivery to Mrs. McCann at the library. Her arthritis is acting up awful bad. I think the kids were headed upstairs," he added, nodding toward the attorney's office.

Upstairs? *Oh, dear God!* Elizabeth breathed a prayer for help as she entered the building, climbed the stairs, and negotiated the dimly lit maze of hallways. If Nick and Montgomery went to see Zachary Chalmers, that could mean only one thing. Nick was on a mission to get himself a father. *Lord, help me to be calm. Help me to be nice. Please direct my words—*

"Nikolai Andrew Hayes!" she shouted as she burst through the door. "What on earth are you doing here?"

"She's yelling now," Nick observed.

"I can see that."

"Montgomery, your mother is—" Elizabeth spotted Phil Fox in the extra chair beside the drafting table. He held a pen with which he'd been sketching. The two children appeared to be drawing something, too. Elizabeth set her hand on the door frame and drew in a deep breath.

"Mr. Chalmers," she said calmly, "I have been searching for these two children for the last half hour."

"They've been right here, safe and sound."

"Did it never occur to you to call me and let me know where I might find my son?"

"Her cheeks always get red when she's mad," Nick informed Zachary. "But they turn pink again after she calms down."

"I've noticed that."

"Nick, you and Montgomery are in big trouble." She reached for her son's hand. "What are you doing here anyway? No, never mind—"

"I came to ask if he would be my daddy. He's going to think about it. He might take you on a date and kiss you."

"Nick!" Wishing she could sink into her shoes, Elizabeth pulled her son upright, knelt on the floor, and took his shoulders. "Nick, your behavior is inappropriate. And as for you, Miss Montgomery Easton, you know you don't have permission to cross the street. Your mommy is very upset."

The little girl's blue eyes filled with tears. "I was just trying to help Nick."

"Don't be too hard on 'em," Phil Fox put in. "They haven't been a bit of trouble the whole time I've been here. Fact is, Zachary was just about to walk the two of them home when I showed up with some business."

"Mr. Fox is going to change the whole town," Nick said. "And Zachary is going to help him."

"Change the town?" She looked at Phil. "How do you plan to do that?"

"Oh, just some rough ideas. You know for a fact we need more parking spaces, Liz. You and Pearlene can hardly handle all the customers you get. Some of the ladies have been parking over at Al Huff's gas station so they can walk to

Pearlene's to shop for their dresses. Al's not real happy about it, I'm telling you. He's thinking of taking up the matter with the city council."

Phil swelled his chest and stuck his thumbs under his suspenders. Elizabeth believed the man had Ambleside's best interests at heart, but she didn't trust Phil Fox. And if Zachary Chalmers went to work designing a new look for the town, there was no telling how things would end up. The architect clearly had no respect for the past—which, in her opinion, was Ambleside's greatest attribute.

"You're working with Phil?" she asked him.

"No," he said.

"Maybe," Phil clarified. "He's thinking about it."

"And he's thinking about being my daddy, too." Nick gave his mother a wet kiss. "Look at this. It's a picture of you, because Zachary wants to put it on his desk so he can think about you."

He held up a drawing of a round face punctuated by a pair of small black eyes, a bulbous nose, and a grin that revealed approximately fifty teeth in two neat rows. This would certainly inspire Mr. Chalmers's affections, she thought, examining the portrait.

"Very pretty, isn't it?" Zachary said, his eyes warm. "Although I've noticed you have a little more hair than the lady in the picture."

"I didn't get to drawl your hair yet," Nick said. "But did you see that Zachary has black hair and green eyes, Mom?"

She pursed her lips. "Yes, I did, and I also see two naughty children who are going home now." With that, she took each child by the hand and marched them out the door.

"How about dinner sometime, Elizabeth?" Zachary called after her. "We really ought to discuss this marriage scenario."

Elizabeth rolled her eyes and kept the children walking.

They turned the corner toward the staircase. The late after-noon sun cast deep purple shadows in the narrow hallway.

She could hear the two men chuckling behind her. Very funny. As if she would go out to dinner with Zachary Chalmers! The architect would be in Phil Fox's back pocket in no time, and the whole town of Ambleside would turn into some kind of neon jungle with glass-walled office buildings and metal modern-art sculptures that looked like flying french fries.

Now which way? Arriving at a fork, she glanced down the halls that led off on either side. This didn't look like the way she'd come in. On the other hand, it was awfully dark.

Gripping the youngsters' small, damp hands, she turned left. "I hope you know you're going to have consequences, Nick," she blurted out. "For one thing, you and Montgomery will not be allowed to play together this weekend."

"Not Saturday *or* Sunday?" her son cried.

"Neither day."

"What about Friday? What about Sunday night?" His voice grew louder and more anguished. "But can I play with Magunnery at church? What about just sliding on the slide? Or the swing? We would be good, I promise."

Elizabeth paused at the darkened end of another long hallway. Nick was doing his orphanage cry, sort of a strangled wail that always sent chills down her spine. She wanted to scream. *I'm lost in this stupid maze of a building with two crying children, and I'm hungry and tired, and I need help! Lord, just get me out of here!*

"Hey now," a deep voice said nearby. "What's all this ruckus?"

Zachary Chalmers's hand touched the small of her back, and Elizabeth felt her shoulders relax. "I turned the wrong way," she said. "I got us lost."

"You're not lost." He paused. "You know the trouble with you, Elizabeth? You try too hard to do everything all by yourself. You know, once in a while it's OK to let someone else take over."

"It's Zachary," Nick said. "You rescued us from the black hallways."

"That's me—your basic knight in shining armor." As he led them forward, he flicked on a switch that lit a bare bulb over the staircase. "There you go. The yellow brick road home. May I walk you there?"

Elizabeth looked into his green eyes, and it occurred to her how comforting it would be to let someone else take responsibility for looking both ways, for walking the children across the street, for warning of cracks in the sidewalk . . . for everything she'd always done because she believed God had given her the job. Her alone.

"Yes," she said to Zachary, "you may walk us home. We'd like that very much."

FOUR

"Sit on the swing," Nick commanded as the group stepped up onto the porch of the apartment behind Finders Keepers. "I will make the tea."

"You will not make tea, Nikolai Hayes." Elizabeth crossed her arms and stared down at her son. "You don't have permission to use the stove, and you're already in big enough trouble, buster. Now, head straight up to your room and put on your jammies. I'll be up in a minute."

"But aren't you going to kiss Zachary?"

"Nick!"

Elizabeth started after her son, who made a beeline for the door that led into their living room. In moments, Zachary could hear the child's small feet pounding up the stairs. A door inside the house slammed shut, and a window overhead slid open.

"Nikolai." Elizabeth spoke the name in a tone of dire warning as she looked up. The window slid shut. "One of these days, that child is going to drive me nuts."

Zachary laughed. "It looks to me like you're one step ahead of his every move."

"One step behind, you mean." She sat down on the swing and dropped her head back, letting out a deep breath. "He scared me to death this afternoon."

Zachary decided to take the place beside her. It hadn't been offered, but it hadn't been denied, either. Maybe he was making progress with the prickly Miss Hayes. As he sat on the swing, the old wood creaked, and the cicadas silenced their song for a moment.

"Magunnery's mom was pretty sick," he remarked, recalling their brief visit at the little girl's house. "You can't really blame Mrs. Easton for taking a nap. She looked like death warmed over."

"It's *Montgomery,*" she corrected him, "and I realize Ellie was sick. Still, she should have been more careful. If anything ever happened to Nick . . ."

"You can't protect a kid twenty-four hours a day."

"I can't lose my son. I just can't."

"That's not a very realistic outlook, is it? I mean, things happen. Accidents, illnesses. We don't own life."

"Oh, what do you know about a mother's love?"

He thought that one over. "Not much, really. My mom was busy a lot."

"Umm, I'm sorry." She fiddled with the links of the chain that held the swing. "I didn't mean to get personal."

"It's OK. I had a lot of little brothers and sisters. I'm not sure Mom really knew I was around."

"Of course she did. I'm sure she loved you deeply. Maybe she felt uncomfortable showing it. Nick is all I have. I had to go through so much to get him that I always feel he's a miracle."

"And you're afraid he'll slip through your fingers?"

"I'm very protective. I won't apologize for that." She hesitated hardly a moment before embarking on her favorite topic. "Now, about Chalmers House—"

"I didn't come to talk about the mansion."

"But as long as you're here—"

"The spider toying with her prey?"

"Am I that bad?"

"Almost." He leaned forward, elbows on his knees. "Look, Elizabeth, I like you a lot. I'd like to spend more time with you. But I don't want to spend it talking about Chalmers House."

"How can you say you like me? The only thing you know about me is my passion to save Grace's home—and you abhor that."

"I don't abhor it. I admire it. But your passion is not going to change my mind." He stuck his thumb in the direction of the ramshackle property next door. "That place is coming down as soon as I get it through probate. I've already drawn the blueprints and lined up a contractor."

When he stopped speaking, he could tell right away he'd said the wrong thing. Elizabeth's walls were up higher than the roofline of Chalmers House—and a lot stronger than the mansion's ivy-eaten bricks. Maybe he should just give up trying to woo the woman. Why did she attract him? And what did he really know about her anyway?

"So, tell me about yourself," he said finally.

She glanced his way, her blue eyes sparking. "I don't hate you, Zachary. I just don't appreciate your attitude. You want to have everything your own way."

"And you don't?"

Crossing her arms, she pursed her lips. "You accuse me of trying to control everything, but you're wrong. I'm doing my best to surrender my life. I'm a Christian, OK? The last thing I want to do is run my own world. In fighting for Chalmers House, I'm trying to respect the wishes of a wonderful old woman. In adopting Nick, I hope I'm following God's will to care for orphans and the homeless. I believe God gave Nick to me to raise—it was a divine commission. In running Finders Keepers, I'm preserving the best of the past, and I'm helping people create warm, cozy homes for their families. I'm just doing my best to live a clean life that mirrors Jesus Christ."

"Whoa." He leaned back and weighed her words. "You've got me beat."

Zachary studied the view from Elizabeth's porch swing, an expanse of lawn leading to the limestone bluffs over the Missouri River. In the gathering darkness, fireflies sparkled like glinting diamonds. The cicadas had quieted, and the moths were beginning to drift toward the porch light. All seemed at rest—outwardly, at least. In truth, Zachary's heart felt as tight as a knot.

He'd never really considered his activities in the context of faith. They had always seemed like two separate things. There was church, where a person did all the things that were required by his religion. And then there was the rest of life, where a man took himself by his own bootstraps and climbed as high as he could go.

But Elizabeth Hayes seemed to filter everything—every choice, every decision, every action—through the screen of her faith. Was this God's will? Did this please Christ? Would this reflect Christianity? It was a new concept, and one that made him more than a little uncomfortable.

"So, you ask God before you make every move?" he inquired. "You prayed about coming to find Nick this evening?"

"I went looking for Nick like a mother tiger in search of a lost cub. I couldn't even think. But as I ran and searched and scoured the neighborhood, I prayed." With her toe, she gave the swing a little push that sent them swaying slightly back and forth. "I'm not perfect, OK? I probably need to stop trying to control things so much. But at least I do my best to act in God's will. Don't you?"

"No. I never think about God's will. I think about Zachary Chalmers's will."

"Well, you should give God a try sometime. Walking in his will helps an awful lot during the rough spots. And you might even begin to see the right way to act on things. Take Chalmers House, for instance—"

"Hold it. You're telling me that God wants that pile of bricks left standing?"

She let out a breath. "I'm not *totally* sure what God wants. I haven't been praying about it as diligently as I probably should. I just know how Grace felt."

"Grace? What does Grace have to do with this? Grace is dead."

"You are a creep!" She jumped to her feet. "You are the most insensitive, mercenary, bloodthirsty—"

"You are selfish," he said, pointing a finger. "Forget all your good-intentioned reasons. Forget God's will, which you just admitted you don't even know. The bottom line is that you want that old house standing so it doesn't mess up business in your musty little junk shop."

"Ohhh!" Clenching her fists, she stormed into the house and slammed the screen door behind her. In a moment she was back outside with a broom. "Get off my porch. Get off, or I'll call Mick and Ben!"

"OK, OK!" He held up his hands in surrender as she prodded him down the steps. "I'm leaving."

He heard the screen door slam again as he headed for the sidewalk. So much for Elizabeth Hayes. So much for romance in Ambleside. So much for—

"Hey, Zachary!" A husky voice called down from an open upstairs window. "Did you kiss my mom yet?"

"Not yet," he called back.

"Not ever!" Elizabeth shouted into the night, and she shut the child's bedroom window with a bang that echoed clear across the Missouri River to the bluffs on the other side.

"Does that help?" Elizabeth adjusted the pillow behind Boompah's head and smoothed the dank-smelling sheet up to his grizzled chin. "You need air-conditioning in here. I'm going to talk to Bud Hoff. He might have a trade-in at the hardware store."

"You fuss over me too much, Elizabeth," the old man said. "I never had air-conditioning before, and I don't need it now that I am sick."

"Boompah, are you going to die?" Nick asked, taking his gnarled hand. "Are you going to get put into a box and buried in the dirt like Grace?"

"Nick!" Elizabeth whirled on her son. "That is not polite, and you—"

"Yes, Nikolai, I am," Boompah said. "I'm going to die one day, just like everybody else. But maybe not right away. I hope Cleo Mueller's medicine will help me live a little longer."

"I don't want you to die, Boompah. I would miss you."

"I would miss you, too, Nikolai. But I'll tell you a little secret. Come here."

He motioned for the boy to move closer, and then he whispered in his ear. Elizabeth watched the two, her heart aching. Nick had insisted on putting Boompah on his family tree in the grandfather's spot. He'd added Grace for the grandmother. Nothing his mother had said to explain the reality of his family situation would deter him from creating a lineage of his own desire.

The father's spot, of course, had been filled by Zachary Chalmers. Elizabeth had told Nick that Zachary was not his father, and he never would be. The man himself was away on his vacation, thank heaven, and neither she nor Nick had seen him since the evening on the porch swing five days ago. She would give just about anything if Zachary Chalmers hadn't stepped into her peaceful life, and she wished her son would get the man out of his fantasies.

But the boy had sketched a round face, a smile with fifty teeth, a pair of green eyes, and a thatch of black hair to match his own right in the "father" spot on the family tree. Then he had labeled it, *Zakry Chamers, my dad*.

The assignment had distressed Elizabeth so much that she'd made an appointment with Nick's teacher, a wonderfully caring woman. Unfortunately, the discussion turned quickly to the usual concerns that Nick was failing to work at grade level, he talked too much in class, and he jumped out of his chair every two or three minutes. The principal had scheduled a meeting for Nick's special-education team, and the matter of the family tree went by the wayside.

"Really?" the boy exclaimed. "Each gate of heaven will be made out of one pearl? They must be really small gates."

"Or really big pearls. I can hardly wait to see them."

Nick pulled up his shirt and scratched his stomach as he pondered. "But will there be volcanoes in heaven? Will they interrupt?"

"Erupt," Elizabeth corrected. "Boompah doesn't know about volcanoes in heaven, and I want you to let him rest. His back is hurting."

"Not so much now, thanks to the pills of Cleo Mueller." He shut his eyes. "Elizabeth, I am thinking of Ruby McCann and her groceries. How will she cook her dinner if the Corner Market is closed?"

"Folks are just going to have to drive over to Russellville for their groceries, and you need to stop worrying about it. I'll check on Mrs. McCann. She can shop with me the next time I go."

"But she likes only the freshest ingredients. Each morning she comes to the market for her milk. She buys every single day from me, Elizabeth. And if the produce is not just so, she gets very unhappy."

"She'll adjust." Elizabeth laid her hand on the old man's frail chest. It worried her that the doctor could find no specific cause for Boompah's immobilizing aches and pains. "We all need to put our faith in God about this. He'll help us through, if we just ask him."

"I will pray," Nick announced, and before his mother

could react, he began. "Dear God, please fix Boompah's
sore back right away. Even though heaven has pearl gates,
we don't want Boompah to go there yet. We aren't finished
with him here. Mrs. McCann needs her groshies, and we
need Boompah because we love him. Thy kingdom kong,
thy will be done, amen."

Nick bent over and gave the old man a loud smacking
kiss on the cheek. "OK, Boompah," he said firmly, "you
don't have to worry anymore. God is the boss. Come on,
Mom, it's time to go home."

Elizabeth sent her son to the kitchen to fetch a glass of
fresh water for the bedside table. "Boompah," she said
softly, "I think Nick is right. We need to trust God with our
worries. He can care for Mrs. McCann, and he'll watch over
you."

"And you too, Elizabeth. I believe God has a good plan
for you, if you can let him take your life."

"He has my life, Boompah."

"Does he?" The old man's eyes slid open, and one thin
eyebrow lifted. "And you are letting God be the boss? I hear
you are having a big fight with that Chalmers boy about
Grace's house."

"Who told you that?"

"Ach. There are no secrets in Ambleside."

"I'm just trying to do what I think Grace would have
wanted, Boompah. Surely you don't think I should give up
and let that self-centered Zachary Chalmers tear down the
mansion. Why would God want that?"

"We don't understand the ways of God. When I was a little Gypsy boy living with my parents, do you think I could
understand why a man like Adolph Hitler came to kill all
the Roma? It seemed wrong."

"It *was* wrong!"

"Ja, but God can make good come out of what seems
very bad. His ways are not our ways. His plans are the best

for us, and we should look always to his path and not our own."

"You think I should just give up?"

"Never give up, Elizabeth." Boompah rested a moment before speaking again. "But I believe that Chalmers boy is not an evil fellow. He thinks his plan is good, and you think your plan is good. Maybe you can pray together to see what is the plan of God."

Elizabeth took the glass from Nick and set it near Boompah's bed. Pray with Zachary Chalmers? That would be like asking Churchill to sit down and pray with Hitler. Hardly possible.

"We'll come see you tomorrow, Boompah," Nick said. "You'll be better."

"I hope so, Nikolai," the old man said. "Thank you for coming."

As Elizabeth and her son made their way down the front porch steps of Boompah's rickety clapboard house, they watched a car pull into the driveway. Someone arriving with a meal, no doubt. She was thankful that Boompah hadn't been forgotten during his time of need. He was always so good to take groceries to the sick or to fill baskets for the hungry at Thanksgiving and Christmas.

"Yoo-hoo!" Pearlene Fox waved as she got out of her car. "Hey there, Liz! How's Mr. Jungemeyer this evening?"

"About the same."

"I brought him one of my tuna casseroles." Balancing on high heels, she crossed the gravel drive. "You know how Phil is always bragging on my cooking. I thought Mr. Jungemeyer could eat what he wanted tonight and freeze the rest. It ought to keep real good. Phil's in the car. Go by and say hello."

Elizabeth's spirits sank as she took Nick's hand and approached the idling automobile. "Hey, Phil," she said through the window. "Nice night."

"You and Zachary Chalmers ever get your problems ironed out?"

"Zachary is going to be my father," Nick piped up.

"Nikolai!"

Phil laughed. "I hear the two of you nearly came to blows the other night. Well, I'll tell you what, Liz. I like that young man. He's a fine fellow. Got a good head on his shoulders. He's volunteered to work with me on the plans for the town."

"What plans?"

"Why, you know, making sure Ambleside goes in the right direction."

"Ambleside is fine just the way it is."

"Sure it is. One old man gets sick, and nobody can even buy a sack of groceries. The whole Corner Market shuts down, and we all have to troop over to Russellville just to keep from starving to death. I'll tell you what, if that don't beat all."

"Mom, are we starving to deaf?" Nick asked.

"We'll all manage just fine until Boompah gets better," Elizabeth told her son. She tried to keep her voice even. "Ambleside doesn't need another grocery store. The Corner Market carries everything a person could want."

"Unless it's closed." Phil smirked as he ran his fingers through his beard. "You've got to admit, Liz, this town is about as efficient as one of them old butter churns you sell. Looks pretty enough, if you like antiques, but it doesn't function all that well."

Elizabeth felt sure he could see the steam rising from her ears. "I moved to Ambleside because I like antiques. My customers drive all the way here from the East Coast because they like antiques. If you and Zachary Chalmers change this town, I could be out of business, and so could half the stores on the square."

"Now, that's plumb wrong—"

"Good night, Phil. And tell Zachary Chalmers he can just rot." Grabbing Nick's hand, she pushed past the forsythia bush that grazed the side of the car. "Doesn't function all that well," she muttered. "This town is more than a hundred years old, and it's functioning just fine. Ambleside ought to keep its character. Tear down the mansion, and then what's next?"

"I will talk to Zachary," Nick said as they set off down the sidewalk toward the square. "I will tell him not to make you mad."

"You stay away from that man, Nick. He's nothing but a bloodsucking leech taking advantage of the kindness and goodness of his aunt. He's going to suck every bit of charm and beauty right out of this town."

As Elizabeth rounded the corner of the park, she stopped and gripped the crusted wrought-iron rail, as if she could somehow hold down the whole town against the winds of change. Why did she feel such a need to cling to the past? Why couldn't she let in the new? What fears kept her bound to this town, to the fragile walls she had built around herself?

Maybe Boompah was right. Maybe she hadn't given the controls of her life to Christ any better than Zachary Chalmers had. The architect had labeled her selfish. If he was right, she had no choice but to admit her own sinful self-centeredness and submit to God's leading. And that might mean letting go of her battle to save the mansion.

❧

Elizabeth flew across Walnut Street in hopes she hadn't missed Pop's daily mail collection from the blue box outside the courthouse. Pop Creighton was as faithful as the clock that chimed the hour in the cupola atop the courthouse, and if a person was a minute late in dropping off mail, well, too bad. It would just have to wait until tomorrow.

Breathless, Elizabeth spotted the man himself striding down the sidewalk toward the box, a grin as wide as the Missouri River across his face. "Gonna beat you!" he threatened.

She made a quick sprint to the box and stuffed in her collection of bills. "Ta-dahh!" she exclaimed, throwing up her arms in a victory cheer. "You're too late, Pop. Better move faster next time."

"Aw, rats. It's those long legs of yours, Miss Hayes. You catch me every time."

With a laugh and a wave, she headed back across the sidewalk. A glance at the Corner Market told her something was amiss. The green striped awning was rolled up as Boompah had left it—but the front door stood ajar, its brass bells jingling in the breeze. A fruit cart filled with fresh cherries brightened the sidewalk. The collection of daily newspapers by the front door had been taken inside. A hand-lettered sign in Boompah's neat calligraphy fluttered from the door handle: OPEN.

"Boompah?" she breathed. He had been bedridden and achy the night before. How could the old man have bounced back so quickly? Though worry tugged at her heart, Elizabeth raced down the sidewalk, eager to greet her friend. He would need to take it slowly, and he shouldn't be rolling his fruit cart outside all by himself, she thought. He'd need help unrolling the awning. He could hardly reach the handle and—

Her breath caught in her throat as Zachary Chalmers stepped outside the Corner Market and stuck a sign into the fruit cart: Farm Fresh Cherries, $1.20 lb. Spotting her, he lifted a hand, and that unexpected grin spread across his face.

"Morning!" he called. "Want some cherries? Better get them now. They're going fast."

Elizabeth hardly glanced at the slow-moving traffic as she crossed the street. "I thought you went on vacation."

"Missed me, did you?"

"No, I—" She let out a breath. "What are you doing here? Where's Boompah?"

"Home in bed. I stopped by to see him on my way out of town last week before I drove down to the lake. The whole time I was at my cabin trying to relax and catch a few crappie, I kept thinking about Boompah and the empty store. You know how Mrs. McCann is about her groceries. So, I came back and opened it for him."

"You did?"

"I did." He shrugged. "Sò?"

"How do you know about Mrs. McCann's groceries?"

"I live here, don't I?"

"Well, I . . . but I didn't think . . ." She could hardly speak. "You'll need to unroll the awning. It'll keep the store cooler inside after the sun hits those windows. Boompah doesn't believe in air-conditioning."

He squinted into the sun and peered at the green-striped canvas. "I guess you turn that handle there?"

"First you have to push the thingie by the door." She went over and moved the mechanism that released the latch. "Now you turn the handle over there. Boompah needs to get this repaired. One of these days he's going to get clob—"

The awning suddenly unrolled like a Japanese fan, the metal ribs clattering open and the canvas giving a loud *foompf*. Zachary winced as he supported the frame on one shoulder while trying to straighten the tangle of canvas with his free hand. Elizabeth leapt to his aid, pushing up to bear some of the weight.

"I think it came unscrewed at the top," she panted.

"Is it still attached to the wall?"

"Barcly. One corncr is swaying . . . and . . . uh-oh!" She

grabbed the awning as it toppled over, knocking the man to the sidewalk and burying him in billows of dusty, sun-bleached canvas. Elizabeth dropped to her knees and pushed at the fabric.

"Are you all right? Can you hear me?"

"I'm seeing stars. Is it night?"

"Oh, thank God you're OK. I can get you out, but I'll need to move this pole here—"

"Elizabeth." His hand emerged from under the awning and grabbed hers. "Get . . . Bud Huff."

"I can do this, Zachary. If I can just lift this off your chest—"

"Get . . . Bud . . . now!"

"OK, OK, just a minute." Heart hammering, she flew across the street to the hardware store. Bud was sorting nails in the big metal bin at the back. "You have to come! The awning fell on Zachary, and I think he's hurt. I tried to move the pole, but there's so much canvas that—"

"Whoa, slow down, Liz. What's the problem?"

"The awning on the Corner Market! It fell on Zachary Chalmers." She grabbed the man's hand and tugged him out the door. As they hustled back to the grocery store, Elizabeth could see that Pearlene Fox and several of the women who'd been shopping at Très Chic had gathered on the sidewalk to gawk at the commotion. Bud's father, Al, had hobbled down to the corner from his gas station. The two men began to lift the metal frame that pinned Zachary.

On her knees again, Elizabeth took Zachary's hand. "Bud's here. Al, too. Are you all right? Can you breathe?"

"I can breathe," he said. "Sort of."

As the frame lifted, she pushed away the canvas that covered his face. He mustered a grin and sucked down a deep breath. She brushed back the dark hair that had fallen across his forehead to examine a scrape near his hairline.

"You tried to kill me," he murmured.

"I did not. It was an accident. I saved you."

"In that case." He edged up on one elbow, cupped her cheek with his free hand, and gave her a firm kiss right on the lips. "Thank you."

At the chorus of delighted *ahhs* that escaped the Très Chic women, Elizabeth scrambled to her feet and set her hands on her hips. "Get up, Zachary Chalmers," she snapped.

He sat up on the sidewalk and rubbed the back of his head. "Anybody want to buy any cherries?" he asked. "They're going fast."

5

FIVE

"My mom says you are a bloodsucking bleach," Nick informed Zachary, who had knelt to greet the child on the sidewalk in front of Finders Keepers. "She says you are going to suck the life right out of the whole town."

The boy's green eyes regarded him seriously, and Zachary did his best to keep a straight face. "A bloodsucking bleach?"

"Yes, and I think if you suck the life out of Ambleside, then we will all be dead and in heaven with the teeny-tiny gate made out of a pearl. How big is a pearl?"

Zachary held up his thumb and forefinger. "Pretty small. But I'll tell you what, Nick, I've never been a bloodsucking bleach, or a bleach of any kind, for that matter. In fact, I think I'm a pretty good guy for the most part." He glanced at the lace-curtained front window. "Is your mom working this afternoon?"

"She works every day except Sunday, and that's when we go to church. Do you go to church? Are you a Christian? I don't think you can be my dad if you're not a Christian."

"You know, if your mother thinks I'm a bloodsucking bleach, she's not going to let me be your dad."

Nick pondered this one. "God can change anybody," he said. "Even you."

"I'll remember that." Zachary stood and gave the boy's hair a rub. "Don't run off, OK? You scared your mom the last time you did that."

"I'm going to get Magunnery. She plays at my house after

school, because her mother is still sick. Boompah's sick, too. Mom says you're running the Corner Market. She says, 'That man ceases to amaze me.'"

Zachary laughed. "I ceased to amaze myself a long time ago. See ya, big guy."

As Nick scampered away, Zachary climbed the old building's limestone steps and pushed open the glass-windowed front door. As before, he was greeted by the mingled scents of beeswax candles, fragrant potpourri, and lemony furniture polish. A fan turning overhead rustled the lace curtains and white linen tablecloths. On a small side table against the wall, a silver teapot sent out a thin drift of steam. Near it, a plate of golden cakes beckoned.

"Be with you in a minute!" Elizabeth called from the back room. "Make yourself at home."

At home. Zachary surveyed the collection of aged furniture, heavy oak tables, simple pine cupboards, worn rocking chairs, and soft-edged footstools. Then he thought back to the crowded trailer in which he'd lived his early life.

Most of his nights had been spent in a sleeping bag on the floor. Meals were consumed from aluminum trays in front of the television set. A brown-and-black shag carpet underfoot had collected the debris of the multitude of children that roamed it—a million crumbs of cookies and potato chips, dozens of sharp-edged plastic blocks, a collection of headless action figures and green army men. Shelves held everything from half-empty cereal boxes to hairbrushes to chewed-up crayons.

That had been home. Nothing like this.

"Oh, it's you." Elizabeth's voice held a note of disappointment. "I see you decided to pay a visit to my musty little junk shop."

A pang of guilt stabbed Zachary as he turned to find the woman crossing the room, her dark brown hair pulled up into a soft bun from which stray tendrils brushed against her neck. In the half light of the shop, her pale blue dress seemed to give off an angelic glow. She reached across a green brocade sofa and switched off a lamp.

"I'm closing for the day," she said. "Do you need something?"

That question could be answered a dozen ways, Zachary thought, and most of them involved Miss Elizabeth Hayes.

"I need to apologize," he said, uncomfortable at the knot that seemed to have formed in his throat. "I shouldn't have insulted your business. Finders Keepers is not a junk shop, and it's definitely not musty. In fact, I came here to pay for my teacup. I picked one out the first time I was here, and then I forgot to take it with me."

"You ought to apologize for your behavior to me on the sidewalk the other morning. Pearlene Fox hasn't stopped jabbering about it. Everyone in town knows what you did."

He lifted an eyebrow. "Apologize for kissing you under the awning?"

"We weren't under the awning. We were out in broad daylight. Al and Bud both saw it. Al thinks it's the funniest thing in the world. He was filling up my gas tank yesterday, and he couldn't stop giggling."

"Giggling?"

"Yes, he was giggling!" She crossed her arms and regarded him.

Zachary took a step closer. "I apologize for kissing you in broad daylight."

"Thank you."

"But," he went on, moving near enough to catch a whiff of the floral scent she wore, "I'm not sorry I kissed you."

A pair of pink roses blossomed on her cheeks. "You didn't have my permission, and I don't like surprises. Besides that, if everybody in town thinks that you and I—"

"When was the last time somebody kissed you, Elizabeth? Not counting me on the sidewalk."

"None of your business."

Her answer told him everything. "You intrigue me. You're a beautiful woman, you're obviously intelligent and ambitious, and you have a good heart. Obviously you want a family, or you wouldn't have adopted Nick. So why aren't you married?"

"That also is none of your business."

She moved past him and picked up the teacup and saucer he had chosen. Vanishing behind a counter, she left only the whisper of her fragrance. Zachary leaned over, elbows on the glass top, as she emerged with a handful of purple tissue paper and a gift bag. He knew he'd be ushered out the door within the space of a minute if he couldn't think of another topic that wouldn't offend her.

Why did he even care to keep this woman talking? She clearly disliked him. Didn't she?

"There you go." She pushed the bag across the counter. "Twenty-five dollars. Plus tax." On an old-fashioned register she rang up the purchase.

"Nick says you think I'm a bloodsucking bleach," he commented as he wrote out a check.

Startled, she glanced up, her blue eyes wide. "Oh, Nick. He's so blunt . . ." She shrugged. "He meant *leech.*"

"So it's true?"

"My opinion of you is not high, Mr. Chalmers. If you and Phil Fox think you can bulldoze this town—"

"Phil Fox came to my office to talk to me. Just like you did. Just like Nick and Montgomery did. That doesn't mean I'm in cahoots with the guy."

"What's he planning to do to Ambleside?"

"Modernize."

"Oh!" She slapped the glass countertop. "You know why I'm not married? Because I don't like change. I want to keep my life calm, serene, and genteel. That's why I moved to Ambleside."

"And you think time should stand still here?"

She sighed, and Zachary felt uncomfortably like a dim-witted schoolboy.

"You see this glass counter?" Her fingertips traced along the surface. "This used to be in a country store in southern Missouri. It's more than a hundred years old. Thousands of people have stood and leaned on it, right where you're leaning. The oak frame is smooth from their touch. They've lived a little bit of life right here—a child chose a piece of penny candy from a glass jar, a gentleman selected a new collar to button onto his shirt for his wedding day, a young mother purchased flannel to sew a blanket for her newborn baby. Those people are all gone now, but the counter remains. If you destroy it—the way they destroyed the country store to make room for a discount mart—then you lose something very special. You lose the chance to touch those people's lives, to think about them, and to learn from them. You lose a little bit of yourself when you destroy the past."

Spellbound, Zachary could almost see the line of customers Elizabeth described. She picked up an old album—a huge velvety thing with a massive brass clasp and thick pages filled with tattered sepia-toned photographs.

"I don't know whose this was," she said softly. "I got it from a man who had bought it at a garage sale for three dollars. Here's somebody's daughter. Here's a grandmother with a baby on her lap. See the names? Hubert, Jeremiah, Ettie. Do you know where your name came from, Zachary Chalmers? Do you know what your great-grandfather looked like? Maybe you don't care, but you should. He was a part of you, and he'll be a part of your children and grandchildren someday."

She shut the old book. "I have to lock up now. Nick and Montgomery will be playing in my yard."

Zachary caught her hand. "This is all about the mansion,

isn't it? That's all you see when you look at me. A
bulldozer."

"Actually," she said, "that was all about me. I was telling
you who I am and what I believe in. For some reason I
can't figure out, I need to make you understand me."

"Do you want to understand me?"

"I already do." She tucked a stray tendril of hair into her
bun. "I resist changing things on the outside—but you don't
want to change on the inside. That would mean trading the
will of Zachary Chalmers for the will of God."

Leaving the counter, she started through the shop, turning
off the array of electric lamps. He watched her figure transform slowly into a silhouette, an ethereal shadow that
seemed to float past the furnishings of yesteryear. He pondered the people whose lives had touched that table, this
chair, the cabinet across the room. The objects weren't junk.
They were treasures. Relics. Pieces of history.

In his own way, Zachary realized, he was creating a heritage he hoped would last beyond his lifetime. The homes
he had designed, the offices and restaurants he had conceived were his legacy. They were a part of him, an
emblem of who he was and what he believed in.

"Good night," Elizabeth said at the door. "At least we
didn't have a fight this time."

Or a kiss, he thought.

"That white cupboard," he said, spotting the piece Phil
Fox had referred to in his diatribe against Elizabeth's
antiques. "How much is it?"

"Two hundred dollars."

"I'll take it."

She set her hand on her hip. "What is this? You haven't
even looked at it. Where are you going to put it? And how
do you know that's a fair price?"

"I need that cabinet."

"What for?"

"For my teacup."

With a laugh, she shook her head. "Maybe I don't understand you as well as I thought."

He walked to the door. "I'll pick it up Saturday morning before I open the Corner Market for the day."

As he passed, she touched his arm. "Zachary, thank you . . . for helping Boompah. It means a lot."

Taking a chance, he bent and kissed her cheek. "And I'm not going to apologize for that one."

He could hear the bells jingle behind him as he descended the limestone steps to the street. Nick and Montgomery waved from the corner where they were chatting with Al, the fellow who ran the gas station up the street. As Zachary passed, he tapped the boy on the shoulder and whispered in his ear.

"I kissed your mom."

The green eyes lit up. "Did she like it?"

"I don't know—but I sure did."

As Nick laughed, Zachary crossed the street toward the Corner Market. For some reason, he felt like his feet were three inches off the ground.

༜

The Saturday morning sunrise cast a pink glow on the ivy-covered brickwork of Chalmers House. Rather than entering Finders Keepers through the door that connected her house to the shop, Elizabeth had chosen to walk the long way around through the yard. She always loved the early hour and the silent peace that accompanied it. This morning, more than any other, she felt the need for divine composure.

Leaning against the shop's wall, she drank in the intricate, white fretwork that graced the mansion's deep front porch. The arched windows with their stained-glass frames glittered like jewels. The iron fretwork of the widow's walk formed a delicate black embroidery on the roofline. The old house was a gem, a masterpiece of Victorian architecture. Elizabeth tried to imagine it gone.

Construction machinery. The pink bricks crumbled to dust. The massive oak staircase smashed and splintered. The sparkling glass windows shattered. The wooden gingerbread tangled on the ground like a heap of fallen lace. Grace's beloved lilacs and forsythias uprooted. The spicy pink dianthus ground under the iron tread of a bulldozer.

And then what? A new building would rise with sharp, modern angles and mirrored windows. The blacktopped parking lot in front of it would be marked with even yellow lines. Boxwoods and yews would be planted along the foundation—easy maintenance and no flowers to litter the tidy lot. A sign would be erected near the street, something bold, graphic, easy to read from a distance.

Elizabeth rubbed her hands over her arms, chilled in the early morning breeze. How could she allow this to happen? How could such destruction be the will of God? And why—in the name of all that was right and sensible—couldn't she get Zachary Chalmers out of her mind?

Closing her eyes to block out the mansion, Elizabeth lifted up a prayer for understanding and peace. Zachary's insight into her life had been uncomfortably close to the truth. She *was* lonely. She *did* long for a family of her own, a normal family with two parents and bunches of children. And she was uncomfortable with change. In fact, she had structured her whole world around the ultimate goal of stability.

But Zachary had come barging in with his new ideas, his charming grin, and his persistent pursuit. The man was competent, wealthy, and handsome enough to attract any woman he chose. So why had he chosen Elizabeth?

If only he would prove to be a bloodsucking bleach! Instead, he knelt to chat with Nick as though the child's conversation genuinely interested him. He stopped by Boompah's house to check on the sick old man, and then he took over running the Corner Market during his vacation. He apologized, drank tea, wore blue jeans to work, toted groceries to Mrs. McCann's house, and generally proved himself totally wonderful in every way.

And those kisses. Elizabeth covered her mouth with her hand. *Oh, God, please help me to remember Grace and her beautiful mansion this morning when Zachary comes to pick up his cupboard. Please don't let me think about his green eyes or his thick hair or—*

"There you are!" The man himself rounded the corner of the store. "I've been waiting out front for you. I was afraid you'd forgotten me."

Not a chance. Elizabeth's heart constricted as Zachary sauntered toward her, mesmerizing in a blue denim shirt and jeans, his dark hair damp from his morning shower, his eyes locked on her face. No man had the right to look that good.

"Am I interrupting something?" he asked. "I don't mean to disturb you."

You do disturb me! she wanted to shout. *You've interrupted my whole life. You've knocked everything topsy-turvy and left me reeling with confusion and uncertainty and feelings I never knew I had! Go away and leave me alone. Let me have my old existence back.*

"You're looking well this morning, Elizabeth." He leaned one shoulder against the brick wall and hooked his hands in his pockets. "I hope I didn't get you out of bed too early."

"No," she managed. "I'm usually up. Nick loves cartoons."

He gave a laugh that curled into her chest and wrapped around her heart. "Me, too. I used to think Saturday mornings were right next to heaven. Popeye, Mighty Mouse, Donald Duck—they were my pals."

"Nick carries around a collection of books with cartoon animals on them. He props them up near him so they can be a part of whatever he's doing. I think it's his way of having secret friends."

"Bobo." With a slightly embarrassed grin, he raked a hand through his hair. "Bobo was this little yellow chicken some lady gave me when I was about five years old. He was real soft, and when you tilted him, he kind of made this *eep eep* sound. I took him everywhere."

"Do you still have him?"

His face sobered. "Nah. Kid's stuff, you know."

"What happened to Bobo, Zachary? Did you lose him?"

Straightening away from the wall, he shrugged. "Hey, I need to open up the market in a few minutes."

Elizabeth frowned. As he turned to go, she touched his shoulder. "Zachary?"

When he swung around, she was struck by the sadness in his eyes. "It was just a dumb stuffed animal."

"Where is Bobo?" Suddenly it seemed the most important question in the world.

He looked away, his focus on the mansion. "When I was thirteen, things got . . . they got a little rough around my house. Financially and in other ways. I moved out. The toy didn't make the transition."

"You moved out of your house when you were thirteen years old?"

"Foster care. The state took over my upbringing. Hey, it happens."

"Oh, Zachary." She ached to throw her arms around him. "I'm so sorry."

"No big deal. You learn to go with the flow. I carved my own path through those years. In a way, it was good for me. I made plans, decided who I wanted to be, what my goals were, and then I set out to make them happen."

"But your parents. Didn't they—"

"No, they didn't. Whatever you were going to ask, the answer is no. They didn't need me, didn't miss me, didn't anything. I was the oldest kid, and I was the one most able to fend for himself. It's OK, Elizabeth. I've put all that behind me."

He turned again and headed for the front of the shop. Elizabeth followed, her thoughts reeling. Zachary's words certainly explained a lot of things about him. His drive to succeed. His affinity for Nick. His lack of tenderness toward things that might evoke the past. Of course he didn't care about his Aunt Grace. Maybe if she'd stepped in with some money when he was a child, he wouldn't have been forced out of his family. Now, her estate probably seemed like too little too late.

"Hey, don't dwell on what I told you," he said, touching her arm and drawing her from her reverie. "A lot of people go through rough times. It was just a toy chicken, anyhow."

She fished her key out of her pocket and opened the door. "Bobo wasn't just a toy," she said softly. "He was your childhood."

Leaving him, she began the familiar ritual of turning on the lamps. As she approached the white cabinet, she realized Zachary was standing beside it, staring at her. She turned the hand-carved wooden latch that opened the matched pair of glass doors. Taking a chamois, she carefully dusted the shelves and gave the cabinet's work surface a polish. She knew Zachary was renting an apartment on the outskirts of town, and she wondered where he planned to display the piece.

"There you go," she said. "Plenty of room for your teacup."

He took her hand and turned her to face him. "Elizabeth, how can I make peace with you about the mansion?"

Her heart began to hammer, and she tried to concentrate on his words. She couldn't think about him as a man. She couldn't think about that kiss. He was her adversary, and he was offering to negotiate a truce. God had presented an answer to her prayers, and now she had to focus on giving the right response.

"It's like a barrier between us," he went on, "and I'd like to resolve it. The fact is, I'd like to see more of you, Elizabeth. Maybe take you to dinner sometime. Go to a movie."

"I don't really have time for socializing—"

"Dating."

"No, I can't. I'm a mother. Nick needs me."

"Maybe I need you."

"You don't need me. You've got your whole life out there, remember? All your plans and goals. Besides, I'm really set in my ways. The proverbial old maid, you know."

"I don't believe that for a second. I think if I asked you out to dinner, you'd say yes."

"Well, I . . ." She looked down at her feet. *Dear God, please help me out here! I'm drowning in this man's green eyes.*

"So about the house next door," he said. "Are you going to be able to let me build my office there?" Suddenly uncomfortable holding Zachary's hand, Elizabeth pulled free.

"Let me buy the mansion from you, Zachary," she said. "I've been wanting to expand. I'd like to put in a small tea shop and carry some new gift items and specialty books. I could expand my inventory and advertise in St. Louis and Kansas City. I inherited some money from my grandmother when she passed away. It's not much, but I can probably manage the down payment. You could use what you make off the mansion to buy a lot and build your dream office."

"But I want the lot next door."

"Why?"

"Location. It's on the town square. It's flat land. It's prime real estate." He let out a breath. "OK, the truth? No one ever gave me anything before, Elizabeth. Other than that toy chicken. My clothes and toys were thrift-shop specials or hand-me-downs. The government paid my foster parents to feed and board me. I worked my way through college. I took out bank loans to start my business. Everything I've ever had as an adult, I've had to work for. But when my aunt died, that little square of land became mine—not because I'd earned it. Because of who I am. It's my little patch of the world, and I'm going to build my dreams on it."

"But Grace didn't leave you just a piece of land. She left you her home."

"I don't want a home. I don't need a home. Please try to see that, Elizabeth."

She closed the cabinet's glass doors and turned the latch into place. "You *do* need a home," she said. "You, more than anyone else, need a home. Maybe Grace heard what happened to you when you were a boy. Maybe that's why she left you the mansion. Remember what she wrote in the note I found in her Bible?"

To her surprise, he dug his wallet from his pocket and slipped out the folded letter. "'I think of my home,'" he read, "'and the many years I have lived within these walls. It is only an earthly treasure, but I do hope it will live on to bless others as it has blessed me. I pray that Zachary . . .'" He lifted his head. "Why would she pray for me?"

Elizabeth smiled. "Nick says it's because she loved you."

"She didn't even know me."

"Are you sure? She was your father's sister. Maybe he never bothered to speak her name, but clearly she knew about you. She cared about you, too. She wanted you to have her most precious treasure."

"If she'd known anything about me, she'd have understood that I wouldn't want a tumbledown old mansion on my hands. It's a money drain. An eyesore. Even a danger

zone. Elizabeth, I intend to establish my future on that lot
next door. Does that goal have to come between you and
me?"

The warmth in his eyes touched her to the core. What
was it in this man that stirred her heart so? They had nothing in common. Nothing but lonely childhoods, the loss of
their parents, the battle for survival, a stubbornness that
refused to bend, an affection for a small town and its inhab-
itants, tenderness for a little green-eyed boy . . .

"Elizabeth, you smell like flowers," he said, stepping
closer and cupping her shoulder in his warm hand. "I try
not to think about you, but that scent—"

"Gardenias and roses."

"It stays with me . . ."

"Lily of the valley, vanilla . . ."

"And then I remember how it felt to kiss you." His gaze
searched hers. "I've never been a patient man."

"But it wouldn't be—"

"Yes, it would. It would be good between us, Elizabeth.
You and me."

She drank down a ragged breath. "Zachary, I never
intended to let anyone into my life. I've been happy. I don't
want to . . . to change."

He gathered her closer. "I think you do," he murmured
against her ear. "I think you want a lot of things. You're just
scared."

"Shouldn't I be?" She put her hands on his arms.
"Zachary, please don't push me. You're right, OK? I'm
lonely and a little tired of managing everything on my own.
I wouldn't mind going out to dinner with you. But where
would that lead? I'm not willing to have a casually intimate
relationship, and I don't want commitment."

"Relationship. Commitment. What about fun? Wouldn't
you like to have a little fun once in a while?"

"Kissing you is not fun." She glanced aside. "It's dangerous."

She could feel the chuckle rise from deep in his chest. "You got that right."

"I never do anything lightly, Zachary."

"Maybe you should."

"Maybe." She moved away from him. "That letter from your Aunt Grace was in her Bible. This Bible." She picked up the heavy leather-bound book that had taken a permanent place on her glass-topped counter. "This is my guidebook. It's pretty serious business, you might recall if you've ever read it."

"I've read it. I'm a Christian, too, Elizabeth. I go to church once in a while. Hey, I even designed a church building in downtown Jefferson City." He walked toward her. "It's not like I've asked you to sin or anything. I said I'd like to take you to dinner. I'd like to kiss you again. Is there anything wrong with that?"

"What's in your heart? Where's your personal commitment? Who's guiding your life? In the end, that's a whole lot more important to me than having fun and eating out and kissing."

"Fine. We won't go out." He searched the room. "You got a dolly so I can move this cabinet out of here?"

"Yoo-hoo!" Pearlene Fox pushed open the front door with a jingle of brass bells. "I thought I'd find you in here, Mr. Chalmers. I was out sweeping my sidewalk, and I spotted Ruby McCann at the Corner Market, banging on the door. You know how she is about her groceries. Likes 'em fresh. And I thought I'd seen you over here in front of Liz's place this morning early. Phil's been so busy getting ready for the city council meeting next week he's hardly taken his nose out of his notes, but he said it was you, all right. I didn't want to interrupt anything, but if Ruby doesn't get her morning milk, she's likely to have a hissy fit."

Elizabeth wheeled the orange dolly up to the cabinet and touched Zachary's arm. Without a word, he loaded his purchase and headed for the front door.

"You weren't interrupting anything, Pearlene," Elizabeth said. "Zachary was picking up his cabinet. That's all."

"You heard the woman," Zachary said to Pearlene. "That's all."

6
Six

"There's Zachary," Nick announced for all to hear as church let out after Sunday morning services. "He came, Mom! I told him he couldn't be my daddy unless he came to church, so he's here."

"Zachary Chalmers is not here because he wants to be your father, Nick." Elizabeth took her son's hand and slipped quickly through the crowd filing out the front door of Ambleside Chapel. "Say hello to the preacher, and let's get going. Boompah's expecting us."

"But I want to talk to Zachary."

"No!" she snapped. Bad enough she'd had to endure Pearlene's lengthy inquiry the day before. Then Bud Huff had commented on his own sighting of Elizabeth and Zachary as he drove out with Al to do some fishing at the family's farm. When Elizabeth stopped at the drugstore to buy party napkins and paper plates for the upcoming church picnic, Cleo Mueller had asked how she and the "new boy in town" were getting along. And Ruby McCann had quirked an eyebrow at Elizabeth as she stepped into the Sunday school classroom that morning. Ruby kept the attendance roster, and she made it her business to know the doings of everybody in town—for ministry reasons, of course.

"Good mornin', Elizabeth," Pastor Paul said, taking her hand. "And how's Nikolai today?"

"The nachos tried to kill Boompah's family," Nick stated.

"Well, well, how about that?" The kindly bald-headed

preacher smiled as if in perfect understanding. His eyes twinkled from behind his round-framed glasses. "You doing all right, Elizabeth?"

"Fine," she mumbled. "I'm fine."

"You know, you could do with a rest, young lady. Why don't you take some time off this summer? Have a little fun."

"I don't need any more fun than I'm already having," she said, her voice harsher than she intended. She shook her head. "I'm sorry, Pastor, I've been stressed out lately."

"The Lord asks to bear the load of the heavy laden, Elizabeth."

"I'll try to give it to him."

"No, *don't* try so hard. That's the idea." With a smile that radiated beyond his heavy brown beard, the pastor turned to greet the next person in line. "Good to see you here this morning, Mr. Chalmers. Did you sign the guest card?"

"Sure did."

"Then I'll be paying you a visit. Better get your ducks in a row."

"My ducks are in a row—and I know how to have fun. Unlike some people."

Elizabeth rolled her eyes as she hurried down the steps to the sidewalk. What was the big deal about having fun? She had always enjoyed running her business, and she loved being a mother. That was fun enough. *Lord, please let that be enough.*

"Hi, Zachary!" Nick called over his shoulder as his mother fairly dragged him across the street. "We're going to Boompah's house to take him some lunch. He's still sick."

"Tell him hello for me. I'll be by to visit him later this afternoon."

Unwilling to even look at the man, Elizabeth hurried her son up onto the sidewalk of the courthouse. She could hear Zachary's footsteps behind them, quickly closing the space.

What did he want now? Hadn't she made it clear where she stood? There would be no more flirtation, no more banter, and no more kisses.

"Hey, Elizabeth," he said, taking his place at her shoulder. "I put the cabinet in my kitchen. The teacup looks great."

"I'm so happy for you."

"Ooo, cold."

She glanced over at him. *Shouldn't have done that!* He was wearing a white shirt, unbuttoned at the neck, his navy-and-gold striped tie hanging loose. A shock of dark hair fell onto his forehead. His green eyes twinkled.

"Did you need to ask me something?" she queried.

"Nope, I just wanted everybody to see the two of us walking together. Sort of spice up the local gossip, if you know what I mean."

"It's spicy enough, thank you." They arrived at the street corner. "Excuse me, but Nick and I have an engagement."

"A date?"

"It's Boompah."

"Well, if he gets to see you, why shouldn't I?"

"Because he's Boompah, and you're you."

"How about Dandy Donuts? You and I could eat breakfast there some morning before we open up our respective places of business."

She paused before stepping down into the street. "Zachary, please."

"It's just a thought. I'm going to take another week's vacation to work at the Corner Market. We've both got to eat breakfast early. Why not do it together?"

"It's a good idea, Mom," Nick put in. "You like donuts. You like the ones with chocolate on top. I know you do, even though you tell me that donuts don't have any tradition."

"Nutrition," Elizabeth corrected. "And Nick, this conversation is not your business, is it?"

"But if Zachary is going to be my dad . . ."

"Oh, Nick!" She glared at her son. "Do you need to sit in time-out for a few minutes?"

"But I didn't mean to block the hole in the drain."

"What hole? Which drain?"

"That drain in the backyard. It was leaking through the hole, so I put a rock in it."

"Drains are supposed to leak! Water drains out of them; that's why they're called drains." Her heart in her throat, Elizabeth gave Zachary a cursory glance. "I have to get home and check my pipes."

She could hear the man chuckling behind her as she hurried her son across the street. So, who needed fun? With Nick, she had about all the excitement she could handle.

❧

Visiting Phil Fox was the last thing Elizabeth wanted to do. The *Ambleside Daily Herald,* which came out once a week these days, had carried the report of the May city council meeting held the past Monday night. As Elizabeth read it, her veins ran with ice. Phil had proposed moving the cannon from the town square, cutting away the entire lawn, and putting in a parking lot. But to Elizabeth, it was an impossible plan.

Summoning her resolve, she pushed open the barbershop/bus-station door and stepped inside. Cavernous, dimly lit, and smelling of old luggage and shaving cream, the building carried a dankness that oppressed the spirit.

"Phil?" She glanced at the line of three swivel barber chairs, upholstered in cracked red vinyl. Empty. Turning, she scanned the bus-station section. Its row of chromed steel chairs joined at the legs was empty as well. The counter was deserted, its surface stacked with bus schedules. On the wall behind it hung torn, dingy maps. The loose linoleum beneath Elizabeth's feet made a slapping sound as she

walked toward the soda machine and blinking pinball game
on the far wall.

"How can I help you?" Phil came through a door she
hadn't noticed. "Oh, hey there, Liz. What's up?" A dollop of
mayonnaise hung from the corner of his mustache. He'd
been eating a chicken salad sandwich, no doubt—even
though he was the one who claimed Ez left the mayonnaise
jar out too long.

"I read the city council story in this week's *Daily Herald*,"
she began. "I don't want anything to happen to the cannon.
I don't want a parking lot at all! If you take out a corner of
the courthouse lawn, Ambleside's not going to have a town
square. It'll have a town *L*."

He laughed and licked at the mayonnaise with his
tongue. "Aw, Liz, you're quite a gal, you know that? An *L?*
Who but you would've thought of that?" He motioned her
toward the ticket counter. "Come here and let me show you
something. Pearlene told me you've been on a tear lately.
She says you're too young for it to be *that* time of life, so it
must be love. Now I know you and Zachary have been having your little troubles, but let me tell you something. He is
one fine young man. Look here at what we sketched out
one day in his office. Come to think of it, it was the day
you came by looking for Nick and his little redhead friend,
remember? Take a look at this, and see if you don't change
your mind about things."

He unrolled a large sheet of paper and spread it across
the ticket counter. Elizabeth leaned over, peering at the grid
work of lines and squares and tiny labels. It was Ambleside.

"Now this here'd be the square with the parking lot," Phil
said, running a stubby finger over the center of the sketch.
"See how many cars a body could fit in there? And then if
we move out some of these businesses that don't have any
place in a modern town, we can move in some up-and-

coming operations, Liz. We don't want Ambleside to fall behind the times."

Elizabeth tried to listen as the man rambled on about his plans for the town, but her focus had wandered to another part of the sketch. Finders Keepers was gone. A sprawling architecture building filled half the block, and a ladies' boutique filled the other half. There was no antiques shop. No attached apartment at the back. No yard with a swing and a sandbox.

"Where's my store?" she cut in, jamming her finger on the Walnut Street location. "What have you done with Finders Keepers?"

He rubbed the back of his neck. "Well, this was drawn in a hurry, Liz. We didn't have time to put in *every* store. I'm sure you'll be there, though. You might want to think about moving out to the edge of town one of these days. You'd catch the traffic going to and from Jeff City. And your customers wouldn't be fighting with Pearlene's for parking spaces."

"Phil, I want you to put me on the agenda for the next city council meeting," she said. "I want to talk to the council about this plan."

"This plan isn't before the council yet, Liz. It's just an idea. Just something Zachary and I whipped out the other day. I thought you'd get the vision for it."

"Put me on the agenda. I've made my home in this town, and I'll fight to keep it just the way it is."

"Drats." He began rolling the paper. "Zachary said you were a pain in the neck, but I didn't believe him till I saw it for myself."

"He said that?"

"Something like it. And Pearlene, too." He wound a green rubber band around his plan. "You know what you need? You need to relax. Have a little fun."

"Fun? I'll tell you about fun. Fun was when Grace was

alive, and Zachary Chalmers hadn't set foot in this town, and you weren't cooking up your ridiculous plans. That was fun, and that's how it's going to be again—if I have anything to do with it."

Tucking her purse under her arm, she swung around and headed for the door.

"You're never going to bring Grace back," Phil called after her. "You know that, don't you?"

☙

Zachary pressed the button that released the newly refurbished green-striped awning and began to roll down the shade over the Corner Market's big windows. Though he had to get up at these early morning hours and he'd given up his vacation in order to help Jacob Jungemeyer out of a bad spot, he actually enjoyed running the little grocery store. Not only was it interesting to keep up with the constantly changing stock and to manage the flow of finances, but he liked the contact with all the folks who stopped by to purchase their groceries each day.

And in Ambleside, people didn't do a week's shopping all at once. They shopped every day.

The morning began with Ruby McCann arriving for her pint of fresh milk. Pretty soon, Ez dropped by to pick up a jar of mayonnaise or an extra can of coffee for the Nifty. Then the stay-at-home moms began to filter in with their preschoolers in tow. Zachary followed Boompah's tradition of giving each child a lollipop.

At noon, people would wander into the market to pick up a newspaper or buy an apple to go with their sack lunch. Teenagers appeared shortly after school let out, and they'd purchase sodas, gum, sticks of beef jerky, and bags of potato chips. In the evening, the working people would make their stops for last-minute dinner needs—a can of peas, a head of lettuce, a carton of ice cream. And then it was time to roll up the awning, lock the doors, and head to the car.

But it was the visits with Boompah that probably meant the most, Zachary realized as he pushed the fresh-fruit cart out the front door. At first, the old man had focused on filling in his substitute on the details of running the market. Before long, however, their conversations had turned to telling stories, trading jokes, and reminiscing on the past. Zachary liked Boompah. Liked him a lot. And he was hoping his friend could get back on his feet before long.

"Umm, hi, Zachary." The familiar voice caught him by surprise. He turned from the fruit cart to find Elizabeth Hayes standing in the pink light of postdawn, her son at her side. "I . . . uhh . . . I was thinking about breakfast."

"We want you to go to Dandy Donuts with us," Nick clarified. "We want to talk to you about the plans for the town. It is not a date. And it is nothing to get excited about."

Zachary smiled down at the little fellow with the shaggy black hair and broad grin. "Hey, Nick. Aren't you going to school today?"

"We need to have breakfast first. I usually go over to Magunnery's house and walk to school with her, but they all went to Texas because they think Magunnery's mommy has cancer."

Zachary glanced up at Elizabeth. "Cancer?"

"They just found out. It's a brain tumor. She's in Houston at M. D. Anderson, and it's apparently pretty serious. Montgomery will be coming back here tomorrow to stay with us while Luke and Ellie are away. We're looking forward to that, aren't we, Nick?"

"Cancer can make you die," the child said. "Is that right, Zachary?"

"Well, a lot of people are cured of cancer these days."

"But you could die."

"Yes, you could."

Nick stared across the street, a forlorn expression on his face. Zachary felt his heart turn over. Losses. This little boy's life had been filled with losses, and now another one loomed on the horizon.

"Dandy Donuts would hit the spot," Zachary said in the most cheerful voice he could muster. "I'll buy."

"I'm buying breakfast," she informed him. "I want to talk to you about something."

"The mansion?"

"Duh," Nick said.

"I was over at the barber shop visiting with Phil Fox a couple days ago," Elizabeth continued, as they strolled toward the donut shop. "He told me about the plans for the town."

"Yeah, I read that in the *Herald*. He wants to put a parking lot where the cannon is now. I don't know about that idea. I think it really does a number on the symmetry of the town square." He shook his head. "It wouldn't even be a square anymore. It'd be an *L*."

Elizabeth's blue eyes widened, and the hint of a smile crossed her face. "That's what I told Phil."

"You mean we agree on something? We'd better call the *Herald* and have them put it in the headlines."

"Seriously, Zachary, I think the parking lot is a terrible idea."

"I don't get the point of it either. The answer to the parking problems in Ambleside is obvious."

"It is?"

"Sure. The parallel spaces around the square are inefficient. What the town needs to do is convert to angled parking. It wouldn't be hard. You'd need to eliminate the strip of grass that runs between the sidewalk and the curb, and then you'd have enough room to repave the streets and paint new parking lines."

"You wouldn't get rid of the sidewalks?"

"A small town has to have sidewalks. Hey, 90 percent of the customer traffic at the Corner Market is walk-in. You can't have all those people roaming the streets. That strip of grass is impractical anyway—too narrow to mow easily. Why not get rid of it? You'd double the parking spaces, and you wouldn't have all the cars running up onto the curb trying to parallel park. You ought to see Ruby McCann maneuvering that big De Soto of hers into one of those spaces. It's a wonder she hasn't run somebody down."

As he opened the door to the donut shop, Zachary realized that Elizabeth's face was lit up like a bonfire. Anyone would have thought he'd just offered her a million dollars. She waved happily at Viola, who ran the little bake shop, and then she practically bounced down onto the booth seat.

"Angled parking!" she said, scooting her son close beside her. "Of course!"

"I would like my usual, please," Nick announced.

Viola scribbled onto her little pad. "How about you, Liz? Chocolate covered? I know, I know, they don't have much—"

"Tradition," Nick butted in. "You better give her two. My mom likes them a lot."

"Two it is, and for you, Zachary?" Viola adjusted her enormous wire-framed glasses and peered down at him.

"Three donuts. Cinnamon sugar, powdered sugar, and one surprise."

"*Your* usual." She laughed. "I'll swan, you folks sure do make a good-lookin' little family. I guess it's true what everyone's been saying. Well, I'll be back in a minute."

Elizabeth's bonfire died out. "I don't know why the people in this town have to gossip about things that are none of their business. What happened to the right of privacy?"

"Not operative in Ambleside." Zachary winked at Viola as she brought their donuts, then poured their coffee and a half cup for Nick. "That's the joy of a small town, you know? Things never change."

Elizabeth stirred her coffee, and Zachary found himself enjoying the sight of her slender fingers. As she absently tucked Nick's napkin into the collar of his shirt and moved his coffee cup away from the edge of the table, Zachary imagined what it would feel like to know this woman's soft touch. She'd laid her hands on his arms once or twice, but her touch was only to push him away.

"Phil Fox showed me a diagram of Ambleside, and he says you drew it. So, did you?"

Zachary took a quick bite of donut. He didn't have any idea what Elizabeth had been talking about. Lost in the image of her caress, he'd drifted off to a place of quiet and warmth, a place in which parking lots had no business.

What was it about Elizabeth that compelled him? Was it the fact that she was a good mother—tender, loving, gentle? He'd missed out on good mothering, so maybe that was all he was looking for. On the other hand, she was incredibly attractive . . .

"Zachary, are you listening to me?" She tapped the side of her spoon on the white coffee cup. "I asked you a question. Did you do that drawing Phil Fox has over at his barber shop?"

He tried to focus. "Um, that day Nick and Montgomery came by . . . yeah, I gave Phil and the kids some paper to draw on. I was in the middle of a project, and I needed to keep them all busy until I finished my work. Why?"

"Then you didn't erase Finders Keepers from Walnut Street?"

"Why would I do that?"

"To put in your office."

"And lose you for a neighbor? No way." He reflected on that afternoon. "Phil has a bunch of ideas about what he'd like to see happen in Ambleside. Computer stores and copy centers—that kind of thing. I don't know. I didn't give him a lot of attention, to tell you the truth."

"You didn't?" Her hand shot across the table and grabbed his. "Oh, Zachary! I'm so glad. I mean, I really believe we need a drugstore, even if Cleo Mueller is getting old. Viola relies on her income from the bakery to provide for her family. Her husband's disabled, you know. And how would we function without the Corner Market?"

"Without the Corner Market? What are you talking about?"

"Phil wants to tear it down and put in a chain store."

He stared at her. "Tear down Boompah's market? Is he nuts? He can't tear down the market. It's one of the corner-stones of this town. People rely on it. Boompah relies on it, and he's not done-for yet."

"Maybe Boompah has a brain tuber," Nick said solemnly. "Maybe he will get sick like Magunnery's mom."

"Boompah doesn't have cancer," Zachary assured him. "He's just feeling his age a little. He'll be back. He's been sitting up in his chair some, and he even hobbles around a little."

Elizabeth's fingers closed tightly around his. "Zachary, lis-ten to yourself. You're talking about the market the way I talk about the mansion. Both of them belong to Ambleside. Both of them need to stay."

"Well, well, well, isn't this a lovely sight?" Ruby McCann folded her hands at the wrist and smiled down at the three people in the booth. Her white hair glowed like a cloud above skin that reminded Zachary of the old leather binding of one of the books in her library. She was wearing a gray jacket buttoned to the throat and pinned with a large brooch of rhinestones and faux pearls.

"Mr. Chalmers, have you forgotten about my milk again this morning?" she asked.

Zachary glanced at his watch. "Whoops, gotta go."

"You know, Grace Chalmers was never tardy with anything," she said. "You certainly don't take after her."

"I guess not." He stood and gave Nick's head a tousle. "But then, I wouldn't really know. I never met my aunt."

"Oh yes you did," Ruby said, turning to go. "You certainly did. On several occasions. And you loved her dearly."

Zachary stared after the old woman. Had he heard her right? Or was she a little confused? Either way, they were going to have to have a talk.

SEVEN

Zachary hadn't been a regular churchgoer for years, but a couple of visits to Ambleside Chapel had reminded him of a few things he had known as a teenager. Church was a good place to hang out if you wanted to be near a gal you had your eye on. Church people—for the most part—had kind hearts and would help you out if they weren't too busy. And church was a great source of food.

Step into a Sunday school room, and you'd be surrounded by the rich aromas of hot cinnamon rolls and percolating coffee. Attend a Wednesday night prayer meeting, and you might be greeted by tables spread with hot casserole dishes containing the most tastebud-tickling treats imaginable. And then there were those church picnics.

Zachary lifted a cooler from the trunk of his car and walked across Mansion Street to the park. He had identified his goals for this Sunday afternoon, and they numbered three. First, eat as much good home cookin' as possible. Second, track down Ruby McCann and get her to explain that comment she'd made on Friday about his Aunt Grace. He'd tried to pin the librarian on it Saturday morning at the market when she came to pick up her milk, but she wouldn't budge an inch. Tight-lipped all the way.

And third, of course, hang around Elizabeth Hayes. At their previous encounter in the donut shop, something amazing had happened between them. They hadn't argued. They hadn't even disagreed. Instead, they'd laughed, discussed the town, chatted like old friends. And Elizabeth had held Zachary's hand.

This chain of events needed to continue, Zachary had decided. He liked it a lot. Liked Elizabeth and her pretty blue eyes. Liked her spunk. Liked her spirit of dedication to a cause and her respect for her faith. And he liked Nick. That was one amazing little kid.

Spotting the boy headed for the swing set, Zachary trotted across the freshly mown grass of the decades-old park. "Hey, Nick!" he called. "How's it going?"

The child's green eyes lit up. He veered from his course toward the swings and raced to Zachary. "You came to the picnic!"

"I had to see you, buddy."

Nick threw his arms around the man and gave him a loud smacking kiss on the arm. "Look, Magunnery came back from Texas! She's staying with us. She sleeps on the couch in the living room."

Zachary knelt. "How's her mom?"

"The brain tuber is very bad. They're going to do research tomorrow."

"Surgery," a gentle voice corrected. "Not *research,* Nick, *surgery.*"

Zachary looked up to find Elizabeth standing beside him, looking great in a pair of denim cutoffs and a simple blue T-shirt, with her hair caught up in a ponytail.

"Hey, Zachary," she said.

She could have knocked him over with a breath. "Wow. This is not what you were wearing at church this morning."

"It's a picnic, silly." She bent over and took Nick's shoulders. "Why don't you go play with Montgomery, sweetheart? She's right over there."

Nick frowned. "But now she's swinging with Herod."

"You can swing with both girls, can't you?"

The boy shrugged. "Herod is not nice to me, but I will try

to be her friend even if she calls me a bad name. And I promise I will not pinch her."

As he ran off, Zachary stood. "Herod?"

"Heather. She's in Nick's class at school. Unlike Montgomery, she's very conscious of Nick's differences. She makes fun of his accent, and she teases him when he says something wrong."

"Herod's a good name for her. I don't like her already."

She smiled. "That's life for Nick, you know. He's going to have to learn to battle his way past the Herods of this world."

"He will. He's tough."

"I'm afraid Montgomery's the one to worry about. Her mom's prognosis is bad. They'll do surgery and radiation, but her dad told me the doctors think this is a fast-growing type of tumor. They don't know if they can eliminate it."

"How's he holding up?"

"Not well." Elizabeth stuck her hands in her back pockets and walked beside him to the picnic tables. "I think his faith is all that's keeping him going. Luke is a deacon at Ambleside Chapel, and he's one of the strongest Christians I know. Everyone at church has been praying for the family."

Zachary set the cooler on a table. He had forgotten that this was yet another aspect of churchgoing. Though he'd heard about such loving care and support, he'd never personally known the touch of a church family. A circle of friends surrounded anyone who was hurting or in need. Prayers would be lifted up, meals brought in, children looked after.

Of course, if you were living in a foster home, wearing hand-me-downs and not bathing on a regular basis, you might find yourself in the same boat as Nick was with Herod. People in church would greet you at the door, maybe smile at you, but they weren't likely to throw their

arms around you and welcome you into their homes. You
were too different.

"Montgomery's father is a carpenter," Elizabeth was saying. "Luke Easton is self-employed. He and Ellie are wonderful people, and so loving and accepting of Nick. Even
though Ellie and I never have become close friends, I'm
very concerned about their future. They're going to be in
big trouble financially, no matter what happens to Ellie. But
if she dies . . ."

"Changes." He touched her arm, wishing he could take
her into his. "They're part of life, Elizabeth, remember?"

"Changes mean losses. Loss of your little yellow toy
chicken. Loss of your family. Loss of Grace and my . . . and
my grandmother." She looked down, her lips pressed
together tightly.

"You've never told me about your grandmother."

"I loved her," she said simply. "She and Grace were a lot
alike. The other day when I went to visit Phil Fox, he said
something I didn't want to hear. It hurt me a lot, but it
explained a few things."

Zachary felt instantly protective, like an angry grizzly
bear. "What did he say to you?"

"He told me I could never bring Grace back." She
shrugged. "He's right. Saving the mansion won't help me
hold onto her. She's gone, and I have to accept that."

"Changes don't always mean losses, though."

She looked up, her blue eyes misty. "How can you say
that?"

"Well . . . I'm here. Maybe it's not the greatest trade-off.
But when my aunt died, that brought me to Ambleside. I'm
glad I came."

"You two lovebirds!" Pearlene Fox exclaimed, clasping
her hands in delight. "Liz, we're going to have to start looking through bridal magazines for a dress for you. Phil said
to me just the other day, he said, 'Pearlene, why don't you

carry any wedding gowns?' And you know, I'd never given it much thought. I mean, I carry a whole range of prom dresses. But wedding gowns? Well, most of the gals just go to Jeff City to buy their bridal outfits. I don't know, though; maybe I should get some for Très Chic. What do you think?"

Zachary thought he'd like to run.

"I'm not in the market for a wedding gown, Pearlene," Elizabeth said firmly. "And you can just tell Phil—"

"Where is Phil?" Zachary cut in, hoping to ward off a storm. "I was planning to talk to him. The other day I was over at the courthouse, and the deeds officer told me Phil had been in there doing some checking on my property."

Pearlene went white. "I'll swan, this town is so full of gossips you just never know what you're going to hear next."

"The mansion's going through probate, but I'm not anticipating any snags. Is Phil?"

"Heavens, how would I know? I just run the dress shop is all."

With a look of mixed annoyance and concern, she turned on her heel and headed off. Zachary watched her go, wondering what shade of bottled blonde she put on her hair. Truth to tell, he had a hard time liking Phil and Pearlene Fox. They considered themselves big fish in this small, pond. But they acted a lot like sharks.

"There's Pastor Paul in the pavilion," Elizabeth said. "I'm going over for the prayer."

Zachary walked beside her, recognizing yet another advantage to church attendance. A good pastor could change lives. In his experience, truly effective ministers were few and far between. But Pastor Paul had a way of reaching out and drawing in his flock that made Zachary open to becoming one of them.

Standing under a grove of towering oak trees, Zachary

bowed his head as the minister offered a prayer of thanksgiving for his congregation, for the beautiful Sunday afternoon, and for the food. It was a simple but sincere prayer, and Zachary found himself imagining how God felt when a faithful man like Pastor Paul spoke with him.

Lonely. The word filled his heart. *Lonely for you, my son*.

Zachary rubbed his eyes, confused at the echoed reverberations inside him. All around, the townsfolk were chattering again, quickly forming a line on each side of the long picnic tables, loading their Styrofoam plates with fried chicken, potato salad, pork steaks, and baked beans.

"Zachary?" Nick's small hand slipped into his. "Are you coming to eat with us? They have workshops here. I love workshops. They smell so yummy that I can almost taste them in my mouth!"

"Workshops?" Still dazed at the powerful realization of God's longing for him, Zachary made his way to the end of the line.

"Pork chops," Elizabeth said softly. "Nick's favorite."

And then Zachary started to laugh. He grabbed Nick around the shoulders and gave the boy a hug. What a cute kid. Challenging, needy, but definitely a charmer.

"Look, there's Mrs. Wrinkles!" Nick exclaimed, darting out of the line and racing across the pavilion toward a lovely young woman seated with her family at one of the long picnic tables.

"Mrs. Winkler," Elizabeth clarified. "She's Nick's English language teacher. She's been with him since the first day of school. Sometimes I think she understands him better than I do."

"Can't she get him to call her by her real name?"

"Oh, she doesn't mind. You know, there are some things about Nick that are very hard to change. He's . . . he's got a lot of special needs. Learning is difficult for him, and his social skills don't match his age."

"You knew that when you adopted him?"

"I knew he was going to have problems. A child can't live five years in a Romanian orphanage and come out unscarred. Nick was severely abused."

Zachary felt his stomach sink. "Abused?"

"Beaten, malnourished—the works. He's a tough little survivor, though. I know God has a great plan for his life. I can't wait to see what he's going to do with Nick."

Zachary followed Elizabeth through the food line, wondering what God had planned for *his* life. Had Zachary lived up to God's dreams for him? Had Zachary even tried to walk the path his heavenly Father had set out for him?

Sure, he'd had a tough childhood, raised in poverty and then sent into the foster-care system. But Nick had faced much worse. If God had a good and perfect plan for this little boy, didn't he have one just as good for Zachary?

"There's a spot over by Mrs. McCann," Elizabeth was saying, as she carried a loaded plate in each hand. "I love to sit near her. She reminds me of my grandmother."

"Does everyone remind you of your grandmother?"

"I miss Gramma a lot." She set off in the direction of a picnic table beneath a tree. Zachary decided he was going to follow, even though he hadn't been invited. He'd been wanting to talk to Ruby anyway. And, of course, there was Elizabeth with her sparkling eyes and sweet smile . . .

"This lettuce is not fresh," Mrs. McCann announced as Zachary and Elizabeth joined her. "I can hardly believe that Mrs. Zimmerman would send a wilted salad to the potluck."

Zachary fought a grin. Kaye Zimmerman ran the local beauty salon. At about five-thirty every evening, she would dash into the Corner Market and breathlessly lament her inability to put a good supper on the table for her family. Kaye's Kut-n-Kurl just took up too much of her time, she told Zachary. That probably explained the wilted lettuce.

"Maybe it's supposed to be wilted," Elizabeth was saying. "I've heard of such a thing as a wilted salad."

"Only when one can't be bothered to select a fresh head of lettuce for one's salad." Ruby McCann's brilliantly white hair gleamed in the afternoon sun, every hair perfectly placed in her curled coiffure. Zachary suspected that the librarian had a regular appointment with Kaye Zimmerman each week. But that didn't stop her from critiquing the salad.

"And how are you, Master Nikolai?" Mrs. McCann inquired as the boy skipped over to the table to take his place. "I see you have been chatting with your teacher."

"I love Mrs. Wrinkles." Nick made the statement and then plunged into his pork chops.

"And Mr. Chalmers, I understand your tenure as our local grocer is at an end?" Ruby asked.

"'Fraid so. I'd keep the market open if I could, but I've got clients waiting. Boompah's been up and about a lot lately, though. I predict he'll be running the place himself soon."

"I cannot imagine what I would do without my morning milk."

"You could buy a larger carton, Mrs. McCann. A half gallon would last you several days."

She looked at him as though he had brought in a stack of overdue books. "I am only one person, Mr. Chalmers. My beloved husband passed away twenty years ago. In case you were unaware, the new subdivision on the outskirts of town is named for him. Yes, Mr. McCann was a generous man, and he was also thrifty. I am quite certain he would agree with me that purchasing an entire half gallon of milk would be wasteful."

"Did you live in Ambleside throughout your marriage?"

"I have lived here all my life. I was born in the very house in which I reside." She held up a gnarled finger.

"Stability is a sacred thing, Mr. Chalmers. Miss Hayes recognizes that fact. You should reconsider her request to purchase the mansion from you. Tearing it down to build your office complex would be a desecration to the town and to your ancestry."

Zachary lifted his brows and had to smile in amazement. Everyone in Ambleside really did know his business. They knew about the mansion, his architectural work, his relationship with Elizabeth—everything. They probably all knew what a lousy Christian he'd been, too. What bitterness he carried toward his parents. What a self-centered, stubborn, and ambitious man he could be.

"The mansion at 100 Walnut Street was built in 1886," Mrs. McCann was saying, her eyes taking on a distant gaze. "The builder was Zachary Chalmers, your great-grandfather. He was a merchant who hailed from the town of Ambleside in northwest England's Lake District. He came to America, founded this town in which we live, and conducted a prosperous mercantile business on the Missouri River. When he was still a young man, he built the magnificent home that bears your family's surname."

Zachary looked across the park at the crumbling old house that was his legacy. "You mean I was named after the founder of Ambleside?"

"Indeed you were. It is a grand heritage you bear, young man. In the year 1890, Zachary Chalmers's wife bore a son. Caleb was your grandfather. A fine gentleman, he was. He carried on the tradition of the family and added to its holdings through his shipping enterprises. He died the year you were born."

"How do you know when I was born?"

"My dear boy, I am the librarian of this town. I make it my business to record the history of Ambleside's prominent families."

"But my family didn't even live here. I grew up in Jefferson City."

"Grace Chalmers was born in 1925," Mrs. McCann went on, seemingly oblivious to her listener. "She was a beauty even as a baby, so they say. Many years later, when Caleb and his wife had given up all hope of a son to carry on the family name, William was born."

"My father."

Mrs. McCann dabbed her lips with a paper napkin. "By then, of course, Grace had made it clear to everyone that she had no desire to ever marry."

"Why not? You said she was beautiful."

"She was unlucky in love," Nick announced around a mouthful of pork. "That's what Grace always used to tell us, huh, Mom? Unlucky in love."

"She loved a young man once, and she had hoped to marry him," Elizabeth recalled, "but her father objected."

"Why?" Zachary demanded.

"The young man was unacceptable," Ruby explained, as though that resolved the matter. "And then William, too, became such a great disappointment."

Zachary reflected on his father, the familiar image of a handsome but unsuccessful man stamped in his mind. How many fledgling businesses had William Chalmers started in Jefferson City? A restaurant, a dry cleaners, a construction company. He'd sold encyclopedias, vacuums, cleaning products, and tinned popcorn. Every time something new came along, he jumped on it, sure it was going to make him rich. Instead, more children were born, the family sank deeper into debt, and the big one never happened.

"Caleb would not have disinherited his son," Mrs. McCann said, "but William walked away from all his family had built for him. He hated Ambleside. Despised his father. Abhorred the family heritage. He was determined to make his own way in the world, young William told his father. He was going to do things *his* way. And, as you know, he did just that."

Zachary looked down at his plate and realized he'd stopped eating. Hadn't he adopted the exact same attitude as his father? William had failed, and Zachary had succeeded. But had such an attitude done either man much good?

"What about my aunt?" he asked. "You told me I'd met her many times. I don't remember that. I don't remember her at all."

Mrs. McCann's paper-thin eyelids slid shut, and she let out a deep breath. "Goodness, I am *so* full! I shall hardly have room for dessert."

"Wait." Zachary reached out and took her thin wrist as she moved to rise. "Please, Mrs. McCann. Tell me about my Aunt Grace."

Cornflower blue eyes regarded him. "When you were a little boy, sometimes your mother would take you to the park and leave you in the company of a kind caretaker. She had lovely eyes and dark hair, and she doted on you. Do you remember her?"

Zachary searched his mind. "Those swings near the trailer park . . . there was a slide . . . and a woman who caught me at the bottom . . . and she always wore a red coat."

Ruby McCann chuckled. "Oh, yes, the notorious red coat. That was her, all right. That was Grace Chalmers."

Rising like a thin wraith, the old woman gave him a half smile and slipped away toward the dessert table.

⌘

Elizabeth took Nick's hand and urged her son and his little friend from the park's playground. The sun was setting, and most of the picnickers had gone home long ago. But Nick and Montgomery were lost in the joy of their playtime, and she didn't have the heart to disrupt them.

Zachary Chalmers had left the picnic not long after he'd eaten, excusing himself quietly and saying he had some business he wanted to take care of. Elizabeth had been sorry to see the man go, but she knew he was preparing to get back to work in his office the following morning. That meant the Corner Market would be closed again, and everyone would start to grumble. Phil Fox would say, "One unreliable grocery store—that's just what's wrong with this town."

She stopped as she spotted Phil himself hailing her from the parking area near the park's gate. Great. Just who she wanted to see. Elizabeth told Nick and Montgomery to stick close as she approached the city councilman.

"Mind if I talk with you a minute, Liz?" he asked. "I felt like we had some harsh words with each other last week, and I don't want to leave things in a bad way between us."

"It's OK, Phil. I'm just concerned about the town."

"Well, I am, too, don't you know? Looks to me like we're on the same side in this matter."

"Maybe so." Elizabeth could see that Pearlene had already gone home. Phil must have returned to the park for the express purpose of having this conversation. "Well, I've got to get the kids into the bathtub, Phil. See you around."

"Just a minute, Liz." He stepped closer, his eyes somber. "I heard you went ahead and got yourself put on the agenda for next month's city council meeting. Are you planning to talk about that parking lot idea of mine?"

"I'm just going to speak on behalf of Ambleside and the town's history. I would hope the council is perceptive enough to see the value in preserving our character."

"You're talking about the square."

"And the mansion, the Corner Market, Dandy Donuts, the drugstore—all the buildings that make Ambleside such a wonderful place to live and raise a family."

"I'll tell you what, Liz; you make a persuasive speaker.

I've been giving our talk the other day a lot of thought. I agree with you that the square needs to stay square. If we move the cannon, no telling who's going to get mad. I think we need to keep our eye on Zachary Chalmers and that mansion, too. If he puts his office right there, downtown's going to get too congested."

Elizabeth held her breath. "Are you saying you don't support Zachary's plan to tear down Grace's house?"

"Not if he's planning to put in an office complex." He smiled. "Are you with me on this, Liz?"

She thought of the handsome newcomer and his dreams for the future. If she and Phil worked against him, they might just be able to put a stop to the demolition. But what would that mean to Zachary? What would it do to the growing sense of unity between the two of them? She liked Zachary Chalmers. In spite of herself, she cared about him. And worst of all, she found herself mulling over the moments of intimacy they had shared—soft laughter, gentle touches, a tender kiss . . .

"Will you work with me to fight this, Liz?" Phil was asking. "Will you help me fight for Ambleside?"

"What are you planning, Phil? I don't see how I can have much influence."

"Zachary likes you—that's plain as day. The town thinks well of you, too. And you're on the city council agenda. You could have a lot of impact." He shifted from one foot to the other. "I was checking the deeds the other day. I talked to some of the folks over at city hall, too. If we push real hard, we might could get that deed locked up for a while."

"How?"

"There's some kind of message about the mansion in the town charter. You know, it was Zachary's great-grandfather who built the house and founded the town, both. Seems he had some things written into the charter to make sure that

his house would never get torn down. Of course, a modern-
day attorney is probably going to find loopholes in that. I
talked to Sawyer-the-lawyer, and he told me those old
charters might not be considered legal documents. Most of
them have been amended and expanded out the kazoo, so
they're not too valid. All the same, we could probably hold
up Zachary's plan for a good while. And maybe we could
talk him out of building that office. We might even get the
city to buy that property."

A ripple of chills raced down Elizabeth's spine. "Are you
telling me you'd work to help the town get ownership of
the mansion?"

"That's what I'm saying."

"Phil! I can't believe you've had such a change of heart."

"I could see my notions about improving the town
weren't getting anywhere, so I decided to try a different
tack. I think this is going to work, Liz, if you'll agree to can-
cel your talk to the council and let me get busy blocking
Zachary Chalmers."

A prickle of wariness took the place of the chills. "I don't
see how it could hurt to let me speak to the council about
the historical preservation of Ambleside."

"But would it help? Don't draw attention to this issue, Liz,
until I've had a chance to get that charter into public view.
Back off, and let me work on this. Will you do that?"

Elizabeth could sense the growing restlessness of the children as they tugged on her arms and played hide-and-seek
around her legs. For some reason, she couldn't make herself trust Phil Fox. On the other hand, he was pledging to
preserve the mansion, wasn't he? What more could she
hope for?

"OK," she said. "I'll call and have my name taken off the
agenda. But I want to see that charter."

"I knew you'd go for this, Liz." He smiled beneath his
beard. "I just knew it."

As he stepped back into his car and pulled out of the parking area, Elizabeth studied the fading red taillights. She had just gained an ally. The mansion had received a stay of execution. So why didn't she feel the least bit victorious?

EIGHT

A crack of thunder rattled the single windowpane in Zachary's tiny upstairs office. He tapped his pen on the blueprint spread across his drafting table and studied the play of lightning that flickered on the brick wall outside. After a few minutes of hard rain, the roof would begin to leak, and he'd need to move his plastic wastebasket under the drip.

The sketch beneath his pen offered a welcome mental reprieve from the musty smell, the seeping water, and the dim light of his current workplace. His future office building displayed every convenience of modern architectural design. Windowpanes could be opened from the inside for cleaning. Closets virtually disappeared into walls. Files hid in false pillars. The heating system ran through the floor. Executive bathrooms sported towel warmers and doorless showers that wouldn't spatter water. The kitchen had roll-away, expandable tables, appliance garages, and a cushioned floor covering that prevented backaches.

His own office on the second floor was to look out over the park—an expanse of oak and maple trees, well-mown lawn, and winding trails. Already most of the other offices in the complex had been spoken for. Acquaintances and business colleagues in Jefferson City had put their names down to rent space in Ambleside. It would be a short drive from the capital, a quiet environment in which to work, and a quaint atmosphere in which to entertain clients.

He had labored for years on this plan, Zachary thought as

he turned to the sketch of the front view of his office. At first, he'd planned it only in his mind—a vague, hoped-for dream. And then his aunt had died and left him Chalmers House.

As he listened to the rain hitting the sidewalks below, Zachary doodled a Victorian curlicue on the post that supported the new office complex's small entry porch. Then he curved the top of each window into an arch and gave it a narrow edging of stained glass. A few more pen strokes transformed the single front door into a pair of tall, narrow doors inset with glass ovals.

He leaned back in his chair and squinted at the modified drawing. Ridiculous! Throwing down his pen, he pushed back from the table and stood. He couldn't transform his new office into a piece of Victorian gingerbread. It would look anachronistic and awkward. People would laugh, and rightly so.

Grabbing his sketchpad and umbrella, he strode toward the door. He couldn't spare the mansion. It would have to come down. The night of the church picnic, he'd gone over to the old building and wandered around inside for nearly two hours. It had been too dark to see details, but the place was clearly mildew ridden, termite eaten, and rotting. The floors squeaked, the windows rattled, doorknobs came off in his hand, the kitchen was cavernous and inefficient. The heater in the basement looked like something out of Dr. Frankenstein's laboratory.

But how could he tear it down? Zachary descended the narrow steps two at a time. Chalmers House had been built by his namesake. The founder of Ambleside had erected that mansion as a statement to the town he had established, and only people bearing the name Chalmers had lived in it. Would a Chalmers now demolish it?

In the pouring, late-afternoon rain, Zachary darted across River Street and splashed down the sidewalk past the cannon. He skirted the pavilion, crossed Walnut Street in front of Finders Keepers, and stopped to stare at his great-grandfather's legacy. As water trickled down the spines of his umbrella, he gazed at the old house, wondering if he could find answers to unspoken questions. Had the first Zachary Chalmers designed the house himself? Had he poured his dreams into its planning the way his great-grandson had planned the mansion's replacement?

Instead of searching for faults this time, Zachary had made up his mind to look for the stamp of his family. He would try to discover his great-grandfather's vision and his grandfather's hopes. Perhaps even a clue to his father's disillusionment. If the auction hadn't completely decimated the place, he might even find his aunt's red coat.

"Hello, Zachary!" Nick Hayes called from the front porch of his mother's shop. "We don't have school today. We get to stay home and play. Do you want to play with me? It's raining."

"I noticed that," Zachary said through the hollow roar of rainwater on his umbrella. "Where's Montgomery?"

"Her daddy came to get her in the middle of the night. They're flying on an airplane back to Texas. Magunnery's mommy might die soon. She doesn't have any hair, but Magunnery is not going to be scared to see her. Magunnery says her mommy is the same even without hair."

Zachary gripped the umbrella in his hand and approached the porch. "Are you sure about Montgomery's mother?"

"I'm sure. They shaved it all off."

"I mean . . . about her dying."

"Oh, yes." The boy nodded solemnly. "My mommy has been crying all day. She cried into the potato salad."

"Where's your mom now?"

"Inside. We're going to visit Boompah after the store closes. You want to come with us?"

Zachary deferred his plan for the moment as he moved into the shelter of the antiques shop's deep front porch. "Let's see if your mom will let you come over to Grace's house with me. Would you like that?"

Nick hopped off the wooden rocking chair. "Is Grace there?"

"Uhh . . . don't you remember about Grace?"

The green eyes saddened. "I remember. But I thought maybe she had come back."

"No, Nick. She's not back." Zachary pushed open the door to Finders Keepers. Death was hard enough for most people to comprehend, but Nick seemed to be having an especially difficult time making sense of it.

"Elizabeth, it's Zachary Chalmers," he called into the large room. "You here?"

She appeared from behind a wardrobe, a tissue pressed against her cheek. "Oh, hey, Zachary. Did you come to talk about the charter?"

"What charter?"

"Didn't Phil tell you?"

"Tell me what?"

"Oh, great." She turned and stared out the window at the rain for a moment. Then she shook her head and shrugged. "Can I help you with something?"

"I'm going over to the mansion for a few minutes. OK if I take Nick along?"

"I guess so. I need him back by five-thirty."

"He told me you're going to visit Boompah." Zachary stepped into the shop. "Elizabeth, I'm sorry to hear about Montgomery's mom. Nick told me."

She nodded, moving the tissue to the corner of her eye. "Ellie's a committed Christian. She'll be OK. It's Luke and Montgomery I'm really worried about."

"Is there anything I can do? I mean, for you?"

A hollow look came across her face. "Are you sure Phil

hasn't talked to you yet? He was going to tell you about the charter."

"I haven't seen Phil since the church picnic the other day. He tried to pin me down in support of his parking lot on the square, but I wouldn't go for it. An *L* is not a square, no matter what Phil says."

"But didn't he tell you he'd found a mention of Chalmers Mansion in the town charter?"

"What town charter?"

"Your great-grandfather wrote it. He put in a statement that requires the mansion to remain standing."

"OK, I'm ready to go," Nick said, taking Zachary's hand and giving it a firm tug. He had donned a yellow plastic raincoat. "I want to see Grace's house. I want to look at what's in the blue vase on the hall table. She always puts flowers in there."

Zachary stiffened. "Remain standing? Are you sure?"

"Of course I'm sure," Nick said. "In the spring she puts in dogwood branches and those yellow flowers. Daffydolls. And in the summer—"

"Elizabeth, do you mean to tell me that Phil is going to try to use this charter thing to block my inheritance of the mansion?"

"Not your inheritance," Elizabeth said. "Just the demolition."

"Then you're with him on it, aren't you?"

She glanced at the window again. "Yes," she said softly.

Biting off the harsh words that rose inside him, he slammed his hand down on the glass-topped counter. "First the letter in the Bible and now some old town charter. You're determined to keep me from my dreams, aren't you?"

"Grace had dreams long before you. Your great-grandfather had dreams when he founded this town."

"They're both dead, Elizabeth!"

"And Montgomery's mommy, too!" Nick cried out. He let out a howl that sent shivers down Zachary's spine. "Everybody's dying!"

"No, no, sweetheart." Elizabeth came across the room, arms outstretched as Zachary knelt beside the little boy.

"I'm sorry, Nick," he began. "I just—"

"But I don't want Grace to die!" Nick wailed. "I don't want Boompah to die! I don't want Ellie to die!"

"Boompah's going to be all right," Elizabeth said, taking her son into her arms. He stood as stiff as a board, his arms straight at his sides and his fingers splayed. "Nick, please try to understand, honey. Mommy and Zachary are talking about—"

"About that Bible!" Nick took a swing and knocked the black book from the counter to the floor. "That Bible makes you yell at each other. It makes you hate each other!"

"No, no, Nick, it's not the Bible. Sweetie, listen to me . . ."

"Hey, Nick," Zachary spoke up. "How about you and I head down to Boompah's store and pick out a new vase for Grace's front hall? We'll get some flowers to put in it, too. I noticed some pink ones growing in the mansion's front yard."

"Dianthus," Elizabeth said. "Grace loved them."

"How about it, Nick? I've got the key to the Corner Market right here in my pocket."

The child's shoulders sagged, and he rubbed his fist hard into one eye. "But don't fight with my mommy anymore, OK?"

"OK."

"You promise?"

Zachary let out a breath, remembering the huge stumbling block that had just been rolled across his path. "I'll do my best, Nick."

"Zachary." Elizabeth laid her hand on his arm as he

stood. "Please try to understand about the charter. Phil's only doing what he thinks is right for the town."

"Phil wants to freeze me out." He took Nick's hand and headed for the door. "The two of you may manage to put my plans on ice. But I'm not the kind of man who can be kept down for long, Elizabeth. No one's ever made me surrender—and no one ever will."

As he and Nick walked out of the antiques shop, Zachary pushed up the umbrella until it clicked open. The little boy turned and waved at his mother through the window. His small face was still pale, his green eyes luminous.

"Surrender is like 'All to Jesus I Surrender,'" Nick said. "We sing that song in church, and I think if you don't ever surrender, you're going to make God very sad, Zachary. He wants to give you the presents, but he can't if you don't surrender to him."

"Presents?" Zachary focused on the sidewalk, his heart heavy. "What presents are you talking about, Nick?"

"'All to Jesus I surrender,'" Nick sang, "'all to him I freely give. I will ever love and trust him, in his presents daily live.' If you surrender, you get the presents, see? You get Jesus to live in your heart every day. Also, you get food to eat, a bed to sleep in, a mommy to love you, and maybe you could even get me to be your very own son. Don't you think you should surrender, Zachary? I think it would be a good idea."

Zachary nodded. Yes, it might be a good idea. It just might.

❧

"Boompah! You're here!" Nick pushed through the front door of the Corner Market and raced across the gray linoleum floor. "You came back! You didn't die!"

Zachary shook the raindrops off his umbrella as Nick threw his arms around the old man, who was seated on a wooden chair behind his cash register. "We came here to get a flower vase, Zachary and me," the boy continued breathlessly. "Zachary has the key in his pocket, and we thought you still would be sick in your bed, but you're not. Are you well? Is your back better?"

"Better, ja." Boompah gave Nick's hair a rub. "And you, my little one? How is Nikolai?"

"It's raining, and we didn't have school today."

"Now they call off the school for rain?" Zachary smiled as Boompah shook his head. He didn't feel like tackling the concept of Memorial Day with the irrepressible child. "These days, they are such weaklings, these modern people," Boompah continued. "I used to ride a horse five miles to school, do you know? And sometimes the snow is up to the horse's stomach. Rain? Bah!"

"I threw up at school one time," Nick confided. "My stomach hurt a lot."

"Nick, why don't you pick out a vase?" Zachary asked, diverting the trend of the conversation as he had seen Elizabeth do so many times. "They're right over there by the school supplies."

"You know my store well now, my friend! Come sit, sit!" Boompah took Zachary's hand in both of his and urged him onto the neighboring chair. "I thank you for stepping into my shoes when I was sick. Now I think I am much better. The doctor says maybe was a little problem with my kidneys. Still is hard to stand up long times, but I need to work. Is my only way to make money, you know? And Ruby McCann needs her milk. Soft bones."

"Osteoporosis."

"She's terrified of it. Ach, getting old is no ball of wax, my son. But you? You're still young and handsome and smart. You have your whole life ahead. How does your business go? How do you and Elizabeth get along these days? And

what are you going to do with all this life God has given
you?"

"Business is good. Elizabeth . . . I don't know." Zachary
linked his fingers together loosely and studied a crack in
the linoleum. "I'm going to spend my life fighting, I guess.
Fighting for what I want—the way I always have." Then he
recalled the words of Nick's song. "Or I could surrender. I
could give up the battle and let God take over. Surrender
my dreams. Surrender my whole future."

"Surrender is defeat?"

"Seems that way."

"You think so? Did Jesus not say the first shall be last,
and the last shall be first?"

"I never understood what that meant."

"Means if you surrender, you win the battle." Boompah
took a cherry-flavored sucker from his shirt pocket and
passed it to Zachary. He unwrapped a lemon sucker and
popped it into his mouth. "Let me ask you this question, my
boy. In this battle you are fighting, is it better to try to be
the general yourself—or to give the leadership to someone
who is smarter, more powerful, and braver than you? Which
way are you more sure to win?"

Zachary shrugged. "You're saying I should surrender the
leadership but not give up the fight?"

"Never give up the battle. Onward Christian soldiers, the
hymn says. Ach, the battle is all around us, and the force of
evil is very great. Myself, I would rather yield to the greatest
leader of all creation than try to fight alone."

Zachary looked up as Nick approached, bearing a large
glass vase. "This is not as pretty as the old blue one Grace
had," he said. "This one is new and ugly."

He set it on the counter and frowned. Zachary picked up
the cheap vase and turned it around in his hands. "But
what's the battle?" he asked Boompah. "Is it a fight to keep
the mansion for myself? Is it a war against the town of

Ambleside? Is it a skirmish against Phil Fox and his loyal troops?"

"Ach, the battle is much bigger than that. Those are small things—little grenades tossed by the enemy onto the field to distract you from the greater war all around. You know this war, Zachary Chalmers. You know it well."

"Are you talking about the nachos again, Boompah?" Nick asked.

The old man took his sucker out of his mouth and gave the child a sticky kiss on the cheek. "I'm talking about the war of good against evil. The war of God against Satan. The war for the soul of every man. And that, my little Nikolai, is a battle much bigger than any battle ever fought against Hitler."

"OK, but I don't want to put Grace's flowers into that ugly vase," Nick said solemnly. "It won't look right in her front hall."

"You want we shall find a better vase for Grace's flowers?" Boompah handed the child a wrapped sucker from his pocket. "Come then. I take you to the back rooms of my market, and I show you the treasures I brought all the way from the old country many years ago. There we find a vase for Grace's flowers."

Zachary stood. "I was hoping to get over to the mansion this afternoon. I need to take a look around."

Boompah smiled around his sucker. "Ja, I know. You go, my son. I keep little Nikolai here with me. We will take a long journey to the land of our birth, he and I, and there we will see many treasures."

"Elizabeth wants Nick back at her shop by five-thirty."

"We do it, don't worry. Go, go!"

Zachary picked up his umbrella and pushed through the door into the driving rain. As he splashed across the street and down the sidewalk toward Chalmers House, he considered the offer Boompah had held out to him. Surrender the leadership of your life. But hadn't he done that years ago as a child? He was a believer already. He was a Christian, wasn't he?

∽ℛ∾

Elizabeth glanced up at the tall grandfather clock near the door. She rolled her eyes and switched off the last lamp in her shop. Leave it to Zachary Chalmers to mess things up. Now she'd have to tramp through the rain to the mansion to retrieve her son. The casserole she had made for Boompah was sitting in her oven, probably getting as dry as shoe leather. Every time she thought of the old man lying alone in that bed, her heart twisted. Was he growing better, as he claimed? Or was it possible his kidney infection might lead to something worse?

She drew a long umbrella from a nineteenth-century stand and stepped outside, pulling the door shut with a jingle of brass bells. It had been a busy day, and with Nick out of school, a tiring one. The child's questions never ended, and his drive to insert himself into every situation exhausted her.

The gloomy weather didn't help. Rain had increased from a mist in the morning to a drizzle by noon. Now it was an absolute torrent as it battered Elizabeth's umbrella, gushed down gutters, and spilled into the streets. She leaped over a small gully that was carving a new path down Grace's driveway. Under the protection of the deep front porch, she could see car lights guiding drivers home from work.

Thanks, Father, that I live behind my store, she offered up as she pushed open the mansion's front door and stepped into the gloom. *Thanks for blessings great and small.*

She could see a light in the upper hallway, so she climbed the long staircase toward it. "Nick?" she called. "It's almost six o'clock. We need to get over to Boompah's house."

"Nick's not here, Elizabeth." Zachary's voice sounded oddly emotionless. "He's with Boompah at the market."

"Zachary?" Concerned, she walked the long hall, peering into every room. "Where are you?"

She turned a corner and caught a glimpse of something red at the far end of a narrow corridor. "I told you he's not here," Zachary said over the rumble of thunder. "Boompah promised to get him home on time."

"What's Boompah doing at the market? And what are you doing there in the dark?"

"I'm just sitting here, OK? If you don't mind, I'd like a little privacy for once."

She bristled. "Have I been bothering you?"

"This whole town has been bothering me. I can't take a step without everybody tracking my footprints."

Pausing, she studied the hunched figure seated at the bottom of the attic steps, his arms wrapped around a bulky red wool coat. "Is that Grace's winter coat?"

"You tell me. I found it in the attic."

She approached him. "Grace wasn't able to get out much the last few years except for church, but I'd recognize that coat anywhere."

"Then she's the one who took me to the park when I was a kid. She's the one who gave me Bobo."

"*Grace* gave you Bobo?" Elizabeth sank onto the dusty step beside him. "Wow. Do you remember her well?"

"No. She stopped coming to see me."

"Why?"

"I don't know. Too busy, I guess." He pushed the coat aside. "But I remembered her after all these years."

"She must have remembered you, too. She gave you her house." Elizabeth looked over his shoulder up the attic stairs. "Did you find anything else?"

"Not much. A couple of pairs of shoes. An old board

game." He stood. "Well, I guess you'll be wanting to get Nick from the market."

She remained seated. "Zachary, I want you to know that Phil Fox and I—"

"Skip it. Doesn't matter."

"It does matter. You and I . . . we were just starting to connect. That morning at the donut shop, I felt like we had an understanding."

"What's to understand? You and Phil are doing everything in your power to block me."

"It's not you personally. It's just that we want to preserve Ambleside's history."

"Don't give me that. I *personally* intend to take down this old house, so I *personally* am the enemy." He leaned one hand on the door frame. "Look, Elizabeth, this is how it is. All my life I've believed in one thing. Tear down the old, and build the new. That's how life taught me, right? The old family structure wasn't working, so my parents put me out into the foster-care system to fend for myself. My heritage said education wasn't important, but I fashioned two college degrees from the rubble of that old image. My father's example taught me not to hold a job more than a few months, so I built myself a business that will withstand anything. That's my experience and my motivation. I don't dwell in the old; I get rid of it and build the new."

"Are you happy?"

"Of course I'm happy." A look of disgust crossed his face as he stared up into the attic gloom. "I don't want this old stuff trying to creep back into my life. I don't want Boompah acting like a father to me, dispensing the wisdom of the ages. I don't want to face a needy little boy day after day, reminding me of the child I used to be. I'm done with that, OK? And I don't want to care about a woman whose whole life is fixated on preserving the past and resisting change.

Old cabinets, old couches, old lamps, old Bibles, old memories . . ."

He lowered his head and shut his eyes. "I can't go backward, Elizabeth. I won't."

"It hurts."

"There's no point."

"Yes, there is. You say you're building on the rubble of the past, but I don't think you're moving forward at all. How can you build these grand worlds all by yourself? You need to let people in. You need to care and hurt and feel all the emotions that real people feel. And you need to quit trying to run your own life."

"Oh, yeah, what about you?" He swung around to face her. "You let people in? Only the safe ones. Only the ones you can control. Only the ones who won't mess up your little comfortable world where nothing changes and everything is tied up in tidy packages."

"Well, I—"

"What about someone like me, huh?" He moved toward her, and she rose and stepped back against the corridor wall. He followed. "You keep me at arm's length because I'm new to town, I have crazy ideas, I'm just too blasted risky. Grace and Boompah and your grandma are safe. They're all either old or dead. They're not going to push you or argue with you. And Nick is safe, too. He's just a kid—moldable, teachable, controllable. What are you afraid of, Elizabeth? Why do I scare you?"

She wedged her hands behind her, wishing she could hang onto something besides cold, crumbly wallpaper. "Because I might lose you," she whispered. "I can't . . . can't lose any more people that I . . . that I love."

"Oh, Elizabeth." He slipped his arms around her and pulled her to his chest. "Boompah says I need to surrender my life, but I've fought so long and so hard I don't know how to do that. I believe in God, in Jesus. I know I do."

"Christ wants more than belief, Zachary. He wants to be in charge."

His cheek brushed her eyelashes. "You're so soft," he murmured. "You're gentle. You make me want things I've pushed out of my life. Tenderness and quiet and intimacy. Hope. Love."

"Zachary." Her mind reeling, Elizabeth lifted her face to his. She felt herself sinking deeper and deeper into this man. How long had it been? How long since she'd let any man this close to her heart? The risk was so great, yet the pleasure felt so intense. So wonderful. "If you lose the battle for the house . . ."

"Then I'll leave town. Why would I stay? Please don't fight me, Elizabeth. Let me stay here and build. Let's see what's up ahead on the road. Maybe there's something for us. For you and me." His lips covered hers, and his hands slid up into her hair.

Go ahead and tear down the mansion, she wanted to cry out as his lips grazed her cheek, her ear, her neck. *Take the house, take everything . . . only don't go! Don't leave, Zachary. Stay forever and forever.*

As she tightened her arms around the man's chest, Elizabeth felt a small hand at her waist and a little head pressing against her hip. With a jolt of dismay, she looked down to find Nick standing as close to her and Zachary as he could get, his arms clutching them both.

"Hi, Mom," he said, his head thrown back and his green eyes shining. "You guys are kissing, huh?"

Zachary stiffened and pulled away. "Nick."

"Hi, Zachary. I brought you a good vase for your mansion. Boompah carried it all the way from the old country, and it's worth about a million dollars."

"I didn't hear you come up the stairs."

"I was very quiet because I didn't want to interrupt the kissing." He grinned from ear to ear. "My plan is going to work really good now, huh? I'm going to get a dad, and we can all live together in Grace's house with Boompah's vase from the old country, and everybody I love will be together."

Elizabeth glanced at Zachary and then quickly sank to her knees. "No, sweetie," she said to her son. "That's not the plan at all. If the mansion stays, then Zachary will have to leave. But if Zachary stays, he's going to tear down the mansion. He's not going to be your dad, and we're not going to live in Grace's house, and where on earth is Boompah? Why did he let you come up here by yourself?"

"He didn't want to interrupt the kissing either. He said, 'I think the surrender is coming.' And I said, 'That means presents!'" Nick looked from one adult to the other. "So what do you think about that?"

NINE

"Liz, I haven't seen hide nor hair of you lately." Pearlene Fox watched as Elizabeth unlocked the front door of Finders Keepers. "Something going on I need to know about?"

Definitely not, Elizabeth thought. She turned the Closed sign to Open and gave the brass bells a quick dusting with the hem of her soft cotton skirt. Pearlene was the last person in the world with whom she would ever share the turmoil inside her.

"Is something bothering you, honey?" Pearlene asked, leaning on her broom. At this point in the summer, there were few fallen leaves or dropped flower petals to sweep up, but Pearlene never missed a morning with her trusty broom. It was said around town that a person could eat off the sidewalk in front of Très Chic.

"I've been busy, that's all," Elizabeth said, hoping to put an end to the conversation. "Well, I'd better—"

"I've seen a fair number of customers going into your shop—which reminds me. Phil said Al Huff was all hot and bothered again about the parking problem. People are leaving their cars over at his gas station so they can shop on the square. You know everybody hates to parallel park if they don't have to. Have you ever seen Ruby McCann trying to get her big DeSoto into one of those little spaces? Anyhow, Al's thinking of taking up the matter with the city council. He wants to put up one of those signs that says No Parking except for Customers of Al's Gas Station and Garage. Or one of those Tow Away Zone signs like they gave Zimmerman on the cannon corner of the square. Anyhow, what have you been up to, Liz?"

"Busy."

"Busy with what?"

Elizabeth selected some news that could be shared. "A couple of days ago, I signed a contract with an interior designer."

"No kidding? What kind of a contract?"

"The woman is refurbishing some of the old houses on the east side of Jeff City. The state bought them, and they're turning them into agency offices. The designer who's doing the interior work subcontracted the antique furnishings to Finders Keepers."

"Who's doing the exteriors?" Pearlene's voice took on a teasing note. "It wouldn't be Zachary Chalmers, by any chance?"

"No. It's another firm." She propped an old iron boot last against the door to hold it open. "Anyway, I've got a lot to do today."

"Well, I think this calls for a celebration, Liz. I mean, it's not every day someone from little ol' Ambleside gets a big Jeff City contract. Why don't you and Nick come over to our house for dinner tonight? I put a roast in the slow cooker this morning. You know how Phil likes his dinner real regular, and all. I mean, it's not like we're just going to up and eat out every night. No, ma'am. I cook. I plan ahead. It won't take anything to open a can of peas and pop some biscuits in the oven. We'll have plenty to eat."

"Thanks, Pearlene, but—"

"I won't take no for an answer. You just pack up that little boy the minute you lock your shop door, hear me? You and Nick drive over to our place, and we'll celebrate that new contract of yours. Besides, I know Phil was wanting to talk to you. He's all worked up over that town charter he found, and the parking problems, and all that city council business. That man is *so* devoted to his elected position. So, can you come?"

Elizabeth glanced down the sidewalk. Boompah had just rolled his little fruit cart out the front door of the market. As Boompah reached for the handle of his striped window awning, Zachary Chalmers rounded the corner. The two men greeted each other with a handshake and a friendly slap on the back. They spoke for a moment, laughed over something, and then Zachary reached up and began to crank down the heavy folds of canvas.

"Liz? Oh, I should have known something more important had captured your attention." Pearlene glanced over her shoulder. "Or maybe I should say some*one.*"

"I'm sorry, Pearlene. I'm just concerned about Boompah."

"Sure you are."

"I am. I really don't think he was ready to go back to work as soon as he did."

"What about that other fellow over there? Aren't you just the teeniest bit interested in him?"

"You know that I like Zachary well enough. But the fact is, his plans don't mesh with mine. Since day one, I've been opposed to Zachary's desire to tear down Chalmers House. And now that Phil has found the old town charter, it looks like we'll be able to block the demolition. I'm not too popular with Zachary these days."

"Hmm. That's not what I hear. Ruby McCann told me she was locking up the library one night last week when she saw you and Zachary come out of the mansion together."

"*And* Nick. I had gone over there to . . . oh, never mind." She set her hands on her hips. "You know, I really wish Ruby McCann would just keep out of my business. This whole town is so nosy; everybody knows what I'm doing even before I do it."

"Don't get all huffy, Liz. It's just that folks think you and Zachary make such a cute couple."

"This isn't high school, Pearlene. We're not cute, and we're certainly not a couple."

"Well, listen to you, Miss High-and-Mighty, picking apart everything I say. If you don't want to come for dinner, so be it. Why didn't you just say so in the first place?"

"Oh, good grief, Pearlene, don't get mad. I'll come to dinner. Thank you for the invitation. Nick will look forward to playing with your puppies."

"Well, if you're sure."

"I'll bring a salad."

The woman's face brightened. "Aren't you just the sweetest thing? Be sure to put fat-free dressing on it. Phil and I are watching our cholesterol, you know."

Swinging around, she gave a cheery wave to Zachary and Boompah. "Hey there, you two! Isn't it a beautiful morning?"

Elizabeth hurried up the steps and into her store. She hadn't talked to Zachary in a week—not since the night they'd been alone together in the mansion. That had been awkward and wonderful and frightening all at the same time. As she organized her cash register for the day, Elizabeth glimpsed Grace Chalmers's old Bible on the glass counter.

Picking it up, she clutched the soft black leather book to her chest and closed her eyes. Sometimes she found it so hard to know what God had planned for her. Surely her heavenly Father didn't want Nick led astray in his desire for an earthly dad. It was up to Elizabeth to protect her son from mistaken ideas and false hopes.

Though his eyes beckoned her and his gentle kisses moved her deeply, Zachary Chalmers would never be Nick's father. He had told her plainly he didn't want a needy little boy around to remind him of his own unhappy childhood. And he didn't want Elizabeth, either. She was too headstrong, too set in her ways, and far too careful to risk letting a man like Zachary into her safe, controlled world.

Lord, she prayed, *please keep me on the right track. On your path. Please help me keep Zachary at a distance, so that I can save the mansion and protect the town and guard my heart. And please help Nick to understand.*

❧

"The Lord works in mysterious ways, doesn't he?" Pearlene opened her screen door to welcome Nick and Elizabeth. "You'll never guess what happened right after I invited you to dinner. Well, I ran into Zachary Chalmers over at the Corner Market, and so I invited him, too!"

Seated on a plaid couch that matched the Foxes' avocado green shag carpet, Zachary watched Elizabeth's focus flick across the room. Her face registered instant dismay when she spotted him. She put a protective arm around her son and turned to her hostess.

"Pearlene, I thought . . . I thought this was a celebration."

"Zachary can celebrate, too, can't you, Zachary?" She swiveled and gave him a wink. "I told you about Liz's big contract, didn't I? Somebody from Jeff City is paying her to furnish a bunch of old houses they're restoring. If you ask me, that just sounds wonderful. Is this the salad? Oh, Liz, you brought your seven-layer extravaganza, didn't you? Phil, she brought the seven-layer salad! He just loves this salad of yours, but you know that cheese will kill us both."

"I went easy on the cheese."

"Zachary brought a loaf of bread from the donut shop, can you believe it? Wasn't that thoughtful? Zachary, you are so thoughtful." Pearlene whisked the salad from Elizabeth's hand and hurried into the dining room. "You all just make yourselves at home. There's not a thing you can do. This dinner has all but made itself. Nick, you want to come with me and see the puppies? They're out in the garage. How's Montgomery? I heard her mother is not feeling well. Not well at all."

As her son left with Pearlene, Elizabeth crossed the room and sat down on the edge of a green plaid love seat near its matching couch. Her softly gathered skirt puddled around her feet as she folded her hands in her lap. "I think we were set up," she said.

Zachary grinned. "What gave you that idea?"

"Listen, about last week—"

"I enjoyed that."

She looked up, startled. "Well, but . . . but you and I are on opposite sides in this town charter thing. And Nick is pretty confused about our relationship. I don't like to have Nick confused. Plus, Ruby McCann saw us coming out of the mansion together, and that's just not appropriate. So from now on—"

"From now on, I think we should go out on real dates. The movies. The Nifty Cafe. That kind of thing. Make it official."

"Zachary, don't be ridiculous."

"What's ridiculous about it? I like being with you. You like being with me. We have some good talks. We enjoy kissing each other."

"Shh!" She practically jumped out of her seat. "For Pete's sake, hush!"

"Nick already knows."

"But it's not going to happen again. I've done a lot of thinking and praying about this. Zachary, I'm going to go ahead and stand with Phil on the matter of the town charter. You'll have to leave Ambleside."

"Chicken."

He leaned back on the couch and eyed her. Elizabeth Hayes was afraid of him. He could see it in her blue eyes.

She was determined to maintain her little town's integrity, and Zachary was the enemy. She was protective of her son's fragile dreams, and Zachary was Nick's hope for a father. Most of all, though, she intended to guard her own heart. And Zachary threatened the barriers she had so carefully erected.

He scared her half to death, and he relished it.

"I have a puffy little fur ball," Nick announced, carrying a small black-and-white puppy into the living room. "Look, Zachary! You can hardly see her tail."

"Be careful, honey," Elizabeth said, coming to her feet. "The puppy's just a baby. You have to be gentle."

His small pale fingers forming a cup for the tiny creature, Nick ignored his mother and made a beeline to Zachary. "It's a girl dog," he said. "Bitsy is the mom, and Booger is the dad. They had five babies. They drink milk right out of Bitsy, but it's not chocolate, because she only makes dog milk. Phil said he's going to sell the puppies for a hundred dollars each. Do you want to buy this one, Zachary? You could keep her forever. You could love her and hug her and give her a home just like my mommy gave me a home."

Zachary stiffened as Nick deposited the wriggling ball of fluff in his lap. He'd never had a dog of his own. There had been plenty of strays wandering around the trailer park where he'd grown up, but he'd never given them much attention. Most were dirty, hungry, flea-bitten. Some were downright dangerous, especially in packs.

"It's bad to take somebody away from their mommy and daddy," Nick was saying as he snuggled onto the couch beside Zachary and the puppy. "But Phil says that's how dogs are. You have to take the puppies away and sell them if you want to make any money off your 'vestment. What's a 'vestment?"

"It's, uh . . ." He looked at Elizabeth. Her eyes had gone

soft as she gazed at her son and the man beside him. "An investment is the money you pay for something. And if you're good at business, you'll earn back the money one day, plus a profit."

"Did my mom pay for me?" Nick focused on his mother. "Did you pay for me? Am I a 'vestment?"

"No, sweetheart." She knelt beside the couch on the green shag carpet. "You're not an investment, and you're not a dog either. You're a boy. A very precious boy."

"Yes, I am." Nick reached over and stroked the puppy's head. "Aren't you going to snuggle her, Zachary?"

Feeling awkward, Zachary scooped up the tiny warm ball of fur and cradled the puppy in one palm. A life so small. Amazing. He touched the puppy's little fuzzy ears and stroked his fingers down her back. She pushed against his thumb, seeking milk as she made small mewling noises.

"You're supposed to cuddle her like this," Nick said, arranging the puppy so that she was tucked under Zachary's chin. "That way she feels warm and safe. Puppies need to feel safe, because they're scared without their mommies and daddies. You have to protect them, see? When I was a baby, I didn't have a mommy or a daddy, but now I have a mommy. Are you going to be my daddy?"

"Nikolai Hayes," Elizabeth blurted out. "We talked about that already, and you know what I told you. Zachary has his own life, his own plans. You can be his friend, but you're not to talk about his being your daddy anymore. Do you understand me, young man? You have a mommy, and that's enough."

"It's not enough," Nick said, his little chin jutting out.

"Yes, it is. Now take the puppy back to the garage."

"Zachary wants it. He wants the puppy, and he wants me!" Nick grabbed Zachary's arm. "Don't you, Zachary? Don't you want me?"

Wedged between the arm of the sofa and the little boy,

Zachary lowered the puppy to his lap. Then he wrapped his arm around the child's small shoulders. "You remember what you told me about surrendering, Nick?" he asked. "Remember how we're supposed to surrender all to Jesus and let him be the leader?"

Nick nodded, his cheek soft against Zachary's arm. "That's how you get the presents."

"Well, I've been doing a lot of thinking lately, and I decided it's time for me to surrender. I have to be willing to give up trying to be in charge, and I need to let God be the boss of my life. You told me I ought to do that. Now I'm telling you the same thing."

"But I really want a daddy."

"There are lots of things I really want, too. Things I've wanted and worked for all my life. But I believe Jesus knows what I need better than I do. So I'm going to let him take over."

"When?"

Zachary swallowed. "Well . . . soon."

"Well, when? You better do it right now before you forget."

Looking into Nick's earnest green eyes, Zachary pulled him into the cradle of his arms. The puppy burrowed into the crevice between the man and the boy. Zachary nodded. "All right."

Turning his focus from small boys, tiny puppies, and the pretty Elizabeth Hayes, Zachary entered the presence of the Lord. "Father," he prayed, "I surrender all control of my life to you. I trust you to guide me and to make your desires my desires. Lord, I believe. Please help my unbelief. In Jesus' name, amen."

"Amen," Nick said. "Me, too, God. I'm going to surrender my wanting a daddy—"

"What a pretty picture!" Pearlene turned and hollered over her shoulder as she returned from the kitchen. "Phil, you should just see these three in here. Four, counting the puppy. Turn off that ball game, and get your hide in here, would you? If that isn't something, inviting people over and then gluing yourself to the TV. Next thing you know, he'll be showing off his World Series baseball. I'll swan."

In a moment, Phil Fox appeared in the living room. "Those Cardinals," he said. "They're at it again. Hey, Zachary, Liz, how are you folks? I couldn't have been more surprised when Pearlene called me up this morning and told me she'd invited you all to dinner."

Zachary stood and shook the man's hand. He had a feeling this whole scenario had been preplanned, but he didn't want to dispute his host. If Zachary had meant his prayer moments before—and he had—he needed to find out what God had in mind for the property he'd inherited. And dinner conversation with Phil and Pearlene would help.

"What are the Redbirds up to?" Zachary asked Phil.

"They need pitching, as usual. I used to get over to St. Louis to watch a game or two every summer, but now that my boys are grown and gone it's easier just to turn on the tube. Liz, did I ever show you my autographed ball from the '64 World Series?"

"Yes, Phil. I've seen it." She smiled indulgently as he removed his prize from its place on the mantel. "Several times."

"Those were the days, yes sir. This here is my pride and joy." He displayed the trophy, though not so closely as to tempt anyone to touch it. "Ever seen anything like it?"

"It looks like a baseball to me," Nick said.

"This is more than a baseball, boy. It's a relic of the glory days. A real treasure. I wouldn't sell this ball for anything." He gazed at the ball for a moment. "How about this, Zachary?"

"That's a valuable ball."

"You bet your bottom dollar." He set the ball back on the

mantel and turned his attention to Elizabeth. "Pearlene tells
me you got a big contract to furnish some old houses in Jefferson City. Congratulations."

"Thanks, Phil."

"Now, here's to show you how little I know about interior design—but why would anybody want to go to all the
trouble of modernizing some old buildings and then turn
around and put antique furniture in them? It'd be like
Pearlene going to the plastic surgeon and paying a small
fortune for a face-lift and a tummy tuck, and then dressing
in some old, wore-out getup her mama used to wear. Poly-
ester double knit, you know what I mean? Seems to me if
you're going to go to the trouble and expense of fixing
something up, you ought to outfit it in new duds."

"Are you saying I need plastic surgery, Phil Fox?"
Pearlene said, setting her hands on her hips. "You always
said you liked how I looked. Was that just for show?"

"I'm not talking about *you,* Pearlene. I'm talking about
those old, broken-down buildings in Jeff City."

"Broken down? Well, if you don't like how I look, why
don't you just come right out and say so? Comparing me to
an old building, I'll swan." She gave him an icy stare before
turning and heading into the dining room. "Come on, everybody, before the dinner gets cold. And Phil, put that puppy
back in the garage before it wets all over somebody."

Zachary found himself seated across the table from Elizabeth. He quickly decided that watching her was going to be
the best part of the evening. The food was delicious, of
course. Hearty Midwestern pot roast sat in a pot filled with
gravy, onions, potatoes, and carrots. Elizabeth's layered
salad and his fresh bread topped off the meal that concluded with bowls of hot peach cobbler swimming in
melted vanilla ice cream.

But if the food was nourishing, the conversation could
have withered the hardiest vine. Pearlene, miffed over the

imagined insult to her appearance, clammed up tight. Phil decided to offer a lengthy oration about the bus station he ran, lamenting the lack of passengers, the dwindling route system, the condition of the vehicles. Nick cut in on Phil's monologue with his usual thousand and one questions, and Elizabeth was kept busy giving her son short, quick answers. Zachary was preoccupied, thinking about his surrender and what it would mean in his life.

"But enough about all that," Phil said, leaning back in his chair and displaying his ample girth. "I'm as full as a tick. Pearlene, that was delicious."

"I'm glad you appreciate something about me."

"Listen to her. Would you just listen to my wife? If she isn't the prettiest gal this side of the Mississippi River, I don't know who is. And the best cook, too." Phil patted Pearlene's hand. "So, Zachary, fill us in on some of the buildings you've designed. I hear tell you are quite the architect. Always in demand, they say."

Zachary laid his napkin beside the empty cobbler bowl. "I do commercial designs, mainly. Offices, stores, churches, that kind of thing. I'm working on a contract for a state office complex right now. It's a big project."

"So, did you design any of the buildings we'd know about? Something we might could recognize?"

"You've probably seen some of my work. I've been designing in Jefferson City for quite a while."

"I love the architecture in the capital," Elizabeth said. "Strolling along High Street and looking into all the shop windows is one of my favorite things to do. The buildings are so quaint. They make me feel like I'm somewhere in Europe."

"It's the German architecture," Zachary said. "Although you'll find some French influence, too—mansard roofs and iron railings."

She nodded. "What bothers me is when someone plops a

modern monstrosity right down in the middle of all that history. I once saw a funeral home that looked like it had been built in the sixties—but when I looked closer, I saw that the newer facade had been constructed right over the lower level of an old Victorian home. The architect had left the second floor intact with all its old brick and gingerbread."

"Bizarre," Zachary said.

"Exactly. It's like people have no problem with erecting some kind of an I. M. Pei or Frank Lloyd Wright type of structure on a block lined with turn-of-the-century town houses."

"Frank Lloyd Wright and I. M. Pei?" Zachary's brows lifted. "You know your architects."

"Buildings are sort of a hobby with me. It's hard to study antique furnishings without developing an interest in architecture. But there are times when I just want to gag. For instance, there's a church near the center of downtown Jefferson City that is the absolute worst kind of aberration. Wright's buildings fit with the landscape. This church is just jarring. It rises up like some kind of homage to Picasso, or something. The stained glass is thick and distorted. It looks like it came off the bottom of broken Coke bottles. The bell tower juts off at a weird angle. And what is that horrible copper thing on the front?"

"That's the awning," Zachary said. "The church's building committee asked for a facade that would work well with the slope of the hill, and the copper awning was the design they liked best."

Elizabeth's lips parted in shock. Pearlene dropped her fork. Phil gawked at Zachary for a moment, and then he began to chuckle. *"You* designed that church?" he asked. *"You* drew the building Liz hates the most in all of Jeff City? Good gravy, Pearlene, did you hear that? While we're at it, Zachary, how do you feel about antiques?"

Zachary studied little Nick, who had paused in his last bite of cobbler and was clearly aware that something had gone wrong with the adult conversation. "I've never been much of an antiques collector," Zachary acknowledged, hoping to calm Elizabeth's fiery pink cheeks. "But I recently bought a white cabinet from Finders Keepers, and I think it's about the best-looking thing in my kitchen. Great for holding my teacup collection."

"Teacup collection!" Phil gave a hoot of laughter. "You're pulling my leg now, Zachary. What a kidder. I'll tell you what; this discussion about old buildings brings me right to the topic of the evening—and that's the Chalmers Mansion."

"Are you going to make Nick sit through this?" Pearlene asked.

"Well, take the boy back out and show him the puppies again, if you want. The adults here have got business to discuss."

Zachary frowned as Pearlene and Nick rose from the table. Not only did he feel ambushed by Phil, but he was uncomfortable at the way Elizabeth was staring blankly at her dessert bowl, her cheeks still looking as hot as fire-crackers. He had the strongest feeling that Miss Hayes was getting mad. And Nick had warned that when his mother got mad, she could yell. Though Zachary didn't like the idea of Elizabeth's anger turned on him, he decided it might be kind of interesting to watch—especially if Phil Fox were to take the brunt of her fiery spirit.

"Now that charter I found in the city's files is as good as gold," Phil began, launching into what Zachary realized was the point of the whole evening's gathering. "Zachary, your great-grandfather meant for that house he built to remain standing. You can't get around it. In fact, Sawyer-the-lawyer tells me that only some kind of a heavy-duty motion approved by the city government can change a legal char-ter. And I'm here to tell you that's not going to happen. You see, those councilmen tend to vote the way I tell them to."

"Is that right?" Zachary said.

"Yes sir, it is. I may not be the mayor yet, but I have an awful lot of influence in this town. Fact is, whatever I say goes. Now, I don't want to cause any more trouble than we've already had over this matter. But I'm going to have to tell you that Liz, here, informed me that you possess a letter from Grace Chalmers. Liz says the letter states as plain as the nose on my face that your aunt wanted to keep the house standing. Is that right?"

"I have the letter here in my pocket."

"I thought you might. Now, Zachary, with all the evidence going against you, I'm sure you're feeling mighty uncomfortable. You own a piece of property that is completely useless to you. Have you thought about that?"

"Day and night," Zachary said, waiting for the final ax to fall.

"Well, I have too, and I think the best course you could take would be to figure out a way to sell off that old place before the city is forced to do something drastic."

"Like what?"

"Well . . . like condemn it."

"You know what, Phil?" Elizabeth said, coming to life. She leaned across the table, her eyes fairly sparking blue flame. "Grace wrote that letter about me and about Zachary. It has nothing to do with you or the city council. The more I've thought about the letter, the more I've realized that Grace focused her whole life on people—not on buildings or town charters or city councils. She cared about Zachary, and she wanted him to have her house."

"That's what I'm saying."

"No, you're not. You don't understand that it was not the *house* Grace wanted to save and protect. It was her *nephew.*" She threw her napkin onto the table. "You want Zachary to give up the house. You want him to turn over that property, don't you?"

"Well, I . . . I don't see what good the old house would do him."

"You're going to prevent him from tearing it down, and you know good and well he can't ever sell it because it would cost the buyer too much to repair. So it's worthless to him."

"Yes, Elizabeth, that's what I'm trying to tell him."

"And how much do you want to pay for it—a dollar?"

"Now, Liz—"

"Tell me if I'm wrong, Phil. You want Zachary to make the Chalmers House a generous transfer of property in exchange for a nominal sum. Isn't that where this is going?"

Phil shifted in his chair. "Actually, I *was* thinking about some sort of transaction along those lines. I mean, if Zachary can't tear down the house and if he can't sell the property, well, why not give such a valuable historic site to the city?"

Elizabeth pushed back from the table and stood. "And what would you do with Chalmers House, Phil Fox?" Without waiting for a response, she turned to Zachary. "I may dislike your architecture, and I may fight you tooth and toenail to keep Grace's house standing. But I'll do all in my power to prevent the Ambleside city council from ever taking over Chalmers House. Excuse me, but I have to get Nick to bed."

Zachary let out a breath as she left the dining room in search of her son. "I don't think she trusts you very much, Phil," he said.

"Aw, Liz is too uppity for her own britches. She can just take her opinions and stick 'em in her ear. What I want to know is what you think, Zachary. What's your opinion on the whole deal?"

Zachary stood. "Well," he said, "what I think is that I don't trust you any more than Elizabeth does. And if you'll excuse me, I need to educate a certain young lady about the basic elements of high-class architecture in Jefferson City, Missouri."

_10_
TEN

Elizabeth lifted the old black Bible and gave the counter a squirt of glass cleaner. As she wiped away the dust, she peered down at her own reflection. How could it be that she was still so young and vibrant—when Montgomery's mother had only a week or two to live? Just this morning, the news had passed through town like wildfire. They were bringing Ellie Easton home to die.

Laying the Bible on the counter, Elizabeth stroked the warm, comforting leather. She had lost both her parents when she was almost the same age as Montgomery. Elizabeth's grandmother had taken the orphan into her home and had done her best to fill the empty spaces in the lonely child's heart. Montgomery would still have a father, but who would do all the 'mommy' things for the little girl? Who would braid her long red hair? Who would kiss her scraped knees? Who would listen as she poured out the joys and sorrows of a first love?

You can do that, Elizabeth.

The words caught her full force in the stomach and filled her heart with conviction. It was true. Montgomery already loved and trusted Elizabeth. Nick's mom provided a safe place to play, lots of yummy snacks, and guidance when things went awry. Elizabeth could help Montgomery adjust to the changes in her young life. And though it might sap the last of her emotional reserves, she would.

Elizabeth let out a sigh as she turned her feather duster to the tea set in her window. She could see Pearlene out

sweeping the sidewalks for the third time that day. It was
almost closing time, and Pearlene would be expecting a
visit from Elizabeth. After all, manners in Ambleside dictated
a follow-up thank-you call or visit the day after a lovely dinner party.

No doubt Pearlene would have realized by now the
hopelessness of her quest to marry off her neighbor to the
new architect in town. Their opposing views on the mansion were clear, and Elizabeth's gaffe the night before had
certainly put a strain on even a comfortable friendship with
Zachary.

How could she have been so blunt about that church in
Jefferson City? On the other hand, how could Zachary have
designed such a monstrosity? The building annoyed her
every time she drove past it. It was ugly and out of place in
the historic capital's downtown. But did she have to lam-
baste it right in front of Zachary? He'd probably never speak
to her again.

The thought of losing his presence in her life sent a curl
of sadness through Elizabeth. She could recall how often
she had wished that Zachary Chalmers had never moved to
Ambleside. Now the possibility of never again looking
deeply into those gray green eyes left a void she was
unprepared to fill. In spite of their verbal jousting—or perhaps because of it—she had come to enjoy Zachary's company. She liked the way he took Nick under his wing. He
was intelligent, hardworking, and—despite that one hideous
church—talented in his profession. She had been touched
by his vocal prayer of surrender to the Lord's leading in the
Foxes' living room last night.

If Zachary was so willing to suppress his personal desires
in order to follow Christ, shouldn't Elizabeth be equally sub-
missive? After all, she was the regular churchgoer. She was
the one who had made such a big deal of her commitment
to God. And yet she held on to her own opinions and her

own plans the way a drowning person clung to a life preserver.

What if she stopped trying to keep herself afloat? What if she let go and took the hand of Christ, relying on him to carry her through every stormy sea in her life? Would she drown? Surely not. She professed to have given her life to Christ many years ago. She had. She truly had. But why was it so hard to actively trust him with each day's troubles?

Elizabeth inwardly winced as Pearlene caught her eye through the shop window and gave her a jaunty wave. No doubt her business neighbor would have an opinion on the previous evening's events. And it looked like Elizabeth was going to have to hear it.

"Hey, there!" Pearlene breezed into Finders Keepers with a jingle of brass bells. "Phil says you-all had words last night while Nick and I were out in the garage with the puppies. Well, I could tell right off he was in quite a mood. Making all those comments about me visiting a plastic surgeon, I'll swan. I've been married to that man for umpteen years, and I never do know what's going to come out of his mouth. Anyhow, I'm sure you're just mortified about what you said about that church Zachary designed in Jeff City, but I think the best thing you can do is just put it out of your mind. Just put it right out of your mind."

"I agree," Elizabeth said. She opened her cash register and began emptying the drawer for the day. "I've decided the most important thing for me right now is to support the Easton family."

"Well, that is so good of you. You know that little girl is just going to be devastated when her mama passes on."

"It'll be rough, but Montgomery is a very resilient child. I think she'll make it through."

"I'm sure she will; it's her daddy I'm worried about. Don't you know Luke Easton just about worships the ground that wife of his walks on?"

"Their love is obvious to everyone."

"And you know what I've been thinking would be the best thing for Luke? To get himself married again as quick as possible after Ellie dies. Just don't even let a month go by. That way he and Montgomery can keep things going along the way they have without hardly a hiccup."

"I doubt Luke will want to marry again anytime soon, Pearlene. He's going to be grieving over Ellie for a long time."

"Not if he finds the right woman. Somebody like you, Liz. Now don't look so shocked. You know Luke thinks a lot of you, and you're practically a second mother to Montgomery already. You could just move right on into their lives like a glove on a hand, don't you know? That would make Nick and Montgomery brother and sister, and I can't think of a prettier picture."

Elizabeth tried to regain control of her heart rate. "Pearlene," she said firmly, "I consider Luke and Ellie my brother and sister in Christ." She jammed the day's earnings into her zippered bank bag. "Luke Easton is a nice man, but I'm not interested in marrying him. I'm not going to marry anyone, OK? This may be hard for you to understand, Pearlene, but I have my own life, and I'm very happy with it. God has given me a wonderful son and a successful business and plenty of things to fulfill me. I don't need a husband. And I sure don't need Zachary Chalmers!"

"Rats." The voice from the front door ricocheted down Elizabeth's spine as Zachary stepped into the shop. "I was hoping we could use the chapel this Saturday."

Pearlene laughed. "Good gravy, it's the man himself. How'd you know we were talking about you, Zachary? Have you got that psychotic energy like they talk about on TV?"

"I doubt it, Pearlene. I don't have to have ESP to know

one thing for sure. That roast beef dinner of yours last night was the tastiest I've ever eaten in my life."

"Aren't you the sweetest thing? Listen, I'm sorry Phil got your back up over that town charter he found. He's such a man of vision, don't you know? And he's sure he is doing what's best for Ambleside. This is a pretty town, but we've got to bring it into the twenty-first century, that's what Phil says. Anyhow, he's got that charter under lock and key, protecting it like a daddy bear with a cub. Do daddy bears protect their cubs, or is it the mama? Whatever, he says nobody's going to pry that charter loose from him until he gets what he's after."

"What's he really after, Pearlene?" Zachary asked.

She swallowed. "Well, I've probably said too much already. Me and my mouth running on and on. I'm sure glad you liked my roast beef, Zachary. Did you drop by just to tell me that? Aren't you the sweetest thing?"

"That, and I needed to buy another teacup or two from Elizabeth. I realized I can't have much of a tea party with just one cup."

"Well, that's right. It sure is, but I don't know who you're thinking of asking for tea. I hope it's not Liz, because let me tell you, she's not just free for the taking, Zachary. I mean there's other men in this town who would be more than happy to snap her up. There are single men . . . and there are men who are *about to be single,* if you know what I mean."

"Is Phil divorcing you?"

"Not Phil! Oh, you are a kidder, I'll swan. I'm stuck with that man for better or worse—and let me tell you there's times I think it can't get much worse. Well, I'll just leave you two to your socializing. See you around, Liz. Don't make yourself a stranger."

Elizabeth followed her neighbor toward the shop door.

"Pearlene, thank you so much for dinner last night. It was truly a wonderful roast."

"I thought so myself," Pearlene said with a wave over her shoulder. "A woman with a nice figure and a good hand in the kitchen is always a hot commodity—now don't you forget that, honey. There's more than one fish in the sea."

Elizabeth stifled a growl of frustration and turned back into her shop. Now what? Why on earth had Zachary come to see her after the things she'd said to him the night before? And how could she apologize for her hasty words—but words she truly had meant?

"I like this one," Zachary said, holding aloft a pink cup decorated with yellow roses and gold trim. "It has kind of a curlicue handle."

"That's Limoges. It's very expensive. You might prefer one of these over here."

"What's the matter? You think I can't afford an expensive teacup?" He set the cup down and leaned across the counter. "Or do you just want to foist one of those ugly ones on me?"

"No, of course I don't—"

"You think I have bad taste, don't you?"

She looked into his eyes and saw the teasing sparkle. "Not where teacups are concerned."

"Just churches?"

"Oh, Zachary, I'm sorry I insulted your design." She pushed the cup at him. "Here, take this. My apology gift."

"You can't buy your way out of this one, Elizabeth, my dear. You're sunk deeper than the *Titanic.*"

"I told you how I felt about that church, and I'm sticking to my guns. I'm just sorry I was so blunt in front of you."

"Better to criticize me behind my back?"

"Oh, take your cup and go!"

"No way. You're not getting rid of me that easily. You criticized my handiwork. My opus. My masterpiece."

"That church is your masterpiece?"

"As a matter of fact, the design won me a couple of awards and moved me into big-time contracts."

She shook her head. "Why? It's so . . . so . . ."

"Ugly, was the word I think you used. But let's not forget that ugly is in the eye of the beholder. You see, I'm a businessman, and I listen to my clients. When I drew up my proposed designs, I knew the congregation of that church had a certain image they wanted to project. They didn't want to blend in with all the quaint old buildings downtown. They wanted to tell people that their faith wasn't something antiquated and passé. Instead, they hoped people would see them as modern, cutting edge, *relevant.*"

"Oh," Elizabeth said softly. "I didn't realize . . ."

"If your building looks old, they reasoned, then folks will think you stand for the old-time religion. Old hymns, old traditions, and lots of old people in your congregation. Nothing wrong with that in my opinion, but this church wanted to reach people of all ages with the new life, new hope, and new promises of Christ's salvation. And they wanted their church building to reflect their aims."

"Well, I didn't think about it that way."

"So why would I design some ancient-looking brick facade that blended right into the background? They wanted to stand out, make a statement."

"They certainly accomplished that."

"I've learned to design what my clients want—even if that isn't necessarily my personal taste."

Elizabeth glanced around at her shop. "All right, I concede your point. I don't always stock antiques I'm crazy about either. Early primitive furnishings aren't my cup of tea, but I know there's a market for them. I have a whole room full of primitives through that door over there. I'm not particularly fond of ornate, dark Victorian furniture, either. And I'm filling three buildings in Jefferson City with it."

"Aha! You're a mercenary."

"I'm a businesswoman."

"And I'm a businessman, which is how that ugly church in Jeff City came to be."

"Do you mean to tell me you don't like the looks of that building any more than I do?"

"Actually, it's a shining example of its style. But personally I prefer designs that fit their surroundings more closely, and I'm something of a traditionalist. On the other hand, the office I'm planning to build next door has the latest in modern conveniences."

His eyes pinned her, willing her to argue. Elizabeth opened her mouth to do just that—and then she shut it again. How could she defy this man any longer? She had insulted and contradicted and fought with him ever since he set foot in Ambleside, and he hadn't backed away one inch from his determination to raze the mansion. Or from his persistent pursuit of her.

If Zachary could surrender, so could she.

"I'd like to see your blueprints sometime," she said.

"Good. Then why don't you and Nick come over to my apartment this evening? We'll have dinner and tea." He grabbed another cup, this one an even more expensive Wedgwood. "Wrap these up for me, would you? You can bring them with you when you come to dinner. I've got to run by the Corner Market and see if Boompah has any fresh asparagus. Wait till you taste my pasta primavera."

Giving her a wink, he breezed out of the shop. As the brass bells ceased their jingling, Elizabeth sank onto the stool behind the counter and shook her head in dismay.

❧

"Boompah?" Elizabeth spotted her elderly friend on the sofa as Zachary opened the apartment door. "Did you come for dinner, too?"

"It looks that way, Elizabeth."

The old man started to rise, but Nick skipped over and gently lowered him back to the couch. "Don't get up, Boompah," Nick said. "It's just mom and me. We've come to eat dinner with Zachary, but we're not going to talk about Zachary being my daddy. That's off lemons."

"Off-limits," Elizabeth said, giving Zachary a sheepish glance. Her son had no filter between his brain and his mouth. If something was on his mind, the whole world soon would know about it. "Nick, why don't you sit down by Boompah and tell him about summer school? You've been doing so well with your reading."

"Oh, yes," Nick said. "I'm a very good reader. I read to Mrs. Wrinkles all the time."

Zachary motioned from the kitchen area of his small apartment. "Come taste this. Tell me if it needs more salt."

Feeling awkward and uncertain, Elizabeth approached the narrow galley kitchen. Though the alcove was open to the living area, it felt somehow intimate to step into Zachary's private realm. But as he lifted a wooden spoon draped with noodles, she pinpointed the right word the moment inspired. It was *homey*. Homey to stand with a man in his kitchen. Homey to lean close to him and sample from the spoon in his hand. Homey to smell the spice bottles open on his counters and to see the suit coat he had casually tossed over the back of a chair.

"I had one foster mom who could cook like nobody's business," Zachary said after Elizabeth had properly oohed and aahed over the pasta. "This lady would have put me into the grave with a blocked artery if I'd stayed with her very long. Everything was butter. Butter, butter, butter. And eggs, too. For breakfast we'd eat sausages, bacon, a couple of eggs fried in butter, and a stack of toast slathered with more butter. At lunch I was on the free-meal program at school. But dinner would be fried pork chops or chicken-fried steak."

Elizabeth watched him stir the saucepan. "How long were you with her?"

"A few months, I guess. About average. Not long enough to form any real attachments. If you want to know the truth, I can't even remember her name. But I did love to eat her cooking."

He opened a narrow pantry and began rooting around in a basketful of linens. Elizabeth felt her heart contract in sorrow. Zachary had been ejected from his birth family and passed through so many foster homes he couldn't even recall the families' names. It was no wonder he had never married or formed any close relationships. It also helped explain his driving determination to possess the legacy of his Aunt Grace. Even though he wasn't aware of his own need for connectedness, he wanted roots.

"Aha. Napkins." He emerged from the pantry and held up a handful of mismatched cloths. "No paper towels for this dinner party."

"Here, let me set up." She took the napkins to the nearby table. "I'm so glad you invited Boompah."

"I thought I might as well make it a foursome."

"This is a lot more comfortable for me. People won't do much speculating about us if Boompah and Nick are here."

"Don't kid yourself. Ruby McCann was at the market when I went in for the asparagus."

"Uh-oh."

He laughed. "I ran into Phil Fox, too. He was buying the *Kansas City Star* and the *St. Louis Post-Dispatch*. A good city councilman has to keep up with the current news, don't you know."

"Well, I'll swan."

Chuckling, she caught his eye and realized that for the second time, they were united. "Phil and Pearlene ambushed us last night," she said. "There's no question about that."

"I think Pearlene's innocent except for her matchmaking. It's Phil who's got the agenda."

"What do you think he's up to?"

Zachary passed her a handful of silverware. "It's pretty clear. He wants the mansion."

"But why? He's never said a positive word about it. In fact, he was originally on your side."

"My side, your side, Phil's side." He set the pasta bowl in the center of the table. "You want to know the truth? I'm tired of playing these games. If Phil tries to hold up the probate proceedings by using that town charter against me, I'm going to take him to court."

Elizabeth straightened. "Are you serious?"

"Why not?"

"Well, people in Ambleside just don't . . . we don't really solve problems that way."

"No wonder Sawyer-the-lawyer spends most of his afternoons asleep on his desk."

"On his desk?"

"Stretched out right across the top, napping like a baby." He leaned toward the living area. "Come on, Boompah, Nick. Soup's on."

"I thought we were having spaghetti," Nick said.

"Pasta," Elizabeth said. "It's kind of like spaghetti, only different."

"But Zachary said *soup*."

"It's one of those American idioms," Boompah explained. "Soup's on. You've got a bee in your bucket. Early bird catches the worm. Deaf as a doorknob. Ach, my little Nikolai, these idioms go on and on, and usually they make no sense. No sense at all."

"Oh, bother," Nick said.

"In Germany we have such sayings: *Der Apfel fällt nicht*

weit vom Stamm—the apple does not fall far from the tree.
Means, the son is like the father, you see?"

"But I don't have a father," Nick said. His big green eyes
turned imploringly to Zachary. "Not yet, anyway."

"Yeah, well . . . uh . . ." Zachary cleared his throat. "Here
in America, the idiom is He's a chip off the old block."

Elizabeth pulled back the chair next to hers. "Sit down,
Nikolai Hayes, and we'll have no more talk of fathers
tonight. I've warned you once, and this is the last time.
You'll lose cartoons tomorrow if you can't obey me."

"Cartoons?" He hopped into the chair and folded his
hands. "Not that! Let's pray. Dear God, please help me to be
a good boy and not talk about fathers, even if I wish I
could be a chip off somebody's old block. Amen."

Elizabeth stared at her son in dismay as Zachary and
Boompah broke into laughter. "Nick, did you realize that
the grown-ups haven't even had a chance to sit down?"

"But I needed to talk to God right then."

"He's got a point, Elizabeth," Zachary said, taking the
chair across from hers. "When you gotta pray, you gotta
pray."

"Amen," Boompah said. "Pass the pasta. I'm so hungry I
could eat a cow."

❧

"How many children do you have, Boompah?" Nick asked
as they sat on Zachary's balcony watching a pink-and-gold
sunset filter across the waters of the Missouri River. "You're
so old, you could be a grandfather."

"Ach, ja, I am very old man," Boompah said. "But I was
never married in all my life. I have not even one child."

Zachary carried his teacup to the green iron bench and
sat down beside Elizabeth. Perfect. For once in Nick's
young life, the little boy had thought ahead. Leaving the

seat beside his mother empty was a stroke of genius, and Zachary would have to give the child a high five for it.

"I wrote your name on my family tree for the grandfather, Boompah," Nick said, "but I'm not telling who I put in the father's place, because I don't want to lose cartoons and be off lemons."

"Well, I can be like a grandfather," Boompah said, taking a sip of tea. "Among the Roma, the old people are respected very much. Not like here in America where the young laugh at an old man and steal gumballs from his machines when he's not looking. Old people have lived many years, and we Gypsies know this means they can be very wise."

"I was a wise man in the Christmas play last year," Nick informed him. "I was supposed to say, 'Mary, the mother of Jesus, I bring frankincense to honor the king.' But I said it all backwards and upside down, and I put in fathers and queens, and everybody laughed."

"Even wise men sometimes make mistakes, Nikolai. Is not a problem, because God always knows what we are trying to say to him."

As the old man and the child carried on their earnest conversation, Zachary studied them. Nick's longing for a father echoed his own heart's desire. In fact, without realizing what he was doing, Zachary had allowed Boompah to take a fatherly role in his life. He enjoyed spending time with the old man, loved listening to his stories, often asked him for advice, and did all he could to help him.

But a person could never depend on an earthly father, Zachary had learned. Nick's father had abandoned his son. Zachary's father had proven himself too lazy and irresponsible to support his children. Elizabeth's father had simply died.

Boompah would die one day. That fact was becoming ever more clear. Nick adored the aging Gypsy, and so did

Zachary. Was it worth the risk of loving someone—even if
you couldn't count on them? Zachary had taken business
risks throughout his career. But to step out in faith with a
personal relationship?

"Why didn't you ever get married, Boompah?" Nick
asked.

"Ach, I was never lucky in love."

"That's what Grace used to say! That very thing, huh,
Mom?"

Elizabeth lifted her head from the back of the iron bench.
"Yes, Nick, that's what she always said."

"Well, Boompah, why didn't you marry Grace?" Nick
demanded. "Then both of you could have been lucky in
love."

"Grace Chalmers was far above me, you know? I am a
poor Gypsy who barely escapes from Adolf Hitler's gas
chambers. I sail to America and sell vegetables that I grow
on my little parcel of land near the Missouri River. But
Grace Chalmers, ach, she is beautiful and rich and very elegant, like a princess. She has fathers and grandfathers who
built the town of Ambleside. Me, I grew up in a caravan."

"But you own the Corner Market."

"Even when I am richer with my own grocery store, I
know Grace lives in that big mansion. No, Nikolai, she is
not for me."

Zachary leaned forward. "Boompah, you've lived in
Ambleside a long time. What do you think I should do with
Chalmers House?"

The old man sat in silence, staring out over the river and
swaying gently back and forth in the green metal rocking
chair. "You ask me a difficult question, my boy," he said
finally. "I cannot know the plans God has for that old
house. But one thing I learned from my years in the old
country. One Roma must not fight against another Roma, or

both might be captured and swallowed by the force of evil that is very great in this world."

"Are you talking about the nachos again, Boompah?" Nick asked.

"No," Zachary said, leaning back on the bench and slipping his arm around Elizabeth's shoulders. "He's talking about your mother and me."

*E*LEVEN

Elizabeth grabbed her broom and headed out the door of Finders Keepers. After last night's dinner at Zachary's apartment, it was clear that her life was a topsy-turvy tangle of confused emotions and uncertain pathways. In the midst of all that mess, only a few things stood out clearly. She must take care of Nick. She must keep her shop running. And, God help her, she must plunge forward into the unknown with Zachary Chalmers.

As she swept the front steps, Elizabeth pondered the effect Zachary might have on Nick's fragile young heart. Was it fair of her to let this man into her son's life, when at any time Zachary could decide to flee? The last thing Elizabeth wanted was to hurt Nick, dash his hopes, and betray his dreams. There was no guarantee that Zachary would ever become a permanent part of their lives. But after last night, how could she turn away from him again?

Pausing in her sweeping, Elizabeth studied the old Chalmers mansion as she reflected on the feel of Zachary's strong arm drawing her close. *Out with the old, in with the new?* Losing that magnificent building filled with memories and traditions would be all but unbearable, Elizabeth realized. But how wonderful it had felt to rest her head on Zachary's chest and hear the solid beat of his heart. Yet it wasn't enough just to revel in the warmth of his embrace or drift off in pleasure at the sound of his voice and the green depths of his eyes. If that had been all there was to the man, she could have resisted him.

No, God had brought Zachary Chalmers into the life of Elizabeth and her son. Of that she was now sure. Zachary matched her in spirit and intellect. The Lord had led them onto the same path, and their faith was growing through their union. Zachary challenged and delighted and restored Elizabeth. And she had made up her mind to stand by his side until God pointed out another path.

Turning away from the mansion, she gave her broom a whack on the curb to shake the dust into the street. *God, please protect my son from harm!* her heart lifted up. *Don't let Zachary abandon Nick, please, Father. I'm not sure either of us could bear the pain of that loss. And Lord, show me how to put aside my hurt about Zachary's plans for the mansion, so that I can be a better—*

"Yoo-hoo!" Pearlene pranced down the sidewalk in the latest summer wear from one of her favorite New York designers. "How are you this morning, Liz? Did I hear that you and Zachary had dinner together last night at his place? Well, that is just so romantic. After the disaster at our house, Phil swore you two would never speak to each other again. But I told him I thought love was more powerful than any argument about a dumb old church in Jeff City. Am I right? Well, am I?"

Elizabeth drank down a breath for fortitude. "It was a foursome, actually. Boompah and Nick were at dinner, too."

"Oh, now don't try to pull that one on me. I know why Zachary had you over, and it doesn't matter who else was there just for show. He's set his cap for you, gal. If you're not the next bride walking down that aisle at Ambleside Chapel, I'll eat my hat."

Elizabeth gave her broom another whack. "Pearlene," she began, and then she looked into the woman's warm brown eyes. *Lord, help me to love Pearlene.*

"Do what, hon?"

"I didn't ask you to do anything."

"You said my name. What did you want?"

"I wanted to . . . to thank you for your friendship." Elizabeth clutched her broom handle. "I wanted to say that you're right, Pearlene. I do care about Zachary."

"I knew it! Good gravy, anybody with two eyes can see that!"

"I guess so."

"Well, sure. I knew that problem over the mansion was going to vanish just like a dandelion in a gust of wind." She took a step closer and leaned over conspiratorially. "If you had ahold of that town charter, you'd see that it's just a piece of dried-up, yellow paper. No judge is going to look at it twice."

"Well, it's very old. I'm sure it's authentic."

"Sure it's old, and so is my husband. That doesn't make either of them worth much." She laughed for a moment. "Phil thinks that charter is some kind of a big deal, but I've signed contracts before, you know, and I understand how things work in the business world. I'm not as dumb as some people might think."

"Of course not."

"I told Phil he ought to leave that charter over at the courthouse where he found it, but no. He's got to treat it like it was some kind of a message from the king of England himself."

"Where's he keeping it?"

"Oh, we've got a safe over at the house. He stores a little cash in there, his fishing license, his mama's wedding ring. Stuff like that. We don't have much that's valuable, don't you know." She smoothed down the linen fabric of her new dress. "I'll tell you what. Just because you're such a good friend, I'll get you that charter and you can make yourself a photocopy. Phil would just kill me if he found out I'd done it, but you know what? I don't much care. I'm tired of all these secret doings of his. He's keeping you and Zachary apart, and that's just not right."

Elizabeth moistened her lips. "Now, Pearlene, I don't want you to get into trouble with your husband."

"Good gravy, I've done a lot worse than raid the safe and give away a stupid old town charter. Do you know one time I washed every one of his white shirts with a brand-new red towel? He liked to died."

"But that was an accident."

"Says who?" She smiled. "We use blue towels in our bathroom, don't you know."

"Oh, Pearlene."

"If you had a copy of that town charter, you'd be able to make sure Zachary can keep the mansion. Then the two of you can figure out what he ought to do with it."

"He's going to build his offices. I can't hope for anything else."

"Good, and then we can just drop the whole subject. There's nothing worse than trouble between a man and a woman. Although it can make for some funny times when you get to thinking about it later." Pearlene got a mischievous twinkle in her eye. "Do you know what I did to Phil one time? I accidentally put a bottle of Nair right where Phil always keeps his shampoo on that little rack in the shower, you know? You should have seen the look on that man's face when his hair took to falling out in big old clumps. I thought I'd about bust laughing. I told him it'd grow back, but he hollered so loud I was scared the whole house would fall down. Now that one was an accident, but I still took the blame for it." She grew serious. "Phil had to wear a hat to work for a good three weeks."

"Wow, that's awful."

"He won't be half as mad about the town charter as he was about the Nair, I'll guarantee." Brightening, she gave Elizabeth a wink. "I'll bring it to you right after lunch."

"That's very kind."

"I'm doing it for love," Pearlene said, turning on her shiny, white patent leather pumps and sashaying back to Très Chic. "All for love!"

❧

Zachary spotted Elizabeth standing on the deep porch of a low, turn-of-the-century bungalow near the town square. As he slowed his car, he recognized the man she was talking to. Luke Easton's head was bent, his hand covering his eyes. He was Montgomery's father and the husband of Ellie Easton, whose life hung by a thread. Elizabeth reached out, slipped her arms around the man, and drew him close.

She's only comforting him, Zachary thought, but he felt a twist in his gut as his foot moved to the brake. *She's mine. Don't get too close, Luke. Elizabeth belongs to me.*

These thoughts rocked him. Wait a minute. Elizabeth didn't belong to anyone. She was a strong, independent woman, and she was merely ministering to a friend.

All the same, Zachary parked, got out of his car, and started across the street. He didn't know the Easton family well, but he'd met little red-haired Montgomery more than once. Surely it wouldn't be out of place for him to extend his sympathies.

Even as he walked up the sidewalk to the house, Zachary had to admit that his motivations were wrong. He suddenly wondered what in the world he was doing. Unbidden, a prayer popped into his mind. *Lord, help me out here. This man is hurting.*

"Hey, Elizabeth," he said, stepping up onto the porch.

She detached from Luke Easton. "Oh, Zachary, I'm so glad you've come." Her voice quavered as she held out a hand to him. "We've just lost Ellie."

In an instant, she was in his arms, her tears wetting his shirt. Luke moved to the edge of the porch, his face in his hands. Zachary drew Elizabeth close and covered her warm, damp hair with his hand. How could he have been thinking only of himself? What if he were Luke Easton now? What if he'd just lost his wife? What if he lost Elizabeth?

"Luke, I'm so sorry," he said, reaching out to the man. "What can I do to help you? Can I call someone?"

"The home health provider is here," Elizabeth answered softly. "They're taking care of things. Oh, Zachary, I'm so worried about Montgomery. She's going to be devastated."

"Where is she?"

"She and Nick are at the library. Ellie slipped into a coma earlier today, and Ruby said she'd watch the children for a few hours."

"I'll go get both kids." He moved away from Elizabeth. "Luke, do you want me to call Pastor Paul?"

The man lifted his head, his eyes red-rimmed. "What for?" he demanded, his voice gravelly. "What good's a preacher going to do me now?"

Zachary drew back at the anguish etched in Luke's handsome face. Anger mingled there with pain, sorrow, torment, agony. The man's thick brown hair was matted and disarrayed, as though he hadn't combed it in days. Bruises of sleeplessness darkened the skin beneath his eyes. Sweat stained the collar of his blue chambray work shirt.

"I've gone to church every Sunday of my life," he said bitterly, "and what did God ever do for me? I begged him to let Ellie live. But she's dead. Dead."

"Luke," Elizabeth said, "I think you ought to sit down."

"You should see my wife in there," he went on, his eyes fiery as he addressed Zachary. "She's got plastic tubes coming out of everywhere, her face is swollen, her eyes . . . they shaved off her hair . . . her beautiful red hair . . . and the scars they left on her head—" He grabbed Zachary's shirtsleeve in his fist and gave it a twist. "You want to go fetch God for me now? You want to bring the preacher over and let him say his prayers? I've been calling out to God for weeks, and he hasn't heard a thing I've said. Nothing!"

"Luke," Elizabeth said, taking the man's shoulders. "Please come over here to the swing with me, and we'll sit together. You haven't slept for days. You need to rest. Come on, now."

Wiping her cheek with the back of her hand, she led Luke across the porch. Zachary watched as she seated him on the old white swing and tucked a pillow behind his back. Taking his hand, she spoke in a low voice for a moment, the voice of a mother to a child.

"Zachary," she said, crossing the porch to his side. "You'd better call Pastor Paul. I don't understand why Luke is acting this way. The things he's saying—he's scaring me."

"He's going through hell."

"But he's a deacon, and he's always been so . . . so . . ."

"He loved his wife, Elizabeth. He's lost the woman he loved."

"I know." She nodded, brushing a tear from her cheek. "She went into a coma, and then she just stopped breathing. She just . . . just didn't breathe anymore."

"Are you OK?"

"I don't know how to make things better."

"Stay here with Luke. I'll go get Montgomery and Nick."

He turned, but she caught his hand and pulled something from the pocket of her slacks. "I'm supposed to give you this. It's the town charter. Pearlene made you a copy of it." She pressed the document into his palm. "Fight for what's yours, Zachary."

"Are you mine?" he asked.

She stared at him, her eyes brimming with tears and confusion.

Never mind her answer, he thought as he turned and headed down the porch steps. The definition of *ownership* had changed. It wasn't so much who or what belonged to him. It was whom he belonged to.

Zachary had surrendered his will to God, and then these people had walked into his heart—Elizabeth, Nick, Montgomery, Boompah, even Ruby McCann and Luke Easton. If they needed protecting, he would guard them. If they needed comfort, he would do his best to provide it. If they needed security, he would become a bulwark against Phil Fox and anyone else who threatened their peace.

Though he couldn't understand exactly how it had happened, Zachary knew the past two and a half months in Ambleside had altered him profoundly. He had become a part of the lives of the people here, and they were now a part of him. No, it was more than that. As he got into his car and shut the door, he knew the meaning of the passion he felt.

This was the place where he had fallen in love.

~

"Shame about Ellie, isn't it?" Phil Fox stood just inside Ambleside Chapel's fellowship hall and swirled red Kool-Aid around in his plastic cup. "And her so young. Really makes you think."

Beside him, Elizabeth stared at the paper plate of uneaten food in her hand. Why did people bring so much food to a funeral? Was there some unwritten law that said a good potluck meal would comfort the bereaved? And why did people say stupid things, making inane comments like those of Phil Fox, who probably had never spoken a word to Ellie Easton?

In the past three days, Elizabeth had hardly eaten or slept. Somehow, Luke had managed to tell Montgomery about her mommy's death. The two children had spent each night since then on Elizabeth's foldout sofa, holding each other tightly and crying themselves to sleep. Zachary had dropped by the shop countless times, asking if there was anything he could do. And Luke . . . oh, Luke Easton had grieved.

Elizabeth closed her eyes. Never had she known a man to be so torn apart by loss. He had raged and wept, he had shouted and stormed, he had curled into himself and sobbed in silence. All she could do was organize the growing supply of food in his refrigerator, vacuum his floor after all the guests had come and gone, and pack away Ellie's things.

"That little gal of hers is going to face a hard life without a mama," Phil said, taking a bite of green bean casserole. "'Course, I guess you'd know more about that than most folks, Liz. Pearlene tells me you lost your parents when you were small."

Elizabeth nodded, unable to speak.

"Myself, I look for Luke to marry pretty quick. I'm with Pearlene on that one. A man like him doesn't need to just sit around, you know. He's young, he's got a good trade with all that carpentering he does, and he's got that little gal to take care of. Beats me why they gave her that weird name. What is it, anyhow?"

"Montgomery."

"That's a city in Alabama, you know. We used to have a bus come in from there of a Tuesday, but not anymore. Things sure do change. This town just isn't the same place." He stuck a bacon-wrapped sausage in his mouth and chewed for a while. "We've got to move ahead with the times, is my motto. I guess you know I'm planning to block Zachary from taking over the old Chalmers house. I've had a meeting with a lawyer in Jeff City."

Elizabeth lifted her head. "A lawyer, Phil?"

"Sometimes a man has to go to extremes." He clamped a hand on his belt buckle and adjusted his trousers. "And I'm willing to go the distance on this one."

"Oh, Phil, why do you want to block Zachary? You know Grace gave him that mansion, free and clear. What are you going to get out of it by talking to a lawyer, for Pete's sake?"

"I'm going to better this town."

"Better it? How?" She was beginning to feel angry now. "Are you planning to preserve the mansion?"

"I'm going to see that the property stays with the city. It belongs to Ambleside, and nobody's going to take it away."

"The *property* isn't going anywhere. The question is the fate of the *mansion*. You've never made any pretense about liking that old house. I've heard you say it ought to be torn down."

"Well, it's an eyesore. You've got to admit that."

"Then why block Zachary? He's planning to tear it down and build an office. Let him have it."

"Nope. That's not what the founding fathers would have wanted."

"How do you know what the founding fathers wanted?"

"Because I have read the charter." He stuffed a hunk of hot roll in his mouth and then punched the air with a buttery finger. "I'm an elected official of this city, and I'm going to do my duty by my constituents."

Elizabeth picked up a sausage ball. "Well, I'm one of your constituents, and I want to know what you're up to."

"None of your beeswax."

"Oh, Phil, good grief!"

"Good grief, yourself. You'll thank me in the end. One of these days, you'll see I'm doing the very best thing for this town, and you'll thank me. You and Pearlene have the most to benefit by what I'm planning, so don't you 'good grief' me."

"You're back to the parking lot idea, aren't you?"

"My lips are zipped."

"We don't need a parking lot. Zachary says all we have to

do is take out that strip of grass around the square and repaint the lines, and we can have angled parking."

"Angled parking?" He picked up a brownie. "And I guess Zachary Chalmers is going to stand there and direct traffic while everybody and their brother tries to back out onto River Street? Angled parking would give us more fender benders than a bumper-car track. Can you just see Ruby McCann trying to back out her big DeSoto from in front of the Corner Market every morning after she's bought her milk? She'll wind up backing through the plate-glass window of Bud Huff's hardware store, sure as shootin'. And then we'll have Bud coming to city council meetings complaining as loud as his father does now."

"The town charter says the mansion should be *preserved*, not torn down to build a parking lot. You're planning to try to get city ownership of that property, aren't you? And then you're going to tear down the mansion yourself."

He pulled a finger across his lips. "As tight as a Ziploc bag."

"Phil Fox, you know that charter orders the mansion be kept standing. 'Preserving the house for perpetuity,' it says. 'A memorial to the Chalmers family and a cornerstone of the town of Ambleside.'"

Phil squinted his eyes. "How do you know what that charter says?"

"My lips are sealed," Elizabeth said, tossing the sausage ball back onto her plate, "as tight as a Ziploc bag."

"Well, I'll be jiggered." He searched the fellowship hall. "Where's Pearlene?"

As Phil left Elizabeth's side and began shouldering his way through the gathering, she sagged against the wall. Zachary emerged from a cluster of townsfolk. "I thought you were going to bean him with the sausage ball," he said.

"I should have. I felt like he was about to eat me alive."

"My hunch is that he wasn't discussing our recent loss in the community of Ambleside."

"He met with a lawyer, and he's planning to get city ownership of the Chalmers House property. Then he's going to tear down the mansion and put in a parking lot."

Zachary took a sip of Kool-Aid. For a moment he didn't speak, his gray green eyes searching hers. "We've just buried Ellie Easton," he said. "In light of that, I don't see that parking lots or office buildings or old mansions matter much at all."

"They don't," she said. "But life does go on, and somehow we have to find purpose in it."

"That doesn't sound very optimistic."

"I don't exactly feel like dancing in the aisle right now."

"How about walking around the square?"

She glanced at the crowded room. "Nick and Montgomery . . ."

"They're playing on the jungle gym outside. I checked on them while you were dueling with Phil."

"They're playing?"

"They're kids. Life does go on, Elizabeth."

"All right." She put her plate in a nearby trash can and joined Zachary, slipping her arm through his. "Once around the square. For life."

∾

Somehow summer had caught Elizabeth by surprise. Nick was still in class, though summer school required only half days. She had turned on the air conditioner in the window of Finders Keepers, but the river breeze had kept the air from feeling too sultry. Now, as she strolled the square with Zachary, she breathed in the dense, humid air of full Missouri summer.

"The statue of Harry Truman," he announced as they drew abreast of the bronze figure of the former president.

"And here we come to the old cannon. I wonder how long those two have graced the southern corners of the square."

"As long as I can remember." Almost too tired to walk, she laid her head against his shoulder. "Grandma and I used to take the bus to Ambleside to shop. I thought of it as a big place."

"You never went to Jefferson City?"

"Not often. Grandma couldn't drive, but she kept Grandpa's old Buick in working order long after he was dead and gone. When she became sick, and I was old enough to get my license, I used to drive her to the doctor in Jefferson City. After her appointment, we'd go over to Zesto and get a vanilla Coke with two straws. We thought we were in tall cotton."

He laughed. "And here we come to the Ambleside pavilion."

"The scene of countless band concerts, church picnics, political speeches, and weddings. Ruby McCann calls this pavilion the social center of the town."

"Does she now? Well, I'll swan."

Elizabeth felt a smile creep across her lips as Zachary escorted her up the pavilion's wooden steps. How long had it been since she'd found anything to laugh about? She felt as though she were carrying a heavy tray on her shoulders, a tray piled high with burdens. Nick needed to learn his addition facts. Montgomery refused to sleep in her own bed. Boompah's back was giving him trouble again. Luke Easton had ordered Pastor Paul out of his house. Twice Elizabeth had found Luke drinking alone. The woman who had contracted Elizabeth to furnish the buildings in Jefferson City was impatient with the amount of time she had taken off during the illness and death of Ellie. And now Phil Fox had reverted to his parking-lot campaign.

"What was that sigh for?" Zachary leaned one shoulder against a white post.

"Did I sigh?"

"It almost blew me over."

"Must have been that garlic cheese dip."

"You didn't eat the cheese dip," he said, slipping his arm around her waist and pulling her close. "You didn't eat anything in there. I was watching."

"It's hard to eat when your stomach is in knots."

"My insides have been tied up ever since I met you, Elizabeth."

She lifted her head and met his eyes. "It's because we've been fighting about the mansion."

"Wrong."

For a moment she couldn't speak as he looked intently into her eyes. "Zachary, that night at the Foxes' house—"

"I don't want to talk about the Foxes."

"That night when you said that prayer . . . that surrender prayer, I realized I needed to let go, too. Right now, I'm not sure what I'm supposed to be doing or where I'm supposed to be going, but I just want you to know that I'm backing off on the mansion. I want you to be happy."

"I'm happy right now." He slipped his hands up her arms and stroked her shoulders with his thumbs. "I'm happy when I'm with you, Elizabeth."

"Oh, Zachary . . ." She tried to suppress the bubble of joy that rose up inside her. "I feel like a teenager who sneaked out of class."

"To go smooch with her boyfriend?"

"We're not smooching."

"Now we are." He drew her close and gave her a long, warm kiss. "Still feel like a kid?"

"Definitely not." She drew in a deep breath. "Zachary, I'm so . . . scared. That's the best word for it. I'm scared."

"Of me?"

"Of this."

"Kissing?" He turned her around so she was leaning

against the post. "Kissing is not scary," he said softly. "Thinking about losing you is."

"I'm not going anywhere, Zachary."

"Luke didn't think Ellie was going anywhere."

"We can't live in fear of loss. We have to let go of the past. We have to keep on living, keep on embracing life and all the things God has given us."

"Is this the same Elizabeth Hayes I talked to at an antiques auction? The woman who reveres an ancient glass-topped counter at which stood countless customers from days of yore? The woman who patiently dusts an old metal coffee grinder that hasn't seen a coffee bean in a hundred years? Is this the woman who never lets go of the past?"

"Out with the old, in with the new," she said, shrugging. Then she stretched upward and brushed a kiss across his lips. "I guess I've changed a little since that morning at the mansion."

"Mmm. Good changes."

"You've changed, too."

"Yep. I've been drawing Victorian curlicues on all my architectural renderings. I actually sketched a cupola on the roof of a nursing home the other day."

"No!" she said in mock horror. "Not a cupola!"

"Indeed. And if I'm going to add cupolas and if you're going to allow kissing, we ought to figure out a way to keep this trend moving forward. Which means I'd better keep my hands on that property over there."

Elizabeth turned in his arms and faced Chalmers House. The heat of summer made the old pink bricks shimmer like a mirage. "Are you saying we should join forces against Phil?"

"How about if we join hands and hearts . . . and see what God has in store for us?"

Elizabeth tried to make herself breathe. She knew he was

asking for a bond that went beyond the casual friendship they had enjoyed. He was asking for a commitment, and with that commitment, he would expect her to risk. Risk her own happiness. Risk the tender heart of her son. Risk losing the comfortable stability of her world and face the possibility of terrible pain.

Without waiting for the storms of fear to assail her, Elizabeth clutched his hands and stood on tiptoe to kiss his cheek. "Yes," she said. "I'm willing."

"Then we'd better haul our backsides over to Sawyer-the-lawyer's office and figure out how to keep Phil Fox away from my property."

"Amen," she said as they linked arms and descended the steps of the Ambleside pavilion.

TWELVE

"Phil Fox, that sly devil." John Sawyer shook his head in admiration. "He's got something up his sleeve, and unless Pearlene spills the beans, you folks had better stay on your toes."

Elizabeth leaned forward and touched the photocopy on the lawyer's desk. "Do you think the town charter is a legal document?"

"I suspect it might hold up pretty well."

He folded his hands, fingertips touching, and leaned back in his big leather chair. Elizabeth fought the urge to jump up. She had left Nick and Montgomery in the care of Boompah, who had taken the children to her house to play on the swing set. Luke Easton had vanished earlier in the day, right after Ellie's funeral service, and no one could find him. The last thing Elizabeth needed to be doing was listening to Sawyer-the-lawyer hem and haw over the town charter.

"It does have Zachary Chalmers's signature," she offered. "But it wasn't voted on, and it doesn't have any seals on it, or anything. So, do you think it's binding?"

"Well, now, that depends." The attorney rocked back and forth, the springs in his chair squeaking loudly. "It's obviously authentic, and a good lawyer could argue its validity either way. A true town charter is a legal document. It's kind of like a constitution, you know."

"So, is it Zachary Chalmers's will?"

"No. And neither is that letter of Grace's you found in her

Bible. As far as the future of the house is concerned, you could argue that they both ought to be thrown out. That would leave only Grace's official last will and testament, which gives the house and the property to Zachary to do with as he sees fit."

"Until Phil stepped in, that's how it stood," Zachary said. "I was going to raze the mansion and build offices."

"On the other hand, both the charter and the letter indicate a strong desire on the part of the property's owners to keep the mansion standing for perpetuity. Phil's lawyer could make a case that if you inherit the mansion, you've got to preserve it."

"How am I supposed to do that, unless they want to provide restoration funds?"

"Well, I think that's what Phil is banking on. He's hoping to wedge you into a tight spot where you can't afford to keep the mansion standing, but you can't tear it down either."

"And then I'll just turn it over to the city."

Elizabeth let out a hot breath. "If Zachary gives Grace's house to the city because the town charter says it's supposed to remain standing, then how is Phil going to get the right to tear it down and put in his parking lot?"

"You've got me on that one," Sawyer said. "I'm stumped. Are you sure he doesn't have some plan to restore the building himself?"

"Every time I talk to him," she replied, "he tells me what an eyesore it is. He makes no bones about his dislike of the mansion. He wants to tear it down, and he wants a parking lot."

"So the congestion around the square won't be so bad?"

"So Pearlene's customers won't keep bothering Al Huff over at the gas station."

"You're saying Phil's got a personal interest in this matter. He's got a lot to gain by putting in that parking lot." Sawyer tapped his fingertips together. "All the same, if Phil's lawyer uses that town charter to keep Zachary from razing the mansion, I can't figure out how Phil thinks he can turn right around and have the city tear it down. It just doesn't make sense."

"Maybe he's planning to move the mansion," Elizabeth offered.

"The cost would be prohibitive," Zachary said. "I've already looked into it."

"You have?" She cocked her head in surprise. "I didn't know you'd thought of anything but tearing it down."

"I've considered it from every angle." He picked up both the photocopy of the charter and the letter from Grace's Bible. "Look, John, see what you can find out for us about these documents. I want that property, and I'm willing to fight to keep it."

"Are you sure? It could cost you a pretty penny in legal fees—and then you'd still have the expense of tearing the thing down and building your new office complex. Maybe you ought to negotiate with Phil."

"What do you mean?"

"Offer him a trade. Tell him you'll give the town the Chalmers property in exchange for a nice piece of acreage at the edge of town. Then he can take a wrecking ball to the old place and pave his parking lot, and you can build your office."

As Zachary pondered this, Elizabeth twisted her fingers together. *No,* she prayed silently. *Don't let him give up, Lord. Grace wanted Zachary to have the house and the land. She cared about him, and she knew he needed roots. In the best way she knew how, his aunt loved him. Give him his birthright, Father, please.*

"No," he said, standing. "I'm not backing down that easily, John. I never understood the value of a legacy before I met Elizabeth. I thought family Bibles were just old books.

And I thought a ramshackle mansion deserved to make way for progress. But that was before I knew that my aunt had always kept a vase of fresh flowers in the hallway—flowers that fascinated a little boy and charmed an old man. It was before I realized that a moth-eaten red coat could bring back the memory of the tender love of a stranger. It was before I recognized that houses and land aren't just the focus of architectural design. They're places where people build their visions and leave their hopes. That land is Chalmers land, John. It's my land. And Phil Fox isn't going to take it away from me."

Elizabeth felt like cheering. Sawyer-the-lawyer grinned from ear to ear. "You ever thought of running for mayor?" he asked. "I'd vote for you."

Zachary laughed. "I think that's Phil Fox's goal, and I'd rather not do battle with him on too many fronts."

"Aw, he's mostly just a big talker. Big schemes, big dreams." He rolled his big chair back and stood. "Head over to Dandy Donuts some morning and listen to him expound. Fancies himself quite the orator, Phil does. One morning he's all hot and bothered to take out a corner of the square for a brand-new parking lot. The next morning, he's up in arms because Jacob Jungemeyer's sick and the Corner Market's been shut down. 'Gotta bring us in a Safeway,' he shouts. 'Gotta keep Ruby McCann in fresh milk.'"

Elizabeth laughed. "I guess Phil's not exactly a fearsome force."

"Well, he's talked quite a few people into thinking he's somebody pretty important. And he has managed to accomplish a few good things during his tenure on the council. The city council rezoned some lots downtown, got some sewer lines put in over on the west edge of the city, fixed up the sidewalks over by Ambleside Chapel. Yeah, Phil has his good points. Like I said, though, you'll have to watch your step with him."

As Zachary thanked the attorney, Elizabeth moved to the window and watched the last cars pulling away from the chapel. Ellie was gone, but Montgomery needed to go on living. Boompah still needed someone to listen to his Gypsy stories. And Ruby McCann still needed her fresh milk each morning. Life had to go on.

"How about dinner?" Zachary asked when they had stepped out onto the sidewalk. "Your place?"

"Inviting yourself over, Mr. Chalmers?"

"It's closer to the action than my apartment."

"What action?"

"Well, I think I'd better eat a quick bite and then start looking for Luke."

"Where do you suppose he could be?" As they walked, she focused on the distant row of shops across the square. Not far from Finders Keepers stood the empty home of Ellie Easton. Empty of her warmth, her tenderness, her love.

"I don't know where Luke is," Zachary said. "But I know if I'd lost someone I loved as much as he loved Ellie, I'd be in bad shape."

He slipped his arm around Elizabeth and drew her close.

❧

"There were bad guys over at Grace's house, Mommy," Nick said, grabbing Elizabeth's hand as she stepped into her living room. "They were walking all around, and they scared me to deaf."

"Bad guys?" She looked at Boompah.

The old man shook his head. "I didn't see anyone, but the children tell me it's a true story. I'm sorry, Elizabeth, but my back doesn't let me walk around very much these days. I watch Nikolai and his friend, but I cannot quickly go all the way to Grace's house."

"Did you talk to the bad guys, Nick?" Elizabeth asked, kneeling to face her son.

His green eyes widened, guilt stricken. "I'm not supposed to talk to strangers."

"I know that, but I think maybe you and Montgomery did talk to them, didn't you?"

Pale faced and clutching the ends of her red braids, Montgomery nodded. "We did, Miss Hayes. We talked to them, but they talked to us first. It wasn't our fault, I promise."

Zachary sat down on the couch and took the little girl on his lap. "Hey, Montgomery," he said. "Were you scared, too?"

"I was brave. I told Nick that I saw somebody walking around over at Grace's house, and we'd better go find out who it was. So we went across the grass to the porch, and that's when the man came out."

"What did he say?"

"He said, 'You kids get outta here.' And I said, 'My mommy died, and you aren't being nice to me, and I don't like you.' And he said, 'We're busy here.' Then he shut the door. So Nick went right up to the door and knocked."

"Oh, Nick, you didn't." Her heart faltering, Elizabeth studied her son. How many times had she prayed for God's protection over this vulnerable little boy? He was so trusting, so innocent. Though she had warned him about strangers, she didn't doubt he would willingly walk into someone's trap.

"Yes, I did," he said, his small chest swelling. "I'm not going to let any bad guys talk mean to Magunnery. She's my friend, and she's sad about her mommy."

"I know she's sad, sweetheart. But those men were strangers."

"Not after I talked to them. They're named Bob and Don, and they live in Jefferson City. Do you know what they do for a job, Mom? They walk around in old buildings to see if they're falling down. And you know what they said about Grace's house? They said it's falling down."

"Inspectors?" Zachary said from the couch. "Phil must have called them in, because I haven't given anyone permission to enter the house."

"What gave Phil the right to let those men walk around in there?" Elizabeth asked.

"Property inspection is city business." He thought for a moment. "And I think I finally know what he's up to. Once I gave the city control of the property, he would have the house condemned."

"Condemned?" Elizabeth tried to process the significance of such a ruling. If the property were condemned, that might supersede the wishes of Zachary Chalmers in the old town charter.

"Is Phil Fox bad?" Nick asked.

"He's difficult," Elizabeth said, standing. "And that's an understatement. I'm going to make some sandwiches for supper."

"What kind?" Nick followed her into the kitchen, his concerns about food immediately taking precedence over anything else. "Not peanut butter. Maybe ham? Or we could have hot dogs, Mom. We had sandwiches last night. Maybe we could have burritos tonight. I like burritos because you can get all the food groups in them, and then you'll be healthy."

"We're having roast beef sandwiches, Nick," Elizabeth said.

"With mayonnaise? I hope not mayonnaise. I could get some mustard out of the refrigerator. We could have ketchup, too. We could put on cheese but not lettuce. Lettuce is leaves, and I don't like to eat leaves. They're revolting and disgusting."

Elizabeth worked on the sandwiches as her shadow trailed her around the kitchen, offering suggestions and trying to change the menu to fit his tastes. She was so accustomed to their nightly routine that she hardly took notice. Her thoughts dwelled on Luke Easton and where he might have gone. Normally, he was such a good father. Though Elizabeth gladly would keep Montgomery at her house for a while longer, Luke was going to have to accept his responsibilities as a single parent. But, oh, the thought of that house without Ellie . . .

"You know, you two are pretty cute," Zachary said, one shoulder propped against the door frame.

Elizabeth stopped and met Zachary's eyes. Nick was standing at her elbow, his chin propped on the counter as he observed the sandwich preparations. She shook her head and lowered the knife coated in mayonnaise. "I'm so upset," she said softly.

Zachary crossed the room and slipped an arm around her. "You know, I could go over to the Tastee Hut and pick up some burgers."

"Not burgers!" Nick said, his small head appearing between them. "I think we could have roast beef sandwiches. I think Mommy has already cut the bread."

"Nick." Zachary cupped the boy's face in his palms. "Go see what Boompah and Montgomery want to drink."

"But what about the burgers?"

"Go."

Nick scuttled out of the room, and Zachary let out a breath. "He's a handful. Persistent little guy."

"Just when I think I can't be patient with him any longer, I remember that his dogged determination is what will get him through life. It's Montgomery who really worries me. Where do you suppose Luke went?"

"Probably someplace quiet."

"Zachary, I'm sure I smelled alcohol on him a few times. That's so unlike him."

"He's grieving."

"You're quick to excuse his behavior."

"I'm quick to remember that he's human." He picked up the knife and began spreading mayonnaise on a slice of bread. "You know, that's the trouble with churchy people. They're human themselves—but they can't let anybody else have a few faults."

"Churchy people?"

"The minute you act like a human, all the churchy people react with horror. OK, so Luke Easton's falling apart a little bit. What are we supposed to do? Reject him? Condemn him? Label him a sinner?"

"I didn't say that."

"All this judging is what keeps people out of church, you know? I figure Luke is about at his wit's end. A few months ago, he had a strong marriage and a sweet kid, and his life looked pretty good. Now he has no wife. He probably doesn't know what to do with his daughter. I'm sure he doesn't want to go to work. And his future looks like a big black hole. So he's not acting like he usually does. Who would?"

Elizabeth crossed her arms and regarded Zachary. "I'm not condemning Luke. I'm worried about him."

"Then let's go find him and bring him here."

"But what if he's been drinking? Montgomery can't see her own father—"

"She can't be sheltered from reality, Elizabeth. Her mom's gone. Her dad's having a rough time. Instead of hiding her and judging him, we need to hold them both. We need to love them."

The defensiveness and anger that had arisen inside Elizabeth began to dissipate. "Is this the Zachary Chalmers I saw that day at the auction? The man who didn't care how anybody felt?"

"I think that guy surrendered over at Phil Fox's house."

Elizabeth finished assembling the sandwiches. "You

surrendered, yes. But you're still hurt. I suspect you must have known a few churchy people in your time."

"Too many to count."

"Then let's not be like them." She picked up the sandwiches and dropped them into a paper bag. "Let's be Christly people, and let's all go together to find Montgomery's daddy."

❧

"This is like *Star Wars*," Nick announced as the group of four walked through Chalmers Memorial Park, eating roast beef sandwiches and drinking sodas. "Remember when they were all looking for that old man in the desert? I am Luke Skywalker, and Magunnery is the princess."

"I don't want to be the princess," Montgomery said as she finished her sandwich. "I want to be Han Solo."

"You can't be him. You're a girl. You have braids like the princess."

"But I want to fly the Millennium Falcon."

"No, I will fly the Lemony Falcon," Nick countered. "You will be the princess, Zachary will be Ham Solo, Boompah will be Yoda, and Mom will be the Wookie."

"Isn't the Wookie that great big hairy creature who growls all the time?" Elizabeth asked over Zachary's guffaws. "Now, wait just a minute here, kiddo."

"And Phil Fox will be Dark Vader," Nick finished.

"He's a bad, bad man," Montgomery announced. "He wants to tear down all the houses in Ambleside. I hate him."

"Now, Montgomery, Mr. Fox is not so bad," Elizabeth said gently. "He cares about Ambleside. He just has his own ideas about what to do with Grace's house."

"If he tries to tear down anything," Nick said, "I will pick up a hammerjack and drill a hole right through him."

"Nick!"

"My daddy uses one of those sometimes," Montgomery said. "But he doesn't tear down houses. He builds them. He's a carpenter. He built my crib and my high chair and Mommy's rocking chair. Mommy says he can build anything. She thinks my daddy is strong and handsome. I do, too, and my mommy is the prettiest lady I ever saw in my whole life."

Elizabeth shone the flashlight on the trail as the four walked along it. Grief clutched at her throat. She remembered so clearly the hours and days after the car accident that had killed her parents. Every time she had turned around, she expected to see her mother hovering nearby or hear her father discussing his day's work. She had spoken of them as though they were alive, thought of them as alive, expected them to come walking through the door at any moment. It took a long, long time before she had realized what death really meant. Death had been so final. So hollow.

But then her grandmother had taken her in, and the two of them had walked to church together every Sunday morning. That's where Elizabeth learned that death was not the end. Death was just a door, and on the other side stretched heaven in all its glory.

"I am Han Solo," Montgomery announced, "and I will defeat the evil empire of Darth Vader."

"I am Luke Skywalker!" Nick cried loudly. "Dark Vader will never defeat us!"

"Hey, Miz Hayes, Mr. Chalmers. Whatchall doing out here in the park?" Ben, the young policeman who patrolled Ambleside's sleepy streets, approached the group, his flashlight swinging from side to side across the path. "The dispatcher got a call from somebody thinking some kids were out here causing trouble again. You know those kids spray-painted their names on the fountain the other night. Pretty dumb, huh? We caught 'em right off."

"We're looking for Luke Easton," Zachary said. "His wife's funeral was this afternoon, and we haven't seen him since."

"Yeah, I know the family. I went over to their house a couple of times when she was having some trouble and they called 911. Nice folks. Too bad about her dying and all. So, you say he's disappeared?"

"My daddy hasn't disappeared!" Montgomery insisted loudly. "My daddy's here. He's here!"

"It's OK, Montgomery," Elizabeth said, slipping her arm around the little girl. "Of course your daddy's around here somewhere. Maybe Ben can help us find him."

"This their little girl?" the young policeman asked, peering at the child in the dim light. "Aw, poor kid. Listen up, honey, we'll find your daddy, sure as shootin'. Anybody been by their house lately?"

"We called about a half hour ago," Zachary said. "No one answered."

"Well, I'll check over there right now. Any other place he might have gone tonight?"

"He likes to go to church," Montgomery said. "He's a deacon."

"Then I'll take a look at church, too."

Elizabeth thought of telling Ben not to bother. Luke had made his feelings of betrayal pretty clear. He felt that God had failed him by letting Ellie die. Elizabeth could understand that, even though she knew God had never promised to keep his flock from the ravages of pain and death. After all, to get to the lap of the Father, they first had to walk through that door of death.

"I'll radio Mick, too," Ben said of the other policeman in town. "He led the funeral procession out to the cemetery today. Maybe he saw where Mr. Easton went."

"Thanks, Ben." Zachary bent down and scooped Montgomery into his arms. "Come here, Han Solo. I'll be the Millennium Falcon for a while."

"I want to ride, too!" Nick said.

Elizabeth reached for her son's hand and spotted a shadowy lump on his back. "Nick, what is this?"

"It's my backpack. I brung all the things we need." He swung it over his shoulder and unzipped the pouch. "Here's a tower—"

"Towel," she corrected.

"And my toothbrush. And some underpants."

At this Montgomery began to giggle.

"I am just trying to help," Nick said firmly. "You shouldn't laugh, Magunnery. It's not nice. And here is the Bible."

He pulled Grace's old book out of his pack and extended it to his mother. With a gasp of dismay, Elizabeth took the Bible and drew it close to her chest.

"Nikolai Hayes, what on earth did you bring this out here for? This is Grace's Bible. It's very fragile. I put it in my shop, right on the counter, and I told you not to touch it. The whole thing could fall apart. See how loose the pages are?"

Nick studied the worn black binding. "Mommy," he said solemnly, "you always told me that the Bible says, 'Seek and you shall find.' How are we going to find Magunnery's daddy if we don't have that Bible?"

She stared into her son's serious eyes. "Oh, Nick . . ."

"He's right," Zachary said. "Seek and you shall find. That's what the Bible says."

"You see?" Nick told her. "I'm right. And now we should pray, because that is how you talk to God if you want to tell him what you're looking for."

She straightened and turned to Zachary. "Out of the mouths of babes."

"OK, I will pray," Nick announced. He took the Bible from his mother and held it in midair. "Dear God, we are seeking for Magunnery's daddy. Please help us to find him, because he's lost. In Jesus' name we pray, amen."

"Amen," Zachary said. "Good prayer, Nick."

"Oh, yes, it was a good prayer," the boy said. "I am very good at prayers. And now I will give everybody my special treat." He reached into his backpack and pulled out a handful of miniature Snickers bars. "Boompah gave them to me."

They walked across the grass to a park bench and sat down, Montgomery on Zachary's lap and Nick snuggled close to his mother. Elizabeth peeled the crinkly paper and slipped the bite of chocolate into her mouth. Leaning back, she gazed out at the darkened forest, its oak and maple trees thick with leaves.

As the chocolate melted, she thought of the oddity of this little group. None of them really belonged together, none were related by blood or genetics. Yet God had drawn them by his invisible threads to this narrow bench in a quiet park.

She looked down the path toward the fountain, and there she spotted a dark shape hunched over, head in his hands. Reaching out, she touched Zachary's arm. In silence, she nodded in the direction of the figure.

"Seek," she whispered.

He nodded. "And you shall find."

THIRTEEN

"Hey, Luke." Zachary approached the silent figure. "It's Zachary Chalmers. We've been looking for you. You OK?"

The man raised his head, his eyes red-rimmed in the soft light of the park's old streetlamps. "Hey, Zachary."

"Montgomery saved you a couple of roast beef sandwiches."

"She with Elizabeth?"

"Yep. Sitting on a bench right down that path. She misses her dad." He sat on the rim of the stone fountain. "Today was rough on both of you, I guess."

Luke lowered his head. "I can't figure how to get through this."

"I doubt there's an easy way."

"You ever lost someone you loved?"

"I never loved anybody."

He gave a low laugh. "Be glad."

"Yeah? All those good years with Ellie weren't enough to outweigh the pain you feel right now?"

"It's hard to think about the good times. When I do, it cuts real hard that she's gone." He let out a breath. "I can't look after Montgomery right now. She's got to stay with Elizabeth."

"You're her dad."

"I don't trust myself." He straightened and stood. "I'm mad. Crazy mad. Yesterday I threw a chair through the kitchen window, you know? I was so glad Montgomery was over at Elizabeth's house. She can't see me like this."

"You think you might hurt her?"

"Not with my hands. But I can't have my little girl seeing me this way. I want everything to be all right again before I take her back."

"What's going to make everything all right?"

"I don't know." He began to pace. "I just don't know. Maybe I need to move out of town. The house is too quiet. Too many memories."

"You've got a lot of friends here in Ambleside. People care about you."

"Yeah, right. They like me when I'm doing my deacon thing—passing around the collection plate, knocking on doors, handing out the church bulletin. But they haven't seen me throwing chairs through the window or drinking so much I can't stand up straight. When everything's OK with you, everything's OK with them. But let a man get in a bad way—"

"I used to think that, too. Sure, some people will always let you down. But I'm starting to find out that there are folks who'll care about you no matter what you say or do."

Luke gave a grunt.

"Don't buy it?" Zachary asked.

"Nope."

"I guess I'm going to have to prove you wrong." Zachary stood and faced the broken man. Even as he spoke, he realized he was taking yet another risk. To love Elizabeth left him open to losing her. And he could get burned reaching out to Luke. Yet his surrender to God's plan had made it impossible to turn away from either of them.

"Let's head over to that park bench and eat those sandwiches Montgomery saved," Zachary suggested. "And tomorrow morning, I'll drop by your place to make sure you've hauled your carcass out of bed."

Luke stared at him. "Why?"

"I guess watching you and Ellie taught me a thing or two.

You may not feel it right now, but the life you shared with your wife was worth every shred of the pain you're feeling now. When Elizabeth told me that Ellie was dying, I thought about the fact that I didn't care about anybody enough to mourn their loss. And nobody cared about me. That's when I realized how empty I felt."

"Look, I don't want anyone's pity."

"I really don't care what you want, Luke. I know what you need—and that's a friend."

"Great." Luke looked away, his large shoulders bent with heaviness. "When you want someone around, you can't have her. And when you don't want someone around, he sticks like a leech."

Stepping over to the man, Zachary laid a hand on his shoulder. "Come on. Your daughter's waiting."

❧

"Where is Zachary?" Nick was sitting beside his mother on the porch swing. The sweltering summer evening had taken its toll on Elizabeth, who felt her patience dripping away with every bead of sweat that rolled down her neck.

Three days had gone by since she and Zachary had walked together to the pavilion following Ellie Easton's funeral. There he had kissed her and held her close. *How about if we join hands and hearts . . . and see what God has in store for us?* His words of commitment had echoed through her heart. Was it possible that God had a future for her with Zachary Chalmers?

"I don't know where Zachary is," she told her son. "How should I know where he is? You know, Nick, it would help me a lot if you would just drop the subject of Zachary Chalmers. The man is not a part of our family. He has his own life, and he can do whatever he wants in the evening. Honestly."

"Are you mad at Zachary? Or are you mad at Mr. Fox for letting the bad guys into Grace's house?"

"I'm not mad at Phil Fox. I'm not mad at anybody."

"You sound mad."

OK, maybe she was a little angry. Why hadn't she heard from Zachary in all this time?

She had almost let herself believe that her heavenly Father could take two adversaries and strip away everything that separated them. In spite of interfering neighbors and a pestering little boy whose matchmaking efforts had nearly derailed them, she and Zachary were finding common ground. And maybe a common future.

So, where was the man?

What was he up to?

Where had he gone?

Why hadn't he shown up at her shop? or on her porch?

Why hadn't he even called?

She brushed her hand down the back of her neck. Why did she care? She'd spent years alone. She didn't need a man. Certainly not. She and Nick had a perfectly happy life together. God had given her more than she could have dreamed. A lovely home. A thriving business. A precious son. She should count her blessings and stop thinking about a man who confused her as much as he thrilled her.

"Zachary doesn't like Mr. Fox very much either," Nick said, swinging his legs back and forth. "I think Mr. Fox is a bloodsucking bleach."

Elizabeth let out a groan and leaned her head against the porch swing's chain. She studied the mansion, its darkened windows ghostly in the bright moonlight. Mosquitoes and moths danced around the single light on its back porch. How often had Grace sat out there in her favorite wicker rocking chair and fanned herself as she sipped a glass of iced lemonade?

"Zachary would never let Mr. Fox—"

"Nick, I asked you not to talk about Zachary. And I don't want to hear about Mr. Fox either."

The boy fell silent. Elizabeth felt the heavy curtain of mother-guilt drift down over her shoulders. She shouldn't be impatient with her son. Nick always had trouble switching from one topic to another. Once his thoughts settled on something like math, or dinner, or Zachary Chalmers, he couldn't let the subject go without fully exploring it. That made school difficult for the child, and it nearly drove Elizabeth nuts. But it was Nick's personality, and she was his mother.

"I will change the subject," he announced. "Mrs. Wrinkles taught me how to do it." He thought for a moment. "It is very hot weather tonight."

"Yes it is. I'll bet the temperature is in the nineties."

"I will check the thermonitor." He jumped off the swing and raced across the porch. Standing on tiptoe, he peered at the little gauge. "Oh, yes, it's very hot. That little silver stuff . . . what do you call it? Mars?"

"Mercury."

"It's high up in the thermonitor." He sauntered back to the swing. "Zachary has air-conditioning in his apartment. He told me it's always cool there, even at lunchtime. Zachary said it's good to stay cool in the summer, because if you get too hot, you can't think straight. Is Zachary right, Mommy?"

Elizabeth rolled her eyes. "I'm sure he is."

"I think that's why Zachary didn't come here tonight. It's too hot. He wants to stay in his air-conditioning apartment. I like his apartment, but I like our house, too. When you get married to Zachary—"

"Nikolai!" Elizabeth turned and took his tiny shoulders. "Please, honey. Don't talk about Zachary. Don't talk about Phil Fox. In fact, don't talk about anything. Just be quiet."

"Maybe I should go and see Magunnery. She says

nighttime is the saddest of all the times without her mommy. That's when she cries."

Pushed to the limit, Elizabeth let out a breath. "You know I don't like for you to go anywhere when it's dark."

"But look at the moon, Mommy. It's not dark at all."

"OK, fine. Go to Montgomery's house. Cross through the Muellers' backyard instead of walking down the sidewalk. You can stay for a few minutes and play with Montgomery, if her daddy says it's all right. But when I call you, I want you to come right home."

"Yesss!" He pumped his fist. "Magunnery will be happy to see me. She loves me."

"I love you, too," she called after him.

Nick paused in his headlong flight down the porch steps. "Magunnery and I will think of a way to make you feel happier, Mom. Don't worry."

"Nick, you don't have to make me happy . . ." She watched him hop down the three porch steps and disappear across the moonlit yard. No one could make her happy. Her joy needed to come from the knowledge that Christ loved her. He had made her whole and complete.

Oh, God, why did you put this awful longing inside me? she prayed. She stretched out sideways on the swing and rested her head on a pillow. *Father, you've given me so much. Please take away this aching desire for human contact. Take away my longing for a man . . . for Zachary. Help me to rest in you.*

She drifted, letting peace slide through her. Snippets of Scripture floated across her thoughts. *My gracious favor is all you need. . . . Yet I am not alone because the Father is with me. . . . I will never forsake you. . . .*

It was true. She didn't need anyone or anything. Whether Zachary came or went was totally in Christ's hands.

Aware of a slight breeze wafting across from the river, Elizabeth focused on her work furnishing the three old houses in Jefferson City. She had less than a month to complete the job, and she still needed to locate quite a few items. Maybe she would take Nick out for an antiquing foray one of these afternoons after his summer-school session was done for the day. He loved to scrounge through the flea markets and junk shops where she often found her treasures. They could take along a picnic supper.

Elizabeth was searching for a hand-hooked rug in shades of taupe and cranberry. And she needed to find a lamp for one of the parlors. Maybe something with a Tiffany-style shade made of intricately leaded stained glass . . .

"Beautiful."

The word shot through Elizabeth like a bolt of lightning. Her eyes flew open to find Zachary Chalmers standing before her, a gentle grin on his face.

"You scared the fire out of me," she said, trying to regain her breath.

"Good. Nick tells me you're too hot, and it's making you grumpy."

Sitting up, she swung her bare feet to the porch floor. "Thank you, Nick. Where did you see him?"

"Over at the Eastons' house."

"You were there?"

"Sure. Luke's been showing me some of his cabinetry work in the evenings. I'm thinking of putting him to work on one of my projects."

"Luke?"

"Easton."

"I know who he is." She tucked her legs under her and smoothed her skirt down over her feet. "So, how's Luke?"

"Not great. He's struggling with the single-parent role. He'd like to move Montgomery in with you for a few weeks, but I think she's keeping him afloat. He can't lose it completely when he's got a responsibility to look after his daughter. He has to function."

"Is he safe?"

"Oh, yeah. Don't get me wrong. He loves Montgomery fiercely. Luke is just real torn up. Did you know he built the bed he and Ellie slept in all nine years of their marriage? It was her wedding present."

"Luke made that four-poster? It's spectacular."

"Yeah. Now he wants to get rid of it."

"I'll put it in my shop for him. It would sell in no time."

"You'd let him sell their bed?" He turned to face her. "With all the memories of his marriage filling it?"

She had to give a little chuckle. "Now you sound like *me* running on about my glass counter. All those memories, all that tradition, all the past wrapped up in an object."

"You convinced me—of a lot of things." He slipped his arm around her shoulders and pulled her close. "Hey, Elizabeth, are we alone?"

"I'm sure half of Ambleside has their binoculars trained on my porch."

He leaned over and brushed a kiss across her lips. "Here's to Ambleside."

She sat breathless for a moment, drinking in the sensation of his hand on her shoulder and his warm breath against her cheek. He smelled of lemons and something else. Pine trees. The T-shirt he'd pulled on over his jeans was soft, a pale cottony blue that molded to his chest.

"How long is Nick going to be at Montgomery's?" he murmured.

"Until I call him."

"Then why don't you and I go inside for a while?"

She moistened her lips, trying to concentrate. One moment, she had been sure Christ was all she needed, all she wanted. And now, with a few whispered words, she was tempted to abandon that security.

"I'd like to be alone with you, Elizabeth," Zachary said against her ear. "I've had to force myself to go over to

Luke's house every day after work. All I can think about is that afternoon in the pavilion and how you stood on tiptoe to kiss me."

"Wait." Hopping off the swing, she grabbed the chain and forced herself to suck down a breath. "Zachary, we can't do this."

"If we go inside, nobody will—"

"I thought you surrendered."

He stared at her, his green eyes depthless. "What are you saying?"

"I'm saying we don't get to pick and choose which parts of the Bible we're going to follow."

"Spending a few minutes alone in a house with a grown woman is a sin?" He stood. "Or are you just worried about what the neighbors will think?"

"I gave up caring what the neighbors think a long time ago. They thought I was nuts to open an antiques shop on the town square. They couldn't believe I wanted to live in the apartment behind it. They called me crazy when I went to Romania to adopt Nick. The residents of Ambleside don't run my life."

"Then why won't you go inside with me? We could sit on the couch and . . . and visit."

She tilted her head and raised one eyebrow. "Visit?"

"OK, I'd rather not kiss you in front of God and everybody."

"God's in my living room, Zachary."

"God doesn't mind when people kiss."

"Is that all you want to do?" She gripped the chain. "Because that's not all I want to do."

He regarded her evenly. "Elizabeth . . ."

"Zachary, I can't. I won't."

He jammed his hands into his pockets and looked away. "I'm not used to this. I mean, a man dates a woman . . ."

"I'm not just any woman." She lifted her chin. "I'll understand if you want to rethink this."

"Well, what are we supposed to do? Sit out here on the
porch swing night after night?"

"I didn't ask you to be a part of my life. I'm telling you
who I am and what I believe. I follow the teachings in the
Bible. I try to stay surrendered. And, yeah, I sit on the
porch swing a lot."

He walked to the white railing that defined the perimeter
of her porch and leaned his hands on it. "This is not the
nineteenth century, Elizabeth. Is it wrong to want each
other, to feel desire?" He gave the railing a smack with his
palm and then swung around to face her. "How much am I
supposed to change who I am, Elizabeth? I want you. I
want to be with you. Am I supposed to give up who I am
and what I need?"

"That's the definition of surrender, isn't it? Give up. Let
go. Become a new man in Christ." She sat down on the
swing. "I didn't say it was easy."

He turned away again, his shoulder against the porch
post. Elizabeth watched him, sure she could read his
thoughts. He probably had known many women, and no
doubt he'd experienced the range of relationships with
them. What was the point of spending time with an
old-fashioned prude who threw biblical admonitions at him?
How boring.

"I don't know," he said. "A few months ago, I was an
award-winning architect with a pretty active social life. Now
I'm supposed to throw in the towel on my dreams for a
new office building. And I'm supposed to sit on a porch
swing with the mosquitoes."

"A few months ago, I was a businesswoman and mother,"
Elizabeth said. "Now I'm supposed to give up my quiet
security, my stability, my risk-free life. And I'm supposed to
sit on a porch swing with the mosquitoes."

"No, you'd be sitting on the porch swing with me."

"And you'd be sitting with me." She crossed her arms. "That's what it all comes down to, you know. Is each of us willing to accept who the other one really is? I'm a porch-swing woman."

"Well, I'm an inside-the-house man."

They stared at each other.

Elizabeth knew it was the end. Zachary had made a lot of changes in his life. But he wasn't going to go this far. This went beyond surrendering dreams and goals. This meant surrendering himself, right down to the core. And she could see in his eyes, he wouldn't do it.

"Boy howdy, ya'll better come quick!" Ben the policeman flew around the corner of the house and leaped onto the porch, his black boots sending up a puff of dust. "We got trouble. Big trouble now."

"Trouble?" Jolted back into focus, Elizabeth stood up. "What's going on, Ben?"

"Lord have mercy, it's them kids."

"The teenagers? What have they done?"

"Not *them* kids. *Ya'll's* kids. Nick and that little red-haired Easton gal."

"What's happened to Nick?" She grabbed the man's arm. "Where's my son?"

"Mick's got the both of them over at the police station."

"Are they hurt?"

"No, ma'am. But they're in trouble. Big trouble. And that boy of yours is hollering like a lonesome coyote. The way he howls sends shivers right down my spine. The little gal is crying her eyes out, too. I felt bad we had to take the both of them over to the station. But what else could we do? Mick said it was protocol. I thought I'd run fetch the redhead's dad, but then I remembered about her mama dying and all. So I came straight over here to get you."

"What did they do, Ben?"

He shook his head. "You ain't gonna believe it. I sure didn't."

"Ben!"

"They went over to Phil Fox's house to look at his puppies, and they up and stole his '64 World Series baseball. Then they took a big ol' rock and threw it right through the plate-glass window of his barbershop. 'Course Mr. Fox realized his baseball was missin' right away, and he figured out who took it. He called us about the time them kids was throwin' that rock through his window. When Mick and I got over to the barber shop, sure enough, they was standin' right there at the scene of the crime lookin' just as guilty as you please. There's glass everywhere, I'm tellin' you. Once I take you over to the station, I got to run back and sweep it up."

Horror and disbelief coursed down Elizabeth's spine. "Why?" she managed. "Why did they do it?"

"Well, that's what we asked 'em, but we couldn't make heads or tails out of what they told us. The little gal took to cryin' so hard she couldn't talk. Your boy just blabbered pure nonsense. I tried to write it down. Lemme see." He pulled his notebook from his back pocket. "Here we go. He said there were some bad guys at Grace's house and they looked like nachos, whatever that means. And then he started talking about foxes, and he was tellin' me how foxes are just like nachos. Now does that make any sense to you?"

"Yes," Elizabeth whispered.

"Then he told me that him and the little gal wanted to make you feel better, Miss Hayes, so they took the baseball for ransom. Ransom—that was his exact word."

"Oh, no."

"I wrote down everything your boy said as best as I could, but it didn't make one lick of sense to me."

Elizabeth folded her hands together and pressed them to

her lips. *Oh, God, please help me. I'm so scared for Nick. I don't know how to help him—*

"Come on," Zachary said, his warm hand covering hers. "Sounds like our little crusaders are about due for a rescue."

She shook her head. "Oh, Zachary, you don't have to—"

"Lead the way, Ben." Zachary cut her off and gave a nod in the direction of the police station. "And while we walk, I'll explain to you about the nachos."

FOURTEEN

Zachary stood to one side as Elizabeth rushed across the front lobby of the police station and scooped her son into her arms. She was crying, and Nick's wails blended with Montgomery's spasmic sobs. Zachary knew he ought to get out of there as fast as he could run. This wasn't his business. All this weeping and turmoil had nothing to do with him. Experience had taught him to detach himself from situations rife with emotion.

Once he had watched his own father and mother shrug and walk away from him. Screaming, crying, he had been gripped by the state social worker assigned to place him in foster care. He could remember the despair that overwhelmed him. Strength and rage poured through his young body, and he had broken free and run to his parents. But his father had turned to him and pushed him away.

No, Zachary. We can't take care of everybody. Be a man.

Zachary, the man, studied the scene unfolding before him. Elizabeth was explaining her son's behavior to the policemen while Mick took notes. Ben had begun dialing Montgomery's father. No longer howling, Nick stood white and trembling at his mother's side. Montgomery had curled into a tiny ball of despair and scooted herself under a desk.

Don't care, Zachary. Walk out. You're not a porch-swing man. You don't need these people and their troubles. You can't take care of everybody.

He slipped his hands into his pockets and turned toward the door. They'd work it out. He would go back to his cool apartment, where he could put on some soothing music and read this week's issue of *Time*. He'd probably plug into the Net and check his stocks. And then maybe he'd dip himself a big bowl of Central Dairy's mint chocolate chip ice cream. The best. He would prop up his feet and—

As he started to push open the glass door, he caught a reflection of Elizabeth's long brown hair. *You've done your part, Zachary. Go home.* Pausing, he glanced over his shoulder at the little ball of whimpering misery under the desk.

"Hey, Montgomery," he said, wheeling around. "What's your favorite kind of ice cream? You like mint chocolate chip?"

Kneeling, he peered under the desk. The child's tearstained, grimy face emerged from the shadows. She sniffled.

"I bet you're a rocky-road gal, aren't you?" he said.

She ran a fist under her wet nose. "Banilla."

"Banana?"

A reluctant smile lifted her trembling lips. She sucked down a shaky breath. "Banilla. It's white."

"Plain ol' white? Listen, have you ever tried mint choco-late chip? I've got a whole box of it in the freezer over at my place. When we get done here, we could all go over there and eat some."

Her face crumpled again. "But we broke the window."

"I know you did, and that was a wrong thing to do." He reached out and took her damp hand. "Guess what. I've done some wrong things, too."

"My daddy's going to be mad."

"Maybe so." He considered the situation. "I reckon it's a daddy's job to help his daughter learn to do the right things. He'll probably be disappointed, but I suspect he'll under-stand that you and Nick thought you were helping out."

"I want my mommy!" She covered her face with her hands and began to sob again.

Zachary reached under the desk, slipped his hands around the little girl, and eased her out into the open. Then he picked her up and held her against his chest. Mick was filling out papers. Ben had left to begin sweeping up broken glass. Nick and Elizabeth were pressed into a single chair as she tried to explain her son's behavior for the police report. When the door burst open, Zachary turned to see Luke Easton barreling into the station like a locomotive.

"Montgomery?" Spotting her in Zachary's arms, he crossed the room in two paces and lifted her into his embrace. "Oh, baby, come here, sweetpea. Don't cry now. Daddy's got you. It's OK, honey, it'll be all right."

As Luke and his daughter joined Elizabeth and her son at Mick's desk, Zachary headed for the door. He would go to his apartment now. The music and magazine and stock market would be there waiting for him. So would his single bowl of ice cream. He'd eat it alone . . . and wish he didn't have to.

❧

"They thought they could defeat Mr. Fox, the barber," Boompah said as he arranged a plate of his day-old muffins on the tea table at Finders Keepers. "It is my fault."

"Your fault, Boompah?" Elizabeth punched a hole in the price tag she had written up for an antique trunk. "I don't see how you can say that. Nick and Montgomery cooked up their little stone-throwing escapade all by themselves."

"But I had told Nikolai the story of how the Jews fought secretly against the Germans in the ghettos of Poland. He believed he could drive away your enemy in the same way."

Elizabeth tied the price tag to the trunk with a narrow white ribbon. "The Polish Jews did not do things like steal a man's prized baseball and try to hold it for ransom."

"Ransom?"

"Montgomery wrote the note. 'Mr. Fox: If you ever want to see your baseball again, you better stay away from Grace's house.'"

"Oh dear."

"And it was some TV show that inspired them to tie the note around a rock and try to throw it through the barbershop door. Of course they missed, and the rock cracked the huge plate-glass window."

"Mmm." Boompah shook his head in dismay.

"Nick and Montgomery both know they are to respect the property of others. I've told Nick a hundred times to use his words and not his hands to solve his problems."

"A very good teaching."

"Well, he forgot all about it, and now he's suffering the consequences."

"What consequences are those?"

"He and Montgomery are performing community service. Luke Easton and I are paying to install a new glass window in the barbershop."

"Community service? But they are only small children."

"There are a lot of things those two small children can do, Boompah. Each afternoon they sweep sidewalks for Pearlene and me. They slide library cards into books for Ruby McCann. They fill napkin holders and saltshakers at Dandy Donuts. And they sort brochures for Phil Fox at the bus station. They start right after Nick gets home from summer school, and they're done by dusk."

"Ach. That Phil Fox, you know, I think he's happy to have all the attention from the stealing of his baseball and the breaking of his window. I hear him at Dandy Donuts this morning talking about the next meeting of the city council. That man can talk and talk until you think you are going to have to throw a jelly donut at him to make him quiet."

Elizabeth laughed. "Don't throw anything at Phil Fox for a while, Boompah. Please! I can't take another episode at the police station."

"OK, OK." Chuckling, the old man bent over and began rearranging the muffins for the umpteenth time. "I tell you what, Elizabeth. I think that Phil Fox is going to try to take Grace's house away from Zachary. This, I believe, is his plan."

"I know he's up to something sneaky. Zachary and I—" She thought of the man who seemed to have vanished from her life almost as quickly as he had appeared. It had been a week and a half since the eventful night at the police station. "It's really none of my business."

"Not your business? And when is the future of Ambleside not the business of everybody who lives here?"

"The mansion belongs to Zachary. He'll have to iron things out with Phil himself."

Boompah was silent as she arranged a collection of fine old crocheted linen pieces in the trunk. She wasn't going to insert herself back into Zachary's life. Clearly they were incompatible. Clearly they had few values in common. Clearly he couldn't be bothered with a woman so rigid . . . so moralistic . . . so "porch swing."

"You better tell Zachary about the city council meeting next week, Elizabeth," Boompah said. "He needs to go there and see what Phil Fox will do."

"You can tell him, Boompah." She smoothed out a set of monogrammed napkins.

"What, you don't talk to Zachary now?"

"Not for a while, really. He's busy and so am I."

"Busy."

"Boompah, Zachary needs a more interesting, more modern sort of woman in his life. I'm just too . . . boring."

"You?" The old man crumpled the paper bag in which he'd brought the stale muffins. "You are not boring! You are smart, beautiful, clever, kind—ach, if I am not such an old man, I try to marry you myself. I better talk to that boy. He can't make a big mistake and be unlucky in love like I was. Certainly not!"

"Boompah, wait." Elizabeth caught his arm as he shuffled toward the door. "Please don't say anything to Zachary about me. He and I have talked things over already. We're very different from each other, OK?"

"No, is not OK." His face darkened. "I don't believe that. To keep away from true love for the reason of being 'different' is stupid! Sometimes different can be very good. Interesting, you know. But you and Zachary are not so different. You are both good people, Christian people, nice people. And you love each other."

"No, Boompah, we don't love each other."

"Don't try to fool this old Gypsy, Elizabeth." He tapped his temple with a fingertip. "I see how you look at Zachary. I watch how he looks at you. I listen to you talk about each other. I know the truth of this thing, and it is called love." He turned to the door. "I go now."

Great. Just great, Elizabeth thought. How could she explain to Boompah all the intricacies of her relationship with Zachary? They held such different moral standards. She had a son he didn't want to bother with. He designed modern churches she could hardly bear to look at. He wanted to tear down antiquities. She wanted to preserve them. They were too different.

"And you better come to that city council meeting, too, Elizabeth," Boompah said over the jingle of brass bells as he stuck his head back through the door. "Zachary needs you."

⁊

"Can Nick come over for supper, Miss Hayes?" Montgomery asked. "Daddy's grilling hot dogs tonight."

"Hot dogs?" Nick poked his head between his mother's

hip and the door frame. "I love hot dogs! Can I have two? Or maybe three? I like them with mustard and ketchup."

Elizabeth regarded her son and his bright, eager eyes. "Nick, you know you're still grounded."

"Oh, bother." He thought for a moment. "But I have not played with Magunnery for a long time, Mommy. All we do every day is eat donuts with Miss Viola and read books with Mrs. McCann. We never get to play together."

"Eat donuts and read books?" She looked back and forth between the two children. "You're supposed to be *working* at the donut shop and the library."

"After we work, we eat the donuts."

Elizabeth sighed. Whatever had made her believe the citizens of Ambleside would be firm with the two wayward children? She should have guessed that Nick and Montgomery would be taken into their wardens' hearts, quickly forgiven their trespasses, and then coddled like a pair of hothouse flowers.

"I have never eaten hot dogs in all my life," Nick said solemnly.

"We eat hot dogs at least once a week, Nikolai Hayes, you little con artist."

"But not with Magunnery. Not hot dogs from the barbecue grill at Magunnery's house."

Elizabeth considered for a moment. Nearly a month had passed since Ellie Easton's death. According to local observation, Luke had been doing better lately. Pearlene had told Elizabeth that Luke was working hard on his construction project at the new McCann subdivision on the outskirts of town. And Ruby had mentioned that Luke and his daughter were seen attending a movie together and walking in the park. Maybe this hot-dog dinner would be a good step toward normalcy for everyone concerned.

"All right," she said. "I'll let you eat supper with

Montgomery just this time. But I'll come by to pick you up at eight."

"Yesss!"

Montgomery did a little twirl across the porch, her red braids flying out to the sides. Hand in hand, the two children skipped down the steps and headed across the back-yard pathway that had been worn between their houses.

Elizabeth sat down on the porch swing and lifted her hair from the back of her neck. Another hot day. To tell the truth, she was grateful to Luke for offering her a break from the constant care of her son. Nick was always a handful, but his confinement following the window-breaking inci-dent had made him more restless than usual.

She shut her eyes and pictured the sleepy little town around her as it basked in the humid heat of midsummer. The aroma of barbecue grills drifted through the air to min-gle with the scent of new-mown grass. In the distance, Eliz-abeth could hear the low buzz of a weed cutter, the murmur of someone's radio tuned to a country music sta-tion, and the metallic thump of car doors shutting. People were parking around the square for the city council meeting.

She wouldn't go, of course.

Turning her thoughts to her latest project, Elizabeth drifted in a sweltery daze. An old walnut sideboard would have to be stripped of its offending 1970s harvest-gold paint. She would remove the hardware . . . check the joints . . . pull on her rubber gloves . . . spread the refinisher . . . wipe and wipe . . . steel wool . . .

❧

"Elizabeth!" Someone shook her shoulder. "It is almost time for the meeting."

She opened her eyes to find Boompah staring down at her. She must have fallen asleep and lost track of time.

"Why you are sleeping on the porch, Elizabeth? Phil Fox has put Grace's mansion into the subject of the 'new business.' The councillors are almost ready to discuss it. There sits Zachary Chalmers all by himself, and you do not stand beside him?"

"Boompah, the mansion is Zachary's heritage. I told you before, it's not my business."

"Bah! Is your business. In Germany we give the town hall the name of *Rathaus*. Means the house of counsel and advice. But in English, is a good name for what happens here in Ambleside tonight. Elizabeth, I think if you will not go and help Zachary, those rats across the street are going to steal his mansion from him!"

"Boompah, one small voice like mine isn't going to make a difference."

"No? Then the biggest rat of them all will gnaw away the heart of Ambleside. You mark my words!"

Still muttering, Boompah turned on his heel and stomped off the porch. Elizabeth leaned back in the swing. She knew what an effort it was for the old man to walk across the street to her house without assistance. Never had she seen him so worked up.

She swung her feet back and forth the way Nick often did. Then she checked her watch. She couldn't make any difference over at the meeting, could she? And if she spoke up for Zachary, what would the town think? What would Zachary think?

Jumping to her feet, she tucked in her blouse and headed across the porch. Why should she care what anyone thought? She wanted to save Grace's home as much as Boompah did. And if she didn't speak out, it might go under the wrecking ball in a matter of days.

Jogging across the street, she tried to calm her heart. She didn't need to pick up Nick from Montgomery's house for at least another half hour. She could slip into the back of the council room and listen to the proceedings. Maybe no one would notice her.

"Now a lot of you know," Phil Fox was saying as Elizabeth opened the door to the basement chambers, "that Ambleside lost a prominent citizen this spring when Grace Chalmers passed away."

An overworked air conditioner pushed the dank smell of rusted pipes into the crowded room as Elizabeth took a chair in the back row near the wall. The council had cancelled its meeting in June due to Ellie's death. Somehow no one in the close-knit community—except maybe Phil Fox—had felt like going ahead with business as usual. And besides, city business in a town as small as Ambleside was rarely a pressing matter. But looking around at the crowd gathered for tonight's meeting, Elizabeth wondered about that.

The room was filled to capacity with townspeople, and all of the city councillors were present. She scanned the fluorescent-lit hall with its ceiling of white plastic tiles and its rows of gray folding chairs. Near the front of the room, Zachary Chalmers leaned forward in his chair, his broad shoulders outlined by the crisp tailoring of his dark suit.

"There's been a lot of talk and speculation as to what ought to be done with Grace's mansion," Phil was saying. "Most folks know Chalmers House has been a part of the history of Ambleside since its founding. But there's not a soul who'd deny that the mansion has fallen on hard times. From the outside, a person can see how the ivy's taken over the walls, a good many of the windows are cracked, and the chimneys are missing some bricks."

He pulled a pair of half-moon spectacles from his shirt pocket and set them on the end of his nose. "Now I've got here an official inspection report that says the heating system is dangerous, the roof leaks, the lower floor's got termites real bad, the stairs are so worn that a body could twist an ankle or maybe even fall right through. The renovation of that building is going to cost a pretty penny, and I'd like to know who's willing to go to such an expense for an old eyesore like that?"

"Eyesore?" Boompah came to his feet, his fist raised. "The building is beautiful."

"Mr. Jungemeyer, I appreciate your comment, but the floor is not yet open for discussion," Phil said.

"And I am not the floor! I am a citizen of the United States of America, and I have the right to give my own opinion."

"In a minute, Jacob," the town's mayor, Cleo Mueller, spoke up. "Let Phil have his say, and then you'll get your turn."

"Thank you, Mr. Mayor." Phil adjusted his spectacles. "Now, in her last will and testament, Grace Chalmers left the mansion to her nephew, Zachary Chalmers. Over the past few weeks, I have spoken at length with Mr. Chalmers, and I believe him to be a fine young man and an outstanding architect. On a number of occasions, Mr. Chalmers and I have discussed the future of the mansion as well as the future of Ambleside itself. Isn't that right, Mr. Chalmers?"

From his chair, Zachary nodded. Elizabeth wondered how he was feeling. Was Phil boxing him into a trap? Or was Zachary a coplayer in this unfolding drama?

"From the day he moved to Ambleside, Mr. Chalmers has made no secret of his desire to raze Chalmers House," Phil stated. A murmur rippled through the crowd, and heads turned in Zachary's direction. "He would like to build offices for his architectural firm on that land. And in a move that could only be beneficial to the city of Ambleside, he plans to rent offices within the complex to other business-men—most of them from Jefferson City."

"How do you know the plans of Zachary Chalmers?" Boompah demanded, again rising from his seat. "He has told you these things? Or you have searched his office and listened to his telephone?"

"I have done nothing of the sort!" Phil retorted.

"Now, Jacob," Cleo Mueller put in. "You've got to stay quiet until Phil gets to the point here. And we're all hoping that will be soon."

To a roomful of laughter, the druggist sat down. So did Boompah. Elizabeth knew the two elderly men were long-time friends, each regularly patronizing the other's place of business.

"All right, I'll get to the point," Phil said. He held up two sheets of paper. "I've got copies here of a couple of important documents, each one plainly stating that the mansion needs to stand. One of them is a letter from Grace Chalmers, and the other is the town charter of Ambleside, Missouri. I'd like to submit them as exhibits one and two."

"Phil, this isn't a court of law," the mayor said. "And nobody's on trial here."

"All the same, I've met with a Jeff City lawyer." Heads turned to stare at John Sawyer as Phil went on speaking. "You folks ought to know that these two documents hold a lot of water. The both of them together make a compelling argument against Zachary Chalmers's tearing down our landmark. In fact, we want to go on record here asking Mr. Chalmers to refrain from demolishing Chalmers House so that we don't have to bring legal action against him."

"Who's *we*, Phil?" Sawyer-the-lawyer stood up. "You got a dead rat in your pocket?"

Amid the chuckles, Boompah rose again. "He's right! The rats are taking over the Rathaus!"

"Now calm down, everybody," Cleo Mueller said. "Let Phil finish, and then we'll open the floor. You'll all get to have your say." The mayor started to sit; then he straightened and focused on Phil. "Get to your point, Mr. Fox,

would you? My ice-cream maker's just about finished churn-
ing, and my wife put fresh peaches in this batch."

Phil gave his fellow councilman a look of scorn. "The
point is, folks, that we don't want Zachary Chalmers to tear
down the mansion. But we doubt that he has the where-
withal or the desire to refurbish it. So we've come up with a
plan to solve the whole problem."

Carrying an easel, he walked around to the front of the
council's table. "My fellow citizens of Ambleside," he
intoned, "what we have here with us tonight is a bona fide
treasure. And I'm not just talking about Chalmers House.
I'm talking about Zachary Chalmers himself."

With a flourish, he set a portfolio of enlarged photographs on the easel. "Mr. Chalmers is responsible for some
of the finest new buildings in mid-Missouri. And I'm going
to show you what I'm talking about. Look here at this
well-known state agency headquarters in Jefferson City.
That's Zachary Chalmers's design. How about these doctors'
offices—recognize them? Sure you do. Here's a restaurant
and a beauty salon. And here's his award-winning church!"

He propped a picture of the ugly church onto the easel.
Elizabeth squinted at it, hoping it might look better than she
remembered. It didn't. Zachary shifted in his chair and
turned to scan the room. His eye fell on her, but his face
registered nothing.

"Now here's my proposal," Phil said.

"'Bout time!" someone hollered.

Phil gave the man a scowl. "If ya'll can't act right while
we do city business, why don't you stay home?"

"We got a right to be here, same as you."

Phil started to reply, but then he took off his glasses,
folded them, and slipped them back into his shirt pocket.
"Since we've got proof that the house ought to remain
standing and we're confident Mr. Chalmers isn't planning to
restore it, I'd like to make a proposal. I hereby propose that

we offer Mr. Chalmers Lots 54 and 55 in the new McCann Estates subdivision, which the city would purchase at a cost of forty thousand dollars. Then he can build his offices there exactly the way he wants. In exchange, Zachary would agree to sign over Chalmers House and the lot it sits on to the city of Ambleside. The city would then restore and preserve a small portion of the mansion as a historical marker in accordance with the desires of its previous own-ers. The city would use the remainder of the land to address a critical need—parking."

At his final word, the room erupted in a buzz of conver-sation. Elizabeth clutched her hands together, trying to keep from speaking out. It wasn't her business. The mansion had been Grace's house, was now Zachary's, and had nothing to do with her. She needed to pick up Nick. Needed to put a load of laundry in the washer. Needed to defrost some ground beef.

"How small a portion?" she heard herself say as she leapt to her feet. "What part of Chalmers House does Mr. Fox intend to leave in place? Are we talking about the front of the mansion, the first floor, the porch, or just a brick?"

"And that subdivision you're talking about, Phil, is zoned for residential use only," John Sawyer declared, rising from his chair. "You can't put an office complex out there with-out changing the zoning to commercial or mixed use."

"I agree with Phil," someone else called. "We do need parking on the square. It's a mess out there."

"Folks keep on parking at my gas station!" Al Huff added, coming to his feet. "Some days I can barely tend to my own customers."

"Let Mr. Fox tear down his barbershop!" Boompah roared. "Most of us have lost our hair anyway, and who rides the bus these days?"

"You leave my business alone, old man," Phil shouted. "Your days at the Corner Market are numbered anyhow!"

"Hey, everybody!" Mayor Mueller stood and banged his gavel on the old steel folding table. "Hold on, now. You folks are all out of order. I can see we've got a lot to consider here. But right now, my ice cream's melting, and I think this meeting's gone on long enough. I move we table any discussion on the future of Chalmers House until the August meeting of the Ambleside City Council."

"Second," another councilman put in quickly.

"All in favor, say aye. All opposed, none. Any other new business? Well, then, that's all for tonight, folks. Anybody who wants to try Ethel's peach ice cream can come over to our place. But talk of the mansion's off-limits." He gave the table a final whack with his gavel, and headed for the door.

Elizabeth glanced at her watch and realized that Luke Easton would be wondering where she was. She would have to hurry if she hoped to beat the crowd out the door. Sidling through the throng, she edged out into the gloomy hallway of the basement and started for the staircase. As she reached the ground floor, a hand caught her arm.

"Elizabeth?"

She swung around to find Zachary Chalmers at her elbow. His green eyes were intense. "Can we have a few minutes alone?"

FIFTEEN

"Alone?"

The look in Elizabeth's eyes spoke volumes. Zachary knew their last conversation had changed things between them. Acting on his desires and his past experiences rather than behaving like a man surrendered, he had driven her away. For a few days he had felt justified, until the solitude and emptiness took over. Maybe he could patch things up. Or at least take a step in the right direction.

"I have to go get Nick," Elizabeth said, glancing out the door as the crowd began to push around them toward the exit. "He's over at Luke's house."

"Luke Easton?" Zachary felt a twinge of queasiness. He knew Elizabeth and Nick had been spending time with the Eastons since Ellie's death. Now he wondered if the relationship between Elizabeth and Luke had gone beyond friendship. Luke was grieving, after all, and Elizabeth was a desirable woman. Through the years, their children had become best friends. All in all, it wasn't that unlikely.

"Excuse me," she said and started for the door.

"Wait." He caught her arm again. "Will you be over at Luke's house a long time?"

"No, I need to get Nick to bed, and I have to do some laundry . . ."

"Then I'll wait for you."

"Zachary, I respect your architectural skills, and I know you want to build your offices across the street. But I'm not going to sit still and watch Phil pull off this con."

He stared at her. "You're talking about the mansion."

"Aren't you?"

"No."

She looked down. "Oh. Well, I'm not sure . . . not sure we have anything else to discuss. I'm sorry I was so blunt with you the other night, but I—"

"I'm not sorry. I needed to hear it."

"I could have been a little more subtle."

"I'm the kind of man who sometimes needs to be hit over the head with a two-by-four."

She struggled to hold back a grin. "I don't think I'd go that far."

"Would you go as far as your porch swing with me?"

Drinking down a deep breath, she met his eyes. "Zachary, I've really got to get Nick and put him to bed."

"And then there's that laundry."

She took a step toward the door. "OK, you can wait for me on the porch."

Before he could respond, she fled. As the last of the crowd filtered out of the building, Zachary spotted Phil Fox heading up the stairs toward him. That was enough motivation to propel him out the door and onto the sidewalk.

"Hey, we don't need any new offices in Ambleside, Zachary Chalmers," someone called out to him. "We want to keep our mansion!"

"I go see my doctor in that professional building you designed in Jeff City, Mr. Chalmers," an elderly lady said, touching his elbow. "I like it real good. The elevators are nice and smooth."

"We need a parking lot!" Al Huff said. "You and Phil have got the right idea. Keep it up."

"I thought that church in Jefferson City was just plain ugly," someone else called. "You better not put up nothin' that ugly here in Ambleside; I don't care how many awards you win."

Zachary jogged across the street and down the side of the Finders Keepers building to the back portion where Elizabeth made her home. As he cut across the grass, he studied the unlit silhouette of the mansion next door. All this hullabaloo over an old house. And yet, it was his heritage, his possession, his future.

On the porch he dropped down onto the swing to wait for Elizabeth. So, he had managed to alienate not only the owner of the local antiques shop but half the town of Ambleside as well. The fate of the old mansion had divided the populace and made him look like either a villain or a hero.

And for what? Did he really even want to live here any longer? Why should he concern himself with the feelings of a group of small-town folks? He didn't owe Elizabeth anything. He hadn't put down any roots here. Didn't own a house. Had no clientele. So what kept him here? He could pack up tomorrow and go back to Jefferson City. No doubt, his former landlord would take him back. His friends would be glad to see him again . . . those few who had even noticed that he'd gone.

Friends? Did he really have friends in Jefferson City?

Women? He couldn't think of anyone he would care to date.

Family? He'd severed ties and then lost track of his parents and siblings years ago. No one else had stepped into his soul the way Boompah, Nick, and Montgomery had. Certainly no one had touched him like Elizabeth Hayes did.

He lifted his feet from the porch floor and tried to swing back and forth the way he'd watched Nick do. Funny little kid. Odd, the way the child had managed to wrap himself around Zachary's heart. Glancing across the porch, he noted the roller skates, the cluster of plastic toy soldiers, the sketch pad and broken crayons.

How could Zachary drive away from all this? Yet how could he stay?

He spotted the old Bible that had belonged to his aunt. It was lying on the small table near the swing; evidently Elizabeth had been reading it. She had left the book open to a passage in the Psalms. He remembered that Nick had insisted that the Bible was the place to turn when you were searching for something.

Seek and you shall find.

Reaching out, Zachary lifted the worn leather book and set it in his lap. He didn't even know what he was searching for. Answers, perhaps. Directions. Connections.

He opened the cover and scanned the tiny notes his aunt had written all over the Bible's title pages. Certainly she had searched throughout this book for answers to the questions in her own life. Flipping through the pages, he watched the faded gold edges flicker and glow in the porch light. In a passage of the first epistle to the Corinthians, he discovered an old pressed flower—a rose, he guessed—though it was brown and crumbly. Then he turned to the central section where the family tree had been printed in a flourish of black script.

Starting at the top, he began to read the names of his ancestors. There was Zachary Chalmers, the founder of Ambleside. Other names followed. Wives and children. Dates of birth and dates of death. Marriages. He located his father's name, and his mother's, and he noted the listing of children beneath, written almost too small to read. Then his eye fell on the name of his aunt, Grace Mariana Chalmers. She had never married, but—oddly—beneath her name in tiny letters was printed another name: Zachary Daniel.

Zachary lifted his head and focused on the yellow porch light. Moths flitted around it, drawn to the pale glow. Zachary Daniel was *his* name. Why had his aunt written his name beneath her own? Looking down at the chart again, he peered at the list of children beneath his father's name. There was no Zachary Daniel among them.

"I ate three hot dogs," Nick said, bounding onto the porch. His mother was right behind him. "Magunnery's daddy said it was OK. I didn't beg for the hot dogs, I promise, Mommy. They were right there on the plate, and Magunnery's daddy asked me if I wanted another one and then another one and then . . ."

"Nick, three is too many," Elizabeth said. "You should know that."

"Hey, it's Zachary!" The boy's face lit up. "Did you come to see us? I ate three hot dogs at Magunnery's house, but I didn't beg. We played in her tepee. She has a tepee in her bedroom, and you can get inside it. It's dark, but we weren't scared because we lit a fire."

"A fire!" Elizabeth gasped and dropped to one knee. "Nick, you're never supposed to—"

"A *pretend* fire, Mommy. We made it out of Magunnery's red sweater."

Zachary stood, feeling as though every ounce of energy had been sapped from his body. "I need to go home," he said.

"I didn't mean to!" Nick cried. "I didn't want to scare you and my mommy about the fire. I won't ever do it again. Please stay here with us!"

"It's not the fire, Nick." Zachary walked toward the steps. "It's, uh, it's the old Bible. I need to . . . need to . . ." He focused on Elizabeth. "You knew, didn't you? You'd read it. How long have you known?"

"Known what?" She rose. "Zachary, what's the matter?"

"Come on, Elizabeth. You must have looked through that Bible hundreds of times. You were reading the Psalms."

"Yes, but . . ." Taking her son's shoulders, she propelled the boy toward the front door. "Nick, go inside and brush your teeth. When you have your jammies on, I'll come up and tuck you into bed."

"What did Grace's Bible do to Zachary?" Nick asked. "What did that Bible say?"

"Go upstairs, Nick," Elizabeth ordered. "I'll be up in a minute."

"That stupid Bible is always making people mad," he retorted, and then he turned on his heel and stomped into the house.

Elizabeth let the screen door fall shut with a bang. "Zachary, I don't have any idea what you're talking about."

"I'm talking about this." He picked up the old book and shoved it toward her. "I'm talking about dear old Grace Chalmers and her life of lies."

"Lies?" She took the Bible.

"Right here." He jammed a finger on his name. "I'm not Grace's nephew. I'm her son."

Elizabeth stared in silence at the crinkled page. "Her son?"

"That's my name. Can you read the chart any other way?"

"Maybe she didn't have room under her brother's name to write—"

"I was their first child," he said. "I'm the oldest, remember? My name should have been at the top of this list. There was plenty of room for Grace to write it—unless it didn't belong there. She put me over here with her. She wrote the right name, the right birth date, everything. Just the wrong mother. And no father."

Elizabeth lifted her head. "Zachary, I had no idea. Grace never said a word about having a son."

"Of course not. Why should she? She wasn't married, and I was a part of her dark past. She'd managed to foist me off on her brother, so why should she ever think of me again?"

"But she did think of you. She came to visit you in her

red coat. She brought you the little toy chicken. And Grace left you the family's mansion."

"Family." He took the Bible and slammed it onto the porch swing. "She kept her mansion until the day she died. Kept her old books. Kept all her china and knickknacks. Even kept her old red coat. She kept everything she ever had. Everything except me."

Feeling as though he might explode, Zachary stormed down the steps. No wonder his parents had held themselves distant from him all those years. No wonder they had found it so easy to place him in state custody and walk away when things got too rough. He wasn't their child.

He was the son of Grace Chalmers, a woman who had abandoned him in order to preserve her reputation. Picking up a stone, he hurled it at the old mansion. The tinkle of breaking glass echoed through the dark summer night.

❧

Elizabeth said good-bye to one of her most loyal customers, and then she stepped outside the open door of her shop to get a breath of fresh air. It had been a profitable Saturday, with a steady stream of customers who had purchased an unusual number of high-ticket items. Her Jefferson City contract was almost complete, which meant yet another influx of cash. Elizabeth glanced across the expanse of lawn at the old Chalmers House. An idea she had toyed with more than once presented itself again. Maybe she could convince Zachary to let her put a down payment on the building. It wouldn't be much, but it might make a difference in the old mansion's fate.

She sighed and leaned against the wall of Finders Keepers. The past few days had been awful. Alone, she had stewed for hours, unable to sleep at night. If she called Zachary, he might think she was intruding on his privacy. After all, the last real conversation they'd had—before the shocking discovery in Graces's Bible—had been a definite severing of any relationship between them.

But at the meeting, he had said he wanted to talk to her—and not about the mansion. What had he been planning to tell her?

Now, because he'd stumbled upon the truth of his background, she might never know. How could she have looked through that Bible so many times and never noticed Zachary's name listed beneath Grace's? And why hadn't Grace told Elizabeth about her son? Who was Zachary's father? Why had Grace given the baby away? Had she known that her brother abandoned Zachary to the foster-care system?

Elizabeth had turned the thoughts over and over in her mind without finding any answers. After reading and rereading the inscriptions so carefully penned in Grace's hand, she had left the Bible on the old porch swing. For some strange reason, she felt as though she, too, had been betrayed by her dear friend.

"Mommy, we're worried," Nick announced, emerging onto the front stoop. He and Montgomery had come through the shop to find her. "Herod is being a pill again."

"What did she do this time?" Elizabeth shook her head in frustration at the annoying little Heather, who seemed to delight in making Nick's life miserable.

"We're supposed to do the play of the practical son in Sunday school tomorrow," Nick explained. "And Herod is supposed to be the father of the practical son, but she says she's going to her grandma's house, and we better just find someone else, so there."

"The practical son?" Elizabeth tried to concentrate.

"You know, Mommy. The practical son takes his daddy's money and goes to a far country and spends it on righteous living."

"Riotous living," Montgomery corrected. "Riotous living is

where you act naughty and go see bad movies and say lots of swear words. You can spend all your money on riotous living. That's what happened to the prodigal son."

"Ah, the *prodigal* son." Elizabeth stifled the urge to laugh out loud.

"I am the practical son in our play," Nick continued, "and Magunnery is my brother. The brother gets angry because the father gives the practical son a fat cow, even though he wasted all that money on righteous living."

"Riotous living," Montgomery corrected him loudly. "Riotous, riotous, riotous!"

"Don't be so picky, Magunnery," Nick replied. "It's just a word."

"You have to talk right, or Heather will keep being mean to you."

Nick weighed this for a moment. "I don't like Herod. We should have given her the part of the fat cow. Then I could say, 'My father has killed the fat cow—'"

"Nick," Elizabeth interrupted, "that isn't nice at all."

"But if Herod won't be our father," Nick went on, "what are we going to do in Sunday school tomorrow?"

"Maybe one of the other children can play the part of the father," Elizabeth said. "We can call someone on the phone, if you want to, Nick. But first of all, I've decided that I'm going to close the store early. I have some concerns that I need to take care of, too."

"Zachary." Nick gave Montgomery a knowing nod. "Like I told you."

"Yes, I am worried about Zachary," Elizabeth acknowledged.

"He was mad because of that Bible."

"Well, he had read something in there that upset him. I feel like I ought to go talk to him, and I want you to come with me, Nick."

The boy's mouth fell open, but no words of protest

emerged. Montgomery looked crestfallen. "OK, I'll go home," she said softly. "Daddy's there."

"Is your father feeling all right today, Montgomery?"

"He never feels all right. On Saturdays he used to work in his shop and build things for my mommy. Now he mostly just sits and stares out the window."

"Why don't you ask if he'll read you a book?"

Nodding glumly, the little redhead plodded off down the sidewalk. Elizabeth turned and locked up her store. In minutes, she and Nick were driving down the road toward the apartment complex where Zachary lived.

A part of her felt sure she was completely nuts. *Leave the man alone,* she told herself. *He's not worth the hours of confusion and turmoil he's caused you already.*

But another part of her ached to take Zachary in her arms and smooth away the lines of pain that had creased his forehead. At least she had known who her parents were. A small box of treasures from their life together lay hidden under her bed—a ribbon with which her mother had tied Elizabeth's hair, a tube of bright lipstick her mother had worn, her father's old brown cardigan sweater, and photographs of their years together as a family. After their deaths, Elizabeth had been taken in by her grandmother and given a life of love and compassion. She could hardly imagine how it would feel to find suddenly that her whole childhood had been a lie.

"Well, here we are," Nick announced for the fifth time as they eased up to a stop sign. "I remember this red sign, Mom. This is the right place, I'm sure of it. I think we must be near Zachary's house."

"Nick, those red signs tell the cars to stop. They're on all the street corners." Elizabeth dreaded the day when her son attempted to learn to drive.

"No, Mommy. Sometimes the corners have lights."

Elizabeth pulled into the parking lot of the apartment

complex and lifted a quick prayer for patience with Nick and for understanding with Zachary.

"See!" Nick said proudly, as they climbed out and began to ascend the stairs to the apartment. "I told you this was the right place."

"You sure did, sweetheart." She knocked and waited. Maybe Zachary had gone out. Maybe he had moved away. Maybe—

The door opened. "Hey, Elizabeth," Zachary said. He had on an old navy T-shirt and a pair of jeans. His hair looked as though it hadn't been combed. "I didn't expect company today."

"I'm here too," Nick spoke up. "We came to see if you were OK, because you got so mad at the Bible the other night."

Zachary studied the child for a moment. Then a grin lifted the corner of his mouth. "You guys want to come inside? I'm afraid I don't have a porch swing."

"Oh, yes, we will come in," Nick said, shouldering his way past the man. "I am not going to ask about any food, Zachary, but I'm just going to tell you that Magunnery says you have a big box of mint chocolate chip ice cream in your freezer."

"Nick!" Elizabeth cried.

"I didn't beg, Mommy."

Zachary laughed. "As a matter of fact, I was just getting ready to throw a burger on the grill. How about if I make supper for all of us, and then we'll eat a bowl of that ice cream?"

"That would be a very good plan." Nick seated himself on the sofa, looking for all the world like a king surveying his realm.

Elizabeth sighed. "Zachary, you don't need to make us supper. I just wanted to drop by and check on you. The other night was so confusing."

His smile faded. "Yeah. I've tried to call my parents . . . my 'whatever they are.' Apparently they moved the whole family out of state. We hadn't spoken for years, but now I don't even know where to start looking."

"Zachary, I've thought a lot about Grace, and—"

"Me, too. And I don't want to think about her anymore." He gestured to the balcony. "You and Nick want to sit outside while I grill?"

Nick made a beeline for the balcony, but Elizabeth refused to be deterred from her mission. "Zachary, there's a lot of this I don't understand, but I do know one thing. Grace cared deeply about you."

Without responding, he moved to the kitchen and began forming two more patties. "Lucky thing they don't sell ground beef in bachelor-sized packets."

Elizabeth followed him. "You know, Nick's birth mother had a tough choice to make, too. Half the time, when I think about her, I get furious. How could she put that precious newborn baby into a cold, gray institution? Didn't she care about him? Didn't she love him at all? She was just thinking of herself, her own needs. She was the lowest form of human being."

"Barbecue sauce?" Zachary asked.

Elizabeth rolled her eyes. "The other half of the time, I have to admit that I don't know this woman at all. I don't know how she became pregnant—was it an act of desperation in exchange for money, was she raped, was it a failed love? All I know is that she chose the best thing she could think of for that little baby. She had to trust that Nick would have food to eat and clothes to wear in the orphanage. He might not have the best life, but at least he would live."

"Onions?" Zachary said.

"In her own way," Elizabeth went on, ignoring his attempts to divert the conversation, "she cared about her son. She didn't abort him before birth, and she didn't throw him into a trash heap afterward. She did what she could."

"Tomatoes?"

"That woman's blood runs through Nick's veins. She's part of who he is and who he'll become someday. The shape of his fingers, the color of his hair, his love of art and music come from her. Sometimes I'm furious with her, and sometimes I even hate her for the pain she caused that precious child. Because of what she did, Nick may never be able to realize his potential. But I am learning not to hate his birth mother, because I know she tried. She tried, Zachary. She gave him life, and her genes, and something of a home. It was the best she could do, and for that I love her."

Picking up the plate of sliced vegetables, Zachary moved past Elizabeth and walked out to the balcony. She stood alone for a moment in the galley kitchen, staring at the bloodied board on which he had formed the patties. Those words had been wrenched from her very soul, and Zachary had ignored them. All the years of anguish she had spent dealing with her feelings about Nick's birth parents had come rolling out in this small room. And now they lay in the cold, empty silence.

Zachary didn't want to hear. And Nick probably wouldn't want to hear, either. When Elizabeth's son was old enough to wonder about the circumstances of his Romanian heritage, she would try to explain. But she had a feeling that the same sense of loss, anger, and betrayal would threaten to overwhelm Nick.

"Aren't you coming outside, Mommy?" the child asked, appearing in the kitchen. "Zachary is cooking the burgers. Smoke is coming out of the top of them. It smells good!"

She tried to smile. "I love you, Nick," she said softly, reaching out to her son.

"I love you, too, Mom, and Zachary's going to let me put

on the barbecue sauce. Do you think I'll like how it tastes? Zachary says it tastes like the sauce on ribs. That sauce is my favorite thing in all the world."

She shook her head as he took her hand and began pulling her toward the balcony. "Your favorite thing?"

He paused. "Oh, bother. I think I like bean burritos better than ribs."

Laughing, Elizabeth followed Nick out onto the balcony. Zachary turned. At the sight of them, the grim line of his mouth softened. "Is Nick trying to change my menu?"

"It's just that I love bean burritos," Nick said.

"Wait'll you taste my burgers," he said, taking a spatula and flipping a patty. "One bite, and you'll forget all about bean burritos."

"Really?" Nick looked at his mother. "But I don't want to forget about burritos. I love them. I was thinking we could eat them tomorrow for lunch right after church. I could have my usual—two bean burritos and water. And that would taste yummy."

"We're not going to plan tomorrow's menu tonight," Elizabeth said.

"But Zachary could come with us to eat at Taco Bell. Because after church, we're going to be very hungry."

He stopped speaking for a moment, and Elizabeth could almost read the direction of his thoughts. Before she could stop him, however, Nick blurted out his latest idea.

"Zachary, you could be the father of the practical son!" The boy leapt from his chair and grabbed Zachary's arm, sending a splatter of barbecue sauce across the wall. "Herod says she won't be the father, so Magunnery and I didn't know who could give me the fat cow, but now it can be you!"

Holding his dripping brush, Zachary gave Elizabeth a quizzical look. "The prodigal son," she explained, "needs a father."

His green eyes deepened as his gaze moved over her face, taking in her eyes, her cheeks, her lips. "Elizabeth . . ." he said.

"Don't shut him out, Zachary. Don't let your pain wound those who care about you the most."

"Are you one of those?"

"I'm here, aren't I?" She swallowed down her own hurt. "I reached out, even though I wasn't able to touch."

"Don't underestimate the power you have over me, Elizabeth," he said. Then he turned and gave Zachary a thumbs-up. "I'd be proud to be the father of the practical son," he said.

Nick pumped his fist. "Yesss!"

Laughing, Zachary winked at Elizabeth. "That kid is determined to turn me into his father."

"One way or another," she said.

Sixteen

Zachary eased his lanky frame down onto a miniature plastic chair in the Sunday school classroom. Once he was reasonably sure it wouldn't collapse under his weight, he focused on the front of the room, where he observed the prodigal son living riotously. Around Zachary the parents of other children leaned forward in anticipation of their little stars' shining moments. Costumeless and cramped in the small room, the players nonetheless performed to perfection.

In place of money, Nick Hayes was handing out colorful beads in exchange for such vices as apple cider, a kiss from the teacher, and a borrowed jacket. "This is a strong drink," he informed the class as he held up the cup of cider, in case they were missing the point. "And this is a wild woman."

At the reference to their sixty-year-old teacher, all the children began to laugh uproariously. Nick didn't crack a smile. This wasn't funny business to him, Zachary could tell. If one were going to live riotously, one must do it in earnest.

"And this jacket is my fancy new clothes." Nick put on the garment, which was a couple sizes too large on the boy's thin frame. "Oh, dear. I have no more money. What shall I do? I'll go home to my father and see if he will give me a fat cow."

"No, Nick, you're supposed to eat with the pigs first!"

Montgomery whispered loudly. "Marnie and Jennifer are waiting for you over in the sty!"

Nick turned to stare at the two girls huddled down on their knees behind a cage made of chairs. "Oops. I forgot to eat with the pigs. Scoot over, pigs."

Amid giggles, Nick wedged himself down between the girls and pretended to eat. Caught up in the play, Zachary hadn't noticed Elizabeth seated on another of the little chairs nearby. When his eyes fell on her, she gave him a shy smile. As Nick gobbled pretend pig food, Zachary thought over the previous evening.

He and Elizabeth hadn't spent long together—just enough time to eat the burgers and a quick bowl of ice cream. She had seemed uncomfortable in his apartment, and he could only assume it was because of their prior discussion. She didn't want to be alone with him, didn't want the town to think there was anything serious to their relationship, didn't want to risk her son's emotional attachment.

All the same, she had come to see Zachary because she was worried about his reaction to the news about Grace Chalmers. Though they hadn't discussed the subject of his parentage any further, he was glad she had cared enough to risk driving out to his place.

"I will go home to see my dad," Nick said. "He might be mad at me because I wasted all his money in righteous . . . rite-u-ous . . . riotous living. But even if I can only be his servant, it will be better than eating this revolting and dis-gusting pig food."

With that, the prodigal son began his journey home. Zachary stood and pretended to search the horizon. "There's my long-lost son," he said, as he had been directed by Nick the evening before. "I'll bet he has wasted all his money on riotous living. I should make him my servant. That's what he deserves. But I—"

"Daddy!" Nick cried, throwing wide his arms and rushing toward Zachary. "There you are, Daddy!"

Zachary caught the little boy up in the air and crushed him against his chest. "Nick, I—"

"I love you, Daddy. I missed you."

"I love you, too, Nick."

"He's not Nick," Montgomery corrected in an even louder whisper. "He's the prodigal son, Mr. Chalmers, and you're supposed to give him the fatted calf so I can get mad."

Nick still in his arms, Zachary looked into the child's bright olive green eyes. "This is my son who was lost," he said. "Now—" To his surprise, Zachary found himself choking up with emotion as he tried to say his line. "Now . . . I've found him."

"Well, I'm his brother, and I say you better not give him that fatted calf," Montgomery shouted, playing her role to the hilt.

"Moo!" called another of the children, who had donned a pair of empty toilet-paper tubes for horns.

Everyone laughed as Montgomery pretended great indignation at the fact that Nick would be honored by the fat cow. At that, the bovine decided it was time to make a run for safety. Montgomery followed in hot pursuit, which sent the other children into a wild scramble around the small classroom.

"Everybody sit down!" the teacher cried, gesturing for order. "Sit down right now, or I'm going to have to take stars away from those crowns on the bulletin board."

At that threat, the children stumbled to their chairs, gasping for breath and giggling as though the parable of the prodigal son was the funniest thing they'd ever heard. Zachary sat down and perched Nick on his lap. For some reason, the story had rocked Zachary to the core. Never had he considered the events from the father's point of view.

In the role of father, he hadn't found it at all hard to

forgive the wayward son. Instead, he had welcomed reunion, restoration, and reconciliation.

"God is your Father," the teacher was saying. "He loves each one of you boys and girls in the same way that the father loved his prodigal son. The son was naughty, just as we can be naughty sometimes."

"Like when Magunnery and me broke Mr. Fox's window," Nick piped up.

"That's right," the teacher acknowledged. "The son made some mistakes, and he did some very foolish things. He hurt the father so much—but the father never stopped loving him. And when the son wanted to come home, his father welcomed him."

"And he gave him the fat cow," Montgomery added.

"The cow was a sign that the father had forgiven the son. But could the brother forgive?"

"No," Montgomery said, tossing a red pigtail over her shoulder. "He didn't forgive. And you know what I think? I think he was the saddest one in the whole story."

"Not sadder than the cow," the cow spoke up. "He got eaten."

⁊

Somehow Zachary had lost sight of Elizabeth in the throng exiting the Sunday school room. He'd spotted her later in church, sitting in the balcony with a very wiggly little Nick. But after the service, she had gotten away again.

Instead of driving home or heading over to the Nifty Cafe to join the usual Sunday after-church crowd, Zachary considered walking to Elizabeth's apartment. He didn't know why he was still so drawn to the woman, when it was obvious she wanted nothing more than a casual friendship with him. He stood on the sidewalk by the Ambleside Chapel and scanned the street for any sign of her.

Elizabeth had looked beautiful that morning, her long

pale pink skirt swishing when she moved. She had pulled her dark brown hair up into a heavy bun near the top of her head, and soft tendrils danced around her neck. This woman, he realized, possessed everything that compelled and fascinated him. She was tender and kindhearted. She loved children, old people, and even glass countertops that reminded her of an era long past. Every time Zachary thought of moving back to Jefferson City and leaving behind his tangled inheritance, he remembered Elizabeth Hayes. And he couldn't go.

Strolling down the sidewalk, he found himself drawn toward her shop. But it wasn't just Finders Keepers and the apartment behind it that beckoned to him. It was Chalmers House. Grace had lived there once . . . his mother.

The thought of her betrayal slammed him in the gut, as it had repeatedly since he found out about it. He paused to catch his breath. A mother who gave away her son. How could she?

And who was Zachary's father? His mind had reviewed the list of Ambleside citizenry and had come up with no one to fit the bill. Why hadn't Grace Chalmers married the man who fathered her child? Why? A hundred thousand whys. And not a single answer.

Though he hadn't planned on it, Zachary found his feet drawn onto the long front porch of Chalmers House. He slipped his hand into his pocket and located the key to the front door. In a moment, he was inside.

The foyer was deeply shadowed and cool in spite of the noontime summer heat. Down at the end of the open chamber stood the large vase that Boompah and Nick had brought to replace the one Zachary had sold at auction that spring.

As Zachary studied the vase standing alone in the empty, marble-floored foyer, he recalled all the things he had been told about Grace Chalmers. She loved beauty, and she was generous to the poor. She liked to sit out on the back porch with her fan, she wore a well-known red coat in winter, and she donned one of her vast collection of hats each Sunday. She had been a member of Ambleside Chapel, Zachary remembered as he wandered through the front parlors and into the large, empty dining room. He turned to stare out a bay window at the thick forest of Chalmers Park. And she had been unlucky in love.

He leaned his palms on the windowsill and shut his eyes. How could he forgive his mother for the selfish act that had destined him to such a lonely, empty childhood? The bitterness that he once felt for those he'd called parents now slipped away from them and wove a tight cord around the woman called Grace.

But even as Zachary's resentment hardened, Elizabeth's words from the night before knocked on the hardened door of his heart. *Forgive. Forgive.* Grace had made a mistake. She had chosen poorly. But like Nick's mother, she had tried to do the best she could. At least she had tried.

"No," he said aloud. Unlike the father he had portrayed that morning in Sunday school, he was a wronged son who found that forgiveness wasn't so easy. He had no mother. He had no father.

God is your Father, the Sunday school teacher had told the children that morning. Zachary shook his head, unwilling to let the concept penetrate. *The son made some mistakes,* the teacher had explained, *and he did some very foolish things. He hurt the father so much—but the father never stopped loving him. And when the son wanted to come home, his father welcomed him.*

Zachary sat down on the sill of the bay window. Without even recognizing it, he had behaved exactly like the prodigal son. Though he had become a child of the Father early in life—and nothing could change that—he had wandered away from that loving home and had spent years following his own willful path. But here in this small town, he had come to realize his emptiness and need. He had returned to the Father, surrendering his life and his daily will.

And God the Father had welcomed him home.

Did that mean he was somehow supposed to forgive Grace? She had walked a path of sinfulness that brought a dire consequence—an unexpected child and an unwelcome choice. Maybe her red-coated visits to him, her gift of the little toy chick, even her bequest of the family mansion were his mother's attempts to seek his forgiveness. But how could he forgive a dead woman? How could he forgive the pain she had caused?

He didn't forgive, Montgomery had said of the prodigal's angry brother. *And you know what I think? I think he was the saddest one in the whole story.*

Feeling as though a whirlwind was raging through his soul, Zachary strode through the empty house, his footfalls echoing in the silence. Stepping out the back door, he paused on the long porch and sucked down a breath of air. Here his mother had sat, fanning herself on long, hot summer afternoons. Zachary sank onto the steps that led to the expanse of back lawn and rubbed his eyes, wishing he could erase that image.

"Zachary?" Elizabeth stood at the foot of the porch steps. "Nick said he saw you come over here after church. And then I spotted you a minute ago when I was out on the swing. Do you want to come over for some apple cobbler?"

He studied her slender figure, outlined by the noon sun that glistened on her hair. She had taken down the bun, and her hair swung to her shoulders, thick and soft. Though she still wore the pink skirt, she had pulled the blouse loose from the waistband, and its hem brushed against her hips. She was barefoot.

"Will you sit down here with me, Elizabeth?"

Without asking for an explanation, she climbed the steps

and settled beside him. Her skirt touched the tips of her
toes as she crooked her legs and wrapped her arms around
them. Closing her eyes, she rested her head on her knees.
The sunshine kissed her cheek in the exact spot where
Zachary wished he could place his own lips.

He didn't want to be bitter. He didn't want to end up as
the saddest one in the story. God had forgiven him, so why
couldn't he forgive? Why couldn't he let go of the pain?

"Elizabeth," he said.

She opened her eyes and gazed at him.

He let out a breath of acceptance. "Will you please tell
me everything you remember about my mother?"

&

"This was where she and I used to sit together on Saturday
mornings," Elizabeth began, pointing to the former location
of the settee in the Chalmers House front parlor. She
wished she could paint for Zachary a perfect word picture
of Grace, but how could she ever recapture the quiet kindness of the woman she had known and loved?

"A Regency-era couch used to sit right here," she
explained. "It was upholstered in gold brocade, and Grace
kept it covered with fringed pillows. She would sit and
spread out her skirts as though she were a sort of Southern
debutante. Her parents had brought her up to use elegant
manners at all times, she told me. Whenever I dropped by
to visit wearing shorts and a T-shirt, she was always gracious. But I could tell that, deep down, she was mortified at
my appearance."

With Zachary following, Elizabeth motioned to another
part of the parlor. "Her tea trolley stood right here, oak with
brass fittings, and Grace would ring a small silver bell to
have the tea brought out. In a few minutes, old Eben Huff,
her butler, would toddle out of the kitchen with a tray in
his arms. Grace told me that Eben's ancestors had been

slaves but that her father had bought the whole family and set them free. Al Huff and his son, Bud, are descendants of that same family. I think Eben was a great-uncle, or something like that. He never married. He wasn't much older than Grace, and they were great friends in spite of their different social roles. He died a few years before she did. After that, I'd bring the tea from the kitchen myself."

"I guess Eben wasn't a candidate for the role of my father," Zachary observed with a slight chuckle.

Elizabeth shook her head. "No, and I can't figure out who was. Grace never spoke fondly of any man other than her father and Eben. She just talked about her family and closest friends—and always with such devoted love. That's how she and I spent our Saturday morning teatimes. Talking."

She pointed across the room. "Gold candelabras stood on a side table over there, and a gold fire screen right here. Your mother loved to light candles and have Eben lay out a fire. I think she secretly enjoyed the fact that the house was a little drafty. It meant she could snuggle right up close to the hearth."

Zachary poked his head into the empty fireplace and peered up the chimney. "Drafty is an understatement. The damper's rusted through. And here's a bad sign," he said, lifting a small blue feather from the iron grate. "Birds must be nesting in the flue. There might even be a few bats up there."

He walked to one of the long double-paned glass windows. When he touched the frame, it rattled. But when he tried to raise it, he discovered that it had been painted shut. Letting out a breath of frustration, Zachary knelt and put his ear to the floor near an outside wall.

"Termites," he said. "They sound like a fizzing Coke. This floor won't hold up long."

He walked around for a moment, locating one squeaky board after another with his foot. With each creak, Elizabeth felt her heart sink. As his practiced eye roved upward to examine the ceiling, she noted for the first time a series of long cracks that had formed around the hanging light fixture. It was the only thing the auctioneer hadn't sold, Elizabeth realized. The heavy chandelier hung with dusty crystals, those that weren't missing. Most of the small, flame-shaped bulbs were gone, too.

"Inefficient heating system," Zachary said, running his hand over the old radiator that had sung and hissed to Grace all winter. "These things put a lot of moisture into the air, which can be good. But most of the heat will rise up to those tall ceilings. Why they built twelve-foot ceilings in a region where the temperature can hover around zero, I'll never understand. The floors probably stay ice cold."

Elizabeth swallowed, recalling the way Grace had lamented her aching feet each winter. Her ankles hurt, she had complained, and her toes were numb. Not even the pair of woolly house shoes Elizabeth had given her one Christmas made much of a difference.

Zachary was peering into a wall switch that had lost its elegant porcelain cover to the auctioneer. "These wires are a fire hazard," he said. "Look at the way they're frayed. One spark and—"

"Did you want me to tell you about Grace?" Elizabeth said. "Or are you more interested in inspecting the house?"

His shoulders dropped, and he shook his head. "I'm sorry. I guess it's a little hard for me to hear you talking about her. It's easier to focus on reality."

"Reality is that Grace was your mother."

He studied the floor for a moment. "I'm trying to accept that."

"Do you need more proof?"

"Maybe."

"Why don't you talk to Ruby McCann? From the things

she hinted about at the church picnic, I have a feeling she knows a lot about Grace Chalmers's past."

"I considered calling her, but if she confirms the truth to me, she might decide she doesn't have to keep her secret any longer. And before I can blink, the whole town will know."

"Are you ashamed?"

He shrugged. "Obviously, my birth was considered a deep, dark, ugly secret. Maybe there's a reason for that."

"Zachary, Grace wasn't married when she conceived you. Of course she felt ashamed. I'm sure her parents were horrified. But that doesn't have anything to do with the man you are today."

"Doesn't it?" He lifted his head and eyed her.

"Not to me."

He nodded. "It's a new concept, though. I spent years trying to accept the fact that my parents had written me off when the house got too crowded. Now I find out I was illegitimate."

"No one can choose the way he comes into this world, Zachary. Your mother's sins don't change who you are. You're legitimately loved by God. Unconditionally forgiven. Completely accepted."

As though this was almost too hard to hear, Zachary walked out of the parlor and into the foyer. "I'm going to keep this property," he declared, turning to Elizabeth. His eyes blazed. "Phil Fox and the city of Ambleside aren't going to get one particle of dust, not one splinter. Nothing. This place is mine."

Without another word, he stalked outside. Elizabeth stared after him. What did he mean? Was he going to keep the mansion standing? Or did he just intend to salvage the property?

She hurried after him. He was already fiddling with his keys, and the moment she exited, he locked the front door.

"Zachary, I hope you're planning to save the house," she said as he strode past her.

"It's in lousy shape." His voice was gruff.

"I realize that, but . . ."

She slowed, realizing that he was headed for her own porch. *Dear God, this man is so confusing!* Elizabeth lifted her head to a patch of brilliant blue sky framed with green oak leaves. *Please give me your words and not my own. I don't know how to talk to him. I don't know what he needs. I care about him, Father . . . no, I love Zachary . . . but he frustrates me so much!*

"Are you coming?" he called. "I need to get into your store."

Shaking herself from her prayer, Elizabeth ran across the grass. "Zachary, it's Sunday. You know I don't do business on Sundays."

"I want my family Bible."

Breathless, she stepped up onto the porch. "It's right there on that little table where I—"

The table beside the wooden swing was empty. Confused, she searched the other furniture on the porch—a pair of old wicker chairs, a bamboo cart, a small table. Certain she had been reading the Bible as she sat on the swing only the day before, Elizabeth frowned.

"Maybe I put it back on the counter in the shop," she said. "I'd been keeping it there earlier, so maybe out of habit—"

"Mommy, are we going to eat the gobbler?" Nick asked, coming out onto the porch. "Oh hey, Zachary! Did you come over to our house to have dessert with us? Mommy made a gobbler out of apples. Gobblers are my favorite food of all."

Zachary smiled. "More than hot dogs and bean burritos?"

Nick pondered this. "But I don't like pizza," he said solemnly. "Not at all."

"Nick, sweetheart," Elizabeth said, touching his cheek to help him focus on her face. "Have you seen that old Bible I used to keep out here on the porch?"

The boy's face flushed instantly with guilt. "That old Bible?"

"Grace's Bible. The one you took to the park in your backpack."

He began to breathe heavily. "You like to read it on the porch, don't you, Mommy?"

"Yes, I do, but now it's not here."

"I think that sometimes you keep that Bible on the counter inside the shop."

"Did you put it there, Nick?"

"I'm not sure . . . but I think I . . . maybe I did . . . or maybe not."

"Nick, good grief, you ought to know if you moved the Bible. I've told you not to touch it anymore. It's very old and fragile."

Irritated, she walked through her living room and down the hall to the door that connected her apartment to Finders Keepers. She could hear two pairs of feet behind her, one firm and masculine, the other practically dancing with nervousness.

She switched on an old beaded lamp and made her way through the familiar clutter of antique cupboards, trunks, and rocking chairs. It didn't take long to recognize the smooth, polished surface of the old glass counter. She could see nothing on it but her cash register.

"Nick?"

"Could I go to Magunnery's house?" he asked breathlessly. "We could play in her tepee, and I won't even mind if I don't get to eat the gobbler. Not at all."

"Nick." Elizabeth put her hands on her hips. "Where is Grace's Bible?"

"Oh, bother," he whispered.

"What did you do with it?"

"Well, I thought that . . . I thought . . . I didn't mean to . . ."

"Didn't mean to what?"

"To . . . to . . ."

Elizabeth knew from experience that this could go on for hours. The more nervous Nick became, the less he was able to speak clearly. She supposed the abuse he had received in the Romanian orphanage had terrified him to such a depth that any confession of wrongdoing was all but impossible.

"Did you move the Bible?" she asked as gently as possible.

"I think I did," he said in an almost inaudible voice. "But maybe not. No, I don't think so. But I might have."

"Is the Bible in the shop?"

His green eyes flicked around the room. "Umm . . . ummm . . ."

"Did you hide the Bible?"

"No." He shook his head violently, clearly thankful that this truth could be told. "No, Mommy, I didn't hide it."

"Nick," Zachary said, crouching down to face the boy at eye level. "I was hoping to take the Bible home with me to my apartment. Do you know where it is?"

Nick gulped audibly. "It's not here."

"And so . . . where is it?"

Another gulp preceded a guttural moan. "I didn't mean to."

"Whatever you did is OK," Zachary said. "Just tell me where you put the Bible."

Nick wrung his hands, glanced at his mother, swallowed three times, and finally mouthed a whispered sentence. "I gave it away."

SEVENTEEN

"Nick, whom did you give the Bible to?" Elizabeth set her hands on her hips and glared at her son. "Do you remember who it was?"

The little boy squared his shoulders. "I don't like that Bible."

"It doesn't matter how you feel about it. That Bible was not yours to give away. You weren't even supposed to touch it. Now who has it?"

"That Bible made you mad at me in the park."

"Only because I'd told you to leave it alone, and you disobeyed me by putting it in your backpack."

"It made Zachary mad, too. I think the Bible made him mad at you, because he threw it on the porch swing, and I saw him do it. It was not a good Bible. It gave us all trouble. I wanted to cut it up with my scissors and burn it in the fireplace or throw it in the toilet and vanish it forever."

"Nikolai Hayes!" Elizabeth tried to control her fury. The old Bible contained the only family record of Zachary Chalmers's birth. It was part of Grace's legacy to her son. Her heart's deepest feelings had been written onto the margins of its crinkled pages. If Zachary were ever to have any hope of understanding his mother, he would need her Bible.

"Nick," she said, "did you cut up the Bible?"

Guilty yet filled with resolve, he avoided this mother's eyes. "That Bible was bad."

"It was not bad. It was Grace's Bible, and I want to know—"

"I'm not talking about the other Bibles in our house, Mom! Those are the good ones, and we take them to church and read them at night. I like those Bibles. But that one of Grace's was bad, Mom, and you should be happy I got rid of it."

"Well, I'm not happy with you. I'm not happy at all."

She looked across at Zachary. He was standing, hands in his pockets, looking as glum as she'd ever seen him. "I'm not sure we're going to get a straight story," she told him. "I've been through this kind of thing with Nick before. Sometimes I just can't understand the logic he uses before he acts."

"He's told you the logic behind what he did. He saw the Bible as the source of trouble. So he got rid of it. Makes sense to me."

"But it might still be around here somewhere, if we could only get him to tell us what he did with it."

"Elizabeth," Zachary said, "your son was right. He saw the truth. That Bible opened a can of worms in my life. I wish I'd never seen the Chalmers family tree. I was better off believing I'd been dumped by my parents. At least that situation was concrete, something I could get fixed in my mind and deal with. Now, all I've got is a mystery about some Southern belle who sat around on a gold settee and drank tea while her servant waited on her."

"But that's not nearly all there was to Grace!"

"It's all I need to know about the woman. All I want to know."

"There's no mystery to Grace. She was wonderful and kind, Zachary. She cared about everyone in this town. She did all she could . . ."

"The mystery is not just my mother. Who was my father? Where did he come from? Where did he go? Why didn't they marry? Too many unanswerable questions. I'll do better if I just forget the whole thing." He reached down and gave Nick's hair a rumple. "Don't worry about the Bible, kiddo. Your mom likes to look backward and hold onto the past. Maybe she even wants to live in the past a little bit, but I learned a long time ago never to do that. The past is gone. It doesn't matter. I've always headed forward with my life. And that's what I'm going to do now."

"Forward?" Nick asked. "Which way is that?"

"Good question."

"Mrs. Wrinkles taught me under, over, inside, outside, upside down, through, around, beside, beyond . . ."

As Nick puzzled over what Zachary had said, Elizabeth knelt and drew her son into her arms. She knew very well what Zachary meant. He was moving on. He would leave the past—including her and Nick—behind him in his quest for a future. Though her heart was breaking, she knew she must concentrate on neither past nor future. Nick was the present, and right now her child needed her.

"Backward is there," Nick said, thrusting a thumb over his shoulder. "Go forward is . . ." He pointed out the window of Finders Keepers. "Are you going away, Zachary? Are you going to leave us?"

For a moment, the only sound in the room was the gentle thudding of Nick's heart against his mother's ear. She knew all too well the pain that this loss would cause the little boy. Somehow he and Zachary had connected from the very beginning. Nick had chosen Zachary to be his father as surely as Elizabeth had once chosen a small, green-eyed Romanian boy to be her son. Such bonds of the spirit were hard to break.

"I'm going back to my apartment," Zachary said. "Thanks for showing me around the mansion, Elizabeth. And for telling me about Grace. And thanks for all the rest of . . . of everything."

She shut her eyes and nodded. "You're welcome."

As Zachary's footfalls echoed through the shop, Elizabeth snuggled her son close. Her frustration and anger with the child seeped away in the sweet boyish smell of his hair and skin. His small fingers began to play with her hair, lifting it up and letting it fall. From the moment God had given her this child, Nick had loved to play with her hair, touching and smoothing and letting it comfort him.

"Mommy?" he said as he picked up two handfuls of her dark hair and pressed them against her cheeks. "Are you still mad at me?"

"I want you to learn to obey me, sweetheart," she said. "But even more important than that, I want you to know that no matter what you do, I'll always love you."

"Always?"

"Always and forever."

"Backward and forward?"

"You bet."

He leaned over and planted a wet kiss on her cheek. "Mommy, why does Zachary always go to his apartment? Doesn't he have a real home anywhere?"

Elizabeth considered the rambling old house across the lawn, the tidy but half-furnished apartment down the road, the series of foster families, the trailer park.

"No," she said finally. "I don't think Zachary has a place he would call a real home of his own. I don't think he ever has."

"I wish we could adopt him to be in our family. Then you could put your arms around him and love him forever and always, backward and forward."

"Well," Elizabeth said, "Zachary is a grown-up, and I don't think he wants to believe that anyone ever loved him—or that anyone could love him now. I really don't think Zachary wants to be in a family, Nick."

"That makes me very sad," he whispered against her neck.

"Me, too, sweetie. Me, too."

Zachary walked down the last three steps in the narrow corridor and pushed open the glass door that led out onto the square. He breathed in a chest full of fresh air to cleanse his lungs of the musty, dusty pall that clung to his office upstairs. It was going to be good to move out of those cramped quarters above Sawyer-the-lawyer's offices and into his own brand-new work space.

As he passed the stores that lined the square, he felt once again the sense of jaunty joy that had given a spring to his step for the past three weeks. He was a man with a plan. His new mission had given him direction and purpose. From the moment he'd figured out the path he was to walk, he had moved forward with all the jet propulsion of a rocket. Nobody and nothing could stand in his way.

And the reason for his inner certainty came from the best place of all.

The night he'd left Elizabeth's place, he had gone home in a funk that wouldn't lift. Unable to sleep, he'd meandered out onto his balcony, and after a while, he'd begun to pray. It wasn't just random praying either. This had been a focused, intent discussion with the Christ to whom he was surrendered. By the time dawn began to send its pink mist across the river, he knew what he was supposed to do.

It was right. It was a plan. And with God's help, he would accomplish it.

"Hey there, Zachary Chalmers!" Pearlene Fox called. She leaned on her broom and gave him a wave. "Long time no see. We've missed you in church. Where've you been keeping yourself?"

"Taking care of business." He crossed the street toward her. "I spent the last couple of weeks in Jeff City."

"Did you? Well, I'll swan. I hope you're not thinking of moving back there after that last council meeting and all. I know folks are all up in arms about the mansion these days, and Phil thinks he's got himself a big enough wave to ride all the way to elections." She rolled her eyes. "As if *parking* was the be-all and end-all of everything in this town."

"I read in the newspaper that parking is the main topic on tonight's council agenda."

"Parking, my foot. Everybody's gearing up to talk about the fate of that old eyesore over there. You want to know what I think? I think there's nobody but Phil Fox himself who gives a rip about the parking situation in Ambleside. I think what everybody wants to talk about is Chalmers House. Who's going to wind up with it, what's going to happen to it, what ought to be done with it—you name it. That place has got folks speculating up one side of the street and down the other."

Zachary nodded. He'd heard more than an earful about it himself. "I guess people have to talk about something."

"In this town? Boy howdy, that's for sure."

He chuckled. "Pearlene, I was wondering if you could help me with something."

"Oh, I don't know if I ought to. I got myself into a peck of trouble by giving Liz a copy of that old town charter. Phil like to killed me. Not really, of course, but he was hoppin' mad. Hoo, was that man steamed!"

"This one shouldn't cause you any problems. It's about Elizabeth Hayes."

"Liz? What about her?"

Zachary tried to steel himself. He knew he was speaking to the queen bee in the gossip hive of Ambleside, Missouri. Once he told her his concerns, his personal business would belong to the town. But no one could help him better than Pearlene, so he'd have to risk it.

"Well," he began, "I've been trying to get in touch with Elizabeth for . . . for a while now. Maybe a week or more. I've called her house, and I tried the shop. She's not answering. I thought I'd drop by and check on her, but maybe you know what's going on."

"Of course I know what's going on. Why didn't you ask me before? Liz and Nick went on a vacation."

"A vacation?" Zachary felt as though the sun had just been knocked slightly off-kilter. Elizabeth Hayes didn't take vacations. She didn't like change. She wanted security and home and the sameness of Ambleside. She was supposed to be right where Zachary had left her last—dependable and certain.

"Liz finished that big Jeff City contract she was working on," Pearlene explained. "You know those three houses she was furnishing? Apparently they liked what she did so well, they gave her another contract. She told me she's going to be doing good to keep her shop open and work on that second contract both. I suspicion she's going to have money flowing in like summer rain in a leaky basement. There was a time when I figured Liz would marry the first man who came along and could offer her and Nick some financial security. But not anymore. No, sir. She's making her own way in this world, and I'm sure proud of her. Any-how, Liz finished her first contract about the same time Nick got done with summer school, which, by the way, turned out real good according to Liz. He's adding double-digit numbers now, did you know that?"

"Double digits," he said blankly.

"And he's been reading almost at grade level, which Liz says is better than everybody expected. She's just as tickled as she can be."

"But . . . about the vacation. Where did she go?"

"Florida."

"Florida!"

"Well, it's not the moon, you know. Liz wanted to show Nick the ocean, which I've got to say is more than I've ever seen of this old world. Anyhow, she packed him up and shut down her shop and off they went. Like I say, they were both at a point where they could take a little break, so they just up and did it. Boompah's checking on her house every other day, bringing in the mail and the newspaper. He's getting around a lot better these days, in case you hadn't noticed that either. Luke Easton is mowing Liz's yard and watering her flowers. And I'm keeping her sidewalk swept."

Zachary stared at the darkened windows of Finders Keepers. Elizabeth couldn't have gone off without telling him. That didn't fit into the plan at all.

OK, so maybe he'd been a little overly focused on putting things in motion. Maybe he'd been a little driven. Maybe . . . maybe he was back to his old way of caring more about things—plans, goals, ambitions—than about people. It's just that he'd counted on Elizabeth staying right where he wanted her until he was ready to tend to that situation.

But Elizabeth wasn't a situation, was she? She was a woman he'd thought he knew pretty well. And he knew she wasn't supposed to change.

"When is she coming back?" he asked.

"Nobody knows," Pearlene said, giving her broom a little whack on the curb to knock off the dust. "She told Boompah she'd come home when she was good and ready. Now, doesn't that beat all?"

Zachary let out a breath. How could it be that just when he thought he'd been getting his surrender to Christ down pat, he had let his focus on people go straight out the window?

He lifted his head and studied the canopy of oak trees

that arched over the rooftops around the square. Though
Elizabeth had warned him of it, he was only just beginning
to realize that this walk along the Christian path wasn't
going to be easy. One slip, and he might lose something—or someone—very important.

"Anyhow," Pearlene said, "if Liz didn't bother to tell you
where she was going, well, I guess that tells the both of us
where you stand in her books."

"It does?"

"At the bottom of the list. 'Course, she wouldn't have
gone off like that if she didn't figure she was at the bottom
of your list, too. And I thought I had you two pegged."

She paused for a moment, gave a shrug, and then went
back to her sweeping.

い **ン**し

Elizabeth helped Nick take off his sneakers, once again
thanking heaven for Velcro, and shook the sand out of
them. "I had no idea you've had sand in your shoes ever
since we left Florida, sweetie," she said as he reached up to
give the Eastons' door his characteristic rapid-fire knock.
"Hasn't it been bothering you?"

"Oh, Mommy, the sand keeps my toes awake. When I
feel the sand, I know my feet are still there."

Elizabeth laughed as the sound of running flip-flops carried through the closed door. In less than a heartbeat, the
door flew open and a swirl of red hair and skinny arms and
legs came flying outside.

"Nick! Nick, you came back!"

"Here I am, Magunnery!" Nick hugged the little girl, doing
his best to pick her up as they danced around and around
on the front porch. "I went to the ocean, and I thought I
would never see you again."

"Can you play?" Her bright eyes focused on Elizabeth.
"Can Nick play with me, Miss Hayes? I want to show him

my new bed. Daddy made me a bed, and you can put stuff
in the drawers underneath, but you can't jump on it, Nick.
Not even if you really, really want to."

"That's fine," Elizabeth said as the pair raced into the
house. "Go ahead."

"Hey, Elizabeth." Luke Easton stepped out of the kitchen
and held up a damp dishcloth in greeting. "Welcome back.
Come on in."

"Thanks. How've you been?"

"Getting by. You?"

"We had fun at the ocean." She gave a little smile. "But
I'm glad we're home."

"Montgomery missed Nick."

"Likewise. How are things in town?"

"About the same. Boompah's getting around better. He's
decided to put in a deli."

"No kidding?"

"You weigh your salad or your sandwich on his little
scale, and off you go. Ruby McCann's already complaining.
She says fresh fruit will weigh more, and that's not fair
because it's so good for you."

Elizabeth laughed. Luke looked a hundred percent better
than he had the day she'd told him she was leaving on a
vacation. Maybe Zachary had been right that he needed the
total responsibility of caring for Montgomery. Keeping his
mind on his daughter seemed to have done Luke a world of
good.

Their house, unfortunately, wasn't faring quite so well.
Elizabeth had never seen so much clutter in her life. Piles
and piles of newspapers, discarded sweaters and jackets,
junk mail, cast-off shoes, cereal boxes, and Little Debbie
wrappers lay scattered on the floors, sofa, and table.

"Uh, sorry about the mess," Luke said, following her
focus around the room. "Ellie was . . . she didn't . . . but I'm
not as . . ."

"It's OK." Elizabeth touched his arm. "So, how's your business going these days? Are you back at work full time?"

"Yep. I just got a good contract." He gave her a sheepish glance. "It's, uh, the mansion. I guess you know about that."

"Zachary indicated he was going to go ahead with the plans for his architectural firm."

"He is—if he can blow past Phil Fox at the council meeting tonight."

"It's tonight?"

"Boy, you are out of touch. Listen, Elizabeth, why don't you leave Nick here and head over there? I'm sure Zachary could use some support—if that's what you could give him."

Elizabeth pursed her lips. "Oh, Luke . . . I really don't think Zachary needs or wants anybody around. In fact, I expected you to tell me he'd moved back to Jefferson City."

"Zachary Chalmers? Why would he do that?"

"The last time we spoke, Zachary told me he was planning to move forward with his life. Conquer new worlds, that sort of thing. You know how he is. He's one of the most single-minded and self-focused men you could ever meet. And he's so driven. I think ambition runs like ice through his veins."

"Are you sure you're talking about Zachary Chalmers? There's not a chip of ice in that man. After Ellie died, he spent hours over here with me. He took time off from work to come check on me. He called at least once or twice a day to make sure I was hanging in OK with Montgomery. Boompah told me Zachary took food over there when he was sick, and he said the two of them have gotten to where they play dominoes together a couple nights a week."

"Zachary plays dominoes?"

"Sure. And Ruby McCann says Zachary started dropping off her fresh milk at the library every morning, so she doesn't have to figure out where to park her DeSoto. I also

know for a fact that he drummed up two or three legal
cases for Sawyer-the-lawyer to work on. The fellow hasn't
been seen sleeping on his desk in the last month. Zachary's
one of the most decent men I ever met."

"Are you sure you're talking about Zachary Chalmers?"

Luke stared at her, and then they both began to laugh.
"But I never saw that side of him!" she protested.

"Well, you've been gone forever and a day."

"I have not." She folded her arms and tapped her foot.
"Look, I know Zachary can be kind. I've seen him reach out
to people in a stiff sort of way. I mean, he did use up his
vacation days to manage the Corner Market for Boompah . . . and he led us all on that search through the park
for you right after Ellie's funeral . . . and he helped out with
the police when Nick and Montgomery threw the rock
through Phil's window . . . and maybe . . ."

"Maybe you don't know the real Zachary Chalmers. He's
a good guy. You ought to go over to that council meeting
and support him."

She glanced at her watch. "Well, it's probably almost
over."

"Nah. Phil's got himself a platform. The meeting could go
on all night."

Letting out a breath of resignation, she gave him a nod.
"OK, but I won't be out long. I'm just going to drop in over
there to show I'm behind Zachary."

Luke grinned. "Yep."

"But I don't like his attitude toward historical preservation."

"Nope."

"And I think he can be very self-focused."

"Uh-huh."

"And bullheaded."

"Bye, Lizzy."

She turned and headed out the door. Why was she going
to the city council meeting? Why? For the past two days, all

the way back from Florida, she'd told herself she wasn't going to think about Zachary Chalmers. Wasn't going to ask about him. Wasn't going to look him up. Wasn't even going to glance in the direction of his office.

As she hurried across the street toward the city hall, she smoothed the wrinkles on her cotton skirt. She'd been driving all day, her hair was a wreck, and she hadn't even thought about makeup or jewelry. Zachary would probably make a face when he saw her . . .

She pulled up short and squared her shoulders. What was she worrying about? She didn't care what Zachary Chalmers thought of her. She just didn't want a parking lot next door.

❧

"All right, you've made your point." Mayor Cleo Mueller was addressing Phil Fox as Elizabeth slipped into the back of the room and found an empty chair. "If you wouldn't mind sitting down, Phil, we might be able to get this meeting finished up by midnight. Viola, read back through Phil's proposal, please."

The plump-cheeked owner of Dandy Donuts, who served as recording secretary, stood and cleared her throat. "Councilman Philip Fox—that's with one *L* in Philip—proposes that the city of Ambleside offer Zachary Chalmers Lots 54 and 55 in the new McCann subdivision in a fair exchange for the property at 100 Walnut Street. Councilman Fox further proposes that Lots 54 and 55 be rezoned from residential use to mixed use. And last, Councilman Fox proposes that the building known as Chalmers House be dismantled except for the front parlor, as per the written requests in the Ambleside town charter and the letter from Grace Chalmers. Both documents are on record. The Chalmers House parlor is to be used as a museum honoring the Chalmers family and as a parking-attendant's office. The grounds of the property are to be paved into a paid parking lot for the use of the citizens of Ambleside and out-of-town visitors."

Viola looked up and blinked. At the sight of the mayor's reassuring smile, she heaved a breath of relief and sat down again.

"Thank you, Viola," Cleo said. "OK, folks, we have a three-part proposal before the council, and we're going to have to take it apart for discussion a little bit at a time. Now, I know a lot of you people want to have your say, so if you'll all be patient, we'll get to you one at a time. The first part of the proposal involves a property exchange. Lots 54 and 55 sit on the edge of the subdivision, right next to the highway. That makes them a logical site for an office complex—"

The mayor halted as Zachary Chalmers stood. Elizabeth had a feeling she'd been through all this before. The hopelessness of saving Grace's home swept over her. Zachary wanted an office. The town wanted a parking lot. One way or another, Grace's legacy was about to end.

"If I might have permission to address the council," Zachary was saying, "I think this matter can be resolved in a very few minutes."

"A few minutes?" Cleo smiled. "Well, now. That's to my liking. What have you got to tell us, Mr. Chalmers?"

"Just this: The property at 100 Walnut Street is mine, and I'm not going to trade it to the city."

As he started to sit, the room erupted. Cleo hammered his gavel on the folding table so hard that Elizabeth feared it might collapse.

"Now hold on a minute there, Zachary!" Phil Fox jumped to his feet. "I thought we had an understanding. You've got a copy of that town charter. You know good and well you can't raze the old mansion for your office!"

"Phil, you're out of order," Cleo bellowed. "Now sit down, and everybody hold your horses!" He grabbed his suspenders and adjusted them angrily. "I haven't even opened the floor for discussion. Zachary, were you finished?"

"I guess not." Zachary pulled a thick legal file from a briefcase beside his chair. "I have various documents here, and I'll make them available to the public. Basically, they reflect a number of legal opinions and a great deal of research. The bottom line is that the document in Mr. Fox's possession was never legally recorded in the records of the city of Ambleside. It may look like a town charter, but it's not. It was never voted on. It was never adopted. Nothing. That's how Phil was able to lay his hands on the thing so easily. What he's been calling the town charter is just an old piece of paper that reflects one man's desires for his property—and it's not any more valid than the letter written by Grace Chalmers. Neither document is a will, and neither will stand up in a court of law."

"Now I don't know about that!" Phil said, again leaping to his feet.

"I also have here," Zachary went on, "the legal will from Grace Chalmers that deeds her property to me. It's been through probate, and not a soul has stepped forward to contest it. A week ago, the matter cleared the courts, and the property was designated as mine. Here's a copy of that document."

Despite Elizabeth's misgivings, a thrill surged through her as Zachary laid one brick after another in a wall that would barricade Phil Fox from the Chalmers property. Zachary was fighting for what belonged to him. Brick by brick, he was building himself a place of his own. And, in spite of her own desires for the mansion, she championed his cause.

"So," Zachary concluded, "the property's mine, and I don't want to exchange it for a lot in a subdivision on the outskirts of town. I'm going to build my architectural firm at

100 Walnut Street. As far as I can see, that settles the situation and makes the proposal of Councilman Fox irrelevant."

Half the room burst into cheers. The other half filled the basement chamber with boos. Zachary strode to the council table and set copies of his documents in front of the mayor. As he returned to his seat, Phil Fox stood.

"There's just one problem, Mr. Chalmers," he said. As the room quieted, he held up a copy of Grace's final testament. "You see, I've got a few documents of my own to show off. This will leaves the property at 100 Walnut Street to Zachary Chalmers, Grace's nephew. But I've done a little research. And what I've learned is that you aren't Grace's nephew at all, are you, Zachary? You're her son."

18
EIGHTEEN

In the hush of the crowded meeting room, Elizabeth suddenly knew victory was in sight. If this revelation about his past crushed Zachary, maybe he would step away from his claim on the mansion. He wouldn't want to live in a town where he was looked upon with disparagement and disgrace. No one would.

With Zachary gone, only Phil and his ridiculous parking-lot idea would block the salvation of the old house. And Elizabeth realized she held the key to its preservation. With her new lucrative contract and her flourishing antiques business to support her bid, she could buy the mansion herself.

She truly could own the place. Had God laid this marvelous opportunity in her lap? Was it his gift? Should she really push through with her own plan?

As she surveyed the roomful of gawking townsfolk, she could see Zachary Chalmers standing alone, his face taut. Phil Fox, eyes blazing, was only just beginning to realize that his action had humiliated and abased Zachary far more effectively than it had done anything to disprove Zachary's claim to the property.

Ruby McCann began to fan herself with the meeting agenda. Cleo Mueller sat with his mouth open. Boompah clutched the back of the nearest seat with whitened fingers.

And just as clearly as Elizabeth knew she might use this moment to save the mansion, she knew she would not.

"May I speak, Mayor Mueller?" Elizabeth heard herself say as she came to her feet.

Every eye in the room turned on her. Cleo nodded. "Go ahead, Miss Hayes."

She swallowed. *Oh, Lord, what do you want me to say? Why am I standing? What am I supposed to do?*

"I'd like to, uh, to say something on behalf of Zachary Chalmers, who is . . . who has become . . . my friend." She tried to breathe. "Since he moved here, Zachary has stirred up some waves in the calm waters of Ambleside. But as a lot of you have discovered in the past few months, he is an honorable and kind gentleman. And he has taught me a few things since I've known him. One of the most important lessons I've learned is to realize when to stop looking at the past and when to start moving forward."

Elizabeth paused to calm herself. As she scanned the room, she noted that Zachary was gazing at her, his green gray eyes bemused. Giving him a half smile, she lifted her chin and continued.

"I'd like to remind you of another little wave in Ambleside's calm waters—my son, Nick." Her words were followed by a chorus of indulgent chuckles. "Everyone knows I adopted Nick from another country, and that the circumstances of his birth are a little cloudy. One of the main reasons I chose to live in Ambleside with Nick is because I believed you folks could help my son move beyond his past . . . and move forward. I'm trusting you to help me give Nick a good future."

Elizabeth clasped her hands together. "Most of you are aware," she went on, "that I oppose Zachary's desire to raze the mansion. But I want him and everyone else in this room to know I stand behind Zachary's right to take possession of the property that was given to him by Grace Chalmers. Not only should he own it, but he ought to be able to do whatever he wants with it. Nothing in his past should make a difference."

She stopped speaking for a moment. "Show Zachary

Chalmers the same measure of kindness that he's shown you," she said firmly. "Give him the same grace that you give to little Nick. Let him move forward."

With a nod to Cleo to show she was finished speaking, Elizabeth headed for the door. She had done what she came to do. She had spoken up for Zachary.

Unwilling to watch the fallout from Phil's heartless statement and her own feeble attempt to mend the hurt, she hurried across the street. The mansion loomed huge and dreary in the last vestiges of the late-summer sunset. Once long ago, the house had been a home. A place of comfort and pleasure and gentility. Now it had become the focus of dissension, quarreling, and cruelty.

Running her fingertips along the brick wall of the parlor Phil had proposed turning into a parking-attendant's office, Elizabeth made her way to the back porch where Grace had always sat to fan herself. As she climbed the wooden steps, she could feel the gentle breath of the Missouri River drift over her, ruffling her skirt and tickling through her hair.

It was time for her to move forward, too, Elizabeth thought as she sat down on the top step and leaned against the porch post. She had to let this mansion go. Had to give to Christ her ambitions and dreams for expanding her business. Had to take Nick by the hand and march him through the future—a future where some would treat him with kindness and others would ridicule and taunt him.

Most of all, she had to relinquish the half-formed hope that Zachary Chalmers had brought to life inside her. Despite her words to Luke earlier that afternoon, she had to admit to herself that she *did* know the real Zachary Chalmers, the honorable and kind man of whom she had spoken at the council meeting. For a few short months, she had even begun to believe that she might have found a true love. Sure, she and Zachary argued a lot and butted heads against their opposing goals. But in the long run, they'd seemed to have a lot in common.

It was hard to give up the idea of having someone to laugh and cry with. Someone to fight with. Someone to depend on. Someone to tease. Someone to dream and plan and hope with.

Hard, too, to surrender the quiet pleasure of a stolen kiss or a reassuring arm around the shoulders. A part of Elizabeth that she'd tried to suppress had awakened to the desire for passion and fulfillment. She wanted to be a woman who knew the ultimate union—spiritual, emotional, and physical—with a man. She wanted to be a wife.

And not just any man's wife. She wanted to be Zachary Chalmers's wife. Through the months, she had grown to love him in a way that went deeper and broader than anything she'd ever hoped to experience.

But it was time to give up that love. Zachary belonged to God, and it was clear that God had other plans for him. Zachary was going to tear down the mansion, build his fancy office, bring in big-city renters, and continue to blaze his trails through the world. Next door, in her quiet little antiques shop, Elizabeth would indulge her clients in the poignant nostalgia of the past. She would continue to be a Christian first, a mother second, an entrepreneur third. Somewhere, far on the back shelf, she would know she was a woman. But that part of herself would remain hidden and mostly forgotten, amid the busyness of her daily life.

And that had to be good enough. With a sigh of acceptance, Elizabeth stood and strolled across the lawn to her own porch. It was time to slip out of her wrinkled skirt and into a pair of shorts before heading along the backyard trails to the Eastons' house. She and Nick would return home, unpack their suitcases, check on the plants, and read the mail. And maybe they'd finish the day with a big bowl

of Nick's current favorite food—mint chocolate chip ice
cream.

As Elizabeth stepped onto the porch, she saw the move-
ment of a shadow on the porch swing. Her heart skipped a
beat in spite of her self-determined calm.

"Elizabeth?" The figure rose slowly and doffed his hat. "I
come from the meeting. Is me, Jacob Jungemeyer."

"Oh, Boompah." Elizabeth couldn't contain her disappointment. Of course it wouldn't be Zachary. He was over at city
hall defending his rights to the mansion. He wouldn't be
coming here.

"Elizabeth, I must talk with you." Boompah hobbled forward, hat in his hand. "I have to tell you something. Something very important."

"Boompah, why don't you sit down on the swing again
for a minute or two? I need to call Luke to check on Nick,
and then I'll see if I can stir us up some lemonade—"

"No, no! Please, Elizabeth!" His gnarled hand gripped
hers with surprising strength. "Is about Grace Chalmers."

"Grace? What about Grace?"

"Maybe you better be the one who is sitting. Is a very
shocking thing I must tell . . . about Grace and . . . Grace
and me. And only this night do I realize the meaning of the
deeds of the past."

"Oh, Boompah."

He hung his head. "You didn't guess before now about
Grace and me?"

"You always said she was beyond you."

"She was. But still . . . somehow . . . we grow to love
each other through the years." He turned his hat brim
around and around in his hand. "I think it is because we
both feel very different, very alone, in this town. I am the
Gypsy, and she is the rich girl. And that difference makes us
somehow the same. Do you understand, Elizabeth?"

"I think so," she said.

"Grace's father forbids me to see her. But we don't listen to him, you know. We are not young, after all. We are adults, and we meet in the grocery when she comes with Eben Huff to shop. Or sometimes I take the groceries to Chalmers House, and I bring flowers for her blue vase. We like to talk, I make her laugh, she enchants me. Somehow, Grace is of the old times. Her ways are gentle and good and elegant. I love her."

"But, Boompah . . ."

"I know. It's wrong, what happened between us." He shook his head. "One night, I am on my way back from Jefferson City with my truck full of groceries, and there I see Grace's little car in the ditch. She was never a good driver, you know. I pull out the car, and then . . . we are alone together . . . and we make a very wrong choice. After that, I don't see Grace for a long time even though I try to call her and bring little notes to the mansion for her. I find out she has gone away to New York to stay with relatives. When she comes back to Ambleside, I don't see her again except from a distance. Now, only Eben comes to my shop for the groceries. Grace goes to the chapel for church, but we never speak. She never leaves her house except to sit on the back porch and fan herself. I know she is very sad, but I cannot reach her."

"You didn't realize Grace had given birth to your son?" Elizabeth whispered.

"How can I know this? Nobody tells me. I try to talk to her, but she will not speak. Eben Huff tells me that sometimes she goes away for a few days to visit her family in Jefferson City, her brother. I try to find him out—his name and house—but I cannot. He has no telephone, and nobody speaks of him. And so I go on living my life, and Grace lives her life until . . . until one day she dies. Never until this night . . . this night . . . I did not know, Elizabeth!"

"Oh, Boompah." Wrapping her arms around the old man,

she held him close. "But Zachary will be thrilled to learn you're his father. He loves you very much."

"You think?"

"I'm sure."

"But all the years when he is a little boy, I never help him. I never teach him. I never protect him. I don't do any of the things a father should do for his son."

"But, Boompah, you couldn't do those things. You didn't know."

"Maybe he is angry with me anyway."

"No, he won't be angry. He'll be surprised . . . amazed . . ."

A footstep on the porch drew Elizabeth's attention. As she looked up, she saw Zachary Chalmers move into the light.

"Uh, excuse me," he said, his eyes narrowing at the sight of the two figures on the porch. "Luke, I didn't mean to interrupt—"

"Zachary," Boompah said, stepping out of Elizabeth's embrace. "Is me, Jacob Jungemeyer."

"Boompah?"

"Elizabeth, maybe I better go now," the old man said. "Maybe you can talk to Zachary and—"

"No, Boompah. This is your business." Stepping back, she decided the time was right to go get her son. Zachary had come to her house, but she didn't trust herself to talk to him. Not now, with her resolve to move forward still so new inside her.

"I'm going on over to Luke's house," she told the men.

"Listen here, Elizabeth." Zachary crossed his arms over his chest, and his voice was hard. "If you and Luke Easton have something going on, I want to know about it right now."

Confused, she tilted her head. "Luke's watching Nick."

"What's he doing that for?"

"So I could . . ." She gestured in the direction of city hall. "Zachary, why did you come here?"

"Because I want to talk to you. You just sashayed out of

town and disappeared. How do you expect me to take care of business when you up and leave without telling anyone?"

"I told lots of people."

"Yeah, well, you didn't tell me."

"Yeah, well, you were busy with your tearing-down business and your moving-forward business, and all that. Now, if you'll excuse me—"

"No, I will not excuse you." He caught her arm and steered her back from the steps. "I want to get to the bottom of a few things around here. I've had it with secrets and lies. It's time for the truth, and I'm going to start with you."

"No, I must be first!" Boompah cried. "Is all my fault that you don't know the truth, Zachary. But how can I tell you the truth, because I don't know it myself until tonight? Now, I will say everything, and may God forgive me for the pain it will cause." He wadded his hat into a ball. "I, Jacob Wilhelm Jungemeyer, am your father."

Elizabeth felt Zachary's grip on her arm go slack. He swallowed hard and dropped his hand. "What?" he mouthed.

"Boompah and Grace," Elizabeth said softly. "They weren't married, and he never knew she'd given birth to his child."

"Me?"

"You are my son," Boompah said, anguish tightening his voice. "And before you become angry, which is your right, let me say that I cannot be more proud of any son than I am of you, Zachary. Even though you and I find out this news only tonight, already in these past months I think of you as my son. I love you."

The silence was punctuated only by the distant horn of a river barge. A moth fluttered past Elizabeth's face and flapped its white wings around the yellow light.

"The last time I stood on this porch," Zachary said, "I

found out Grace Chalmers was my mother. And now I have
a father."

"But you do not need to tell anybody this thing,"
Boompah said. "I know is not something to be proud of,
the way you came into this world with such sin and decep-
tion. And I am not a father for any man to boast about, only
an old Gypsy who runs a grocery store and cannot talk
good English after all these years. Don't worry, Zachary.
This knowledge among us can stay a secret—"

"No more secrets," Zachary said, stepping away from Elizabeth. "Of all the men I've ever met, there's not one I'd
rather claim as my father than you."

"Yes?" The old man's eyes glistened.

"Yes." Zachary gathered Boompah into his arms and
pulled him close. "With your permission, I plan to tell the
whole world that I am the son of Jacob Jungemeyer."

"Ach, God is too good to me," Boompah mumbled as his
gnarled hands slipped around the broad back of his son.
"Even from my sin, he can bring a blessing."

"And speaking of blessings," Elizabeth said as she
brushed at her damp cheek, "I'd better go get Nick."

"Not so fast." Zachary caught her hand. "Boompah, wait
here. Elizabeth, come with me."

"But I promised Luke—"

"This way," he said, tugging her down the porch steps
and across the lawn to the back of the old mansion. "I've
got something for you, and at the rate things are going
tonight, I might never get around to giving it to you."

"Zachary, what's going on?"

"You'll see." He led her up the steps. "Now sit down."

"Are you bossing me around?"

"Yes." He pressed her shoulder until she was forced to
sit. "I had this made for you almost three weeks ago, and
I've been more than a little irked that you went off to
Florida without it."

"Well, excuse me. It appears Boompah and Grace weren't the only ones with a few secrets."

"All right, close your eyes."

Her heart hammering, Elizabeth shut her eyes and took a deep breath. What could this be? She could hear him huffing a little as the sound of scraping moved across the porch behind her.

"OK," he said. "Open your eyes and turn around."

As she swiveled on the porch step, Elizabeth saw that Zachary was supporting a large wooden sign complete with a pair of heavy brass chains. Coming to her feet, she moved to where she could see the inscription more clearly in the dim light.

"Finders Keepers," she read aloud. "100 Walnut Street. Elizabeth Chalmers, Proprietress."

For a moment she couldn't speak. Again, she read the sign, this time in silence. Finally, she lifted her head.

"100 Walnut Street?" she whispered.

"Just the downstairs, though." He was grinning that lopsided grin she had come to love so much. "That other sign will direct my clients upstairs."

Her focus shifted to a smaller, neatly painted sign leaning against the balustrade. It read Zachary Chalmers, Architect.

"You mean you aren't going to tear the house down?" Elizabeth asked, almost afraid of the answer.

"Nope. I've hired Luke Easton to restore the entire building. The house will look exactly like it did when it was originally built, but it will be structurally sound and have all the modern conveniences—plus updated heating, cooling, plumbing, and electrical systems. So . . . what do you think?"

Elizabeth looked into his eyes. "But this sign says my name is . . . is . . . isn't Hayes."

"Well, that part is negotiable."

"Negotiable?"

"If you put it in business terms." He laughed "Which it isn't."

"No?"

"Nope." Dropping to one knee, he took her hand. "Miss Elizabeth Hayes, I profess to you my undying love. I promise faithfulness, honor, protection, and—" he paused—"I'm no good at doing things the old way, Elizabeth."

Standing, he took her into his arms and kissed her lips with all the passion she felt in her own heart. "I love you, Elizabeth," he murmured, his breath warm against her ear. "I love you, and I want you. That's all I know. I want you past, present, and future. You certainly don't need me, and the Lord knows I'm far from perfect. But if you can see beyond my bullheadedness and . . . and my occasional cockiness . . . and even that ugly church in Jefferson City . . . I want you to be my wife."

"Oh, Zachary." The tears of her pent-up loneliness finally pushed past the dam she had built, and Elizabeth wept on his shoulder. "Zachary, I gave you up. I surrendered us to God. I didn't believe we could ever find a place of common ground, a place where we could touch each other. Somewhere between the past and the future—"

"And it was right here under our noses the whole time," he said. "So what do you think about the new sign? And, uh, the new name?"

"Yes," she said, her cheek pressed against his and her fingers threading through his hair. "Elizabeth Chalmers. I like that."

"Finders Keepers," he said. "I like that even better."

Arm in arm, Elizabeth and Zachary climbed onto the porch behind the antiques shop. Seated together on the swing, Boompah and Nick were each enjoying a bowl of mint chocolate chip ice cream. The boy glanced up and gave his mother a sly smile.

"Mommy, you were kissing Zachary," he said. "Boompah came to Magunnery's house to get me because he said you were busy. And when we got here to the porch, I saw that you were busy kissing."

"Well, that's rather nosy, Nick." Elizabeth considered moving toward her son, but she decided she liked her current location better. "You're not supposed to spy on people."

"I'd say he's observant," Zachary countered. "And that is a very good thing."

Nick giggled. "You look happy, Mommy."

"I am happy." She looked at the man she loved. "Zachary asked me to marry him."

"Did you say yes?"

"I certainly did."

"That's what I told Magunnery!" Nick cried, nearly upsetting the ice-cream bowl. "I told her a long time ago that Zachary was going to be my dad. Remember, Mom? I put Zachary on the family tree for the father, and you for the mother, and Boompah was the grandfather, and Grace was the grandmother and—"

"Oh, Zachary!" Elizabeth gasped. "He did write all that down!"

"That's my boy," Zachary said with a laugh. "I wonder if he somehow knew."

"He knows that God's plans are greater than our own," Boompah said. "And in Christ, we are all one family, no matter who is our father or mother."

"That's why Magunnery told me to write my family down in Grace's old Bible with the other names on the list," Nick said. The moment the words were out, he clapped his hand over his mouth. The ice-cream bowl tumbled off his lap, splattering green droplets across the porch.

"Nikolai Hayes," Elizabeth said, finally stepping out of Zachary's embrace. "Where did you write down your family tree?"

"On a paper," Nick whispered, his green eyes growing round.

"You said you wrote it in Grace's Bible. You said Montgomery told you to do it."

Nick nodded.

"Is Grace's Bible at the Eastons' house?"

Nick nodded again.

"Young man, I want you to march right over there this minute and get that Bible. It belongs to Zachary."

Nick gulped and slid down from the swing. "Mommy, I should never disobey you, but I can't get the Bible. It doesn't belong to Zachary or you anymore. It belongs to Magunnery."

As Elizabeth's ire rose, she felt Zachary slip a calming arm around her shoulders. "You gave your friend the Bible?" he asked. "How come?"

"Because she needed it. But it's OK because I wrote down everybody from my family tree on the page with all the lines. I wrote down Elizabeth Hayes for my mother, and Zachary Chalmers for my father, and Boompah—"

"Nick, you shouldn't have written in the Bible," Elizabeth said.

"No, it's all right." Zachary took the child's hand and pulled him close. "Boompah's right. We're all in the family of God, aren't we, Nick? And I guess Montgomery needs that old Bible right now a lot more than we do."

"Oh, yes," Nick said. "She does. You see, she remembered that when I took the Bible to the park, it helped us find her father. So now that Bible is going to help Magunnery get a new mother."

Elizabeth gazed into her son's eyes as Zachary drew the three of them close. There had been so many surprises on this night of wonder that she would believe almost anything. Two sons on this porch had found fathers. Two fathers had welcomed sons. And a man and a woman had been blessed with love beyond imagining.

Perhaps an old Bible inscribed with the names of those whom God had chosen to form into a family could somehow bring a little girl a brand-new mother. And maybe, just maybe, it could lead a broken man into the arms of a forgiving grace and a healing love.

Dear Friends,

I write these words in my office—a turreted room inside a beautiful brick mansion much like Chalmers House. My windows look out on blossoming dogwoods and fragrant lilacs. Gentle breezes drift across the nearby Missouri River.

When I moved into this office three years ago, I decorated the limestone walls with sprays of ivy, lengths of crocheted lace, and photographs of my family and friends. This is my creative cocoon.

Last weekend I learned the building had been put up for sale, its future undecided. My first reaction, of course, was total panic! My second was to remember my favorite verse: Jeremiah 29:11. Like Elizabeth Hayes, I've learned that God knows the plans he has for me, plans for good and not for evil, to give me a future and a hope. Though it's not always easy, I surrender my own will in the matter of my little office, my writing, my family, my future. And I lay all these things in the lap of Christ, my Savior.

My deepest thanks to those of you who faithfully read each of my books and to those who write to share such wonderful words of encouragement. I praise God that my stories touch your lives and help you grow in your faith walk.

Watch for my first hardcover novel, due out in the summer of 2000. The sequel to *Finders Keepers,* to be titled *Hide and Seek,* is due for release soon after that. Meanwhile, be sure to read my novellas in *With This Ring* and the Victorian Christmas series: *A Victorian Christmas Cottage, A Victorian Christmas Quilt,* and *A Victorian Christmas Tea.* We're also planning a Prairie Christmas anthology for Christmas 2000, in which you'll be able to get reacquainted with the characters from A Town Called Hope.

May God Bless you with peace of mind and heart,
Catherine Palmer

About the Author

Catherine Palmer lives in Missouri with her husband, Tim, and sons, Geoffrey and Andrei. She is a graduate of Southwest Baptist University and has a master's degree in English from Baylor University. Her first book was published in 1988. Since then she has written thirty books and published more than twenty. Catherine has also won numerous awards for her writing, including Most Exotic Historical Romance Novel from *Romantic Times* magazine. Her novel *Prairie Fire* was a finalist for both the Holt Medallion Award and the *Romantic Times* Reviewer's Choice Award. Total sales of her novels number close to one million copies.

In addition to *Finders Keepers,* her Tyndale House books include *Prairie Rose, Prairie Fire, Prairie Storm, The Treasure of Timbuktu, The Treasure of Zanzibar,* and novellas in the anthologies *A Victorian Christmas Tea, With This Ring, A Victorian Christmas Quilt,* and *A Victorian Christmas Cottage.* Catherine welcomes letters written to her in care of Tyndale House Author Relations, P.O. Box 80, Wheaton, IL 60189-0080.

Current HeartQuest Releases

- *A Bouquet of Love*, Ginny Aiken, Ranee McCollum, Jeri Odell, and Debra White Smith
- *Faith*, Lori Copeland
- *Finders Keepers*, Catherine Palmer
- *Hope*, Lori Copeland
- *June*, Lori Copeland
- *Prairie Rose*, Catherine Palmer
- *Prairie Fire*, Catherine Palmer
- *Prairie Storm*, Catherine Palmer
- *Reunited*, Judy Baer, Jeri Odell, Jan Duffy, and Peggy Stoks
- *The Treasure of Timbuktu*, Catherine Palmer
- *The Treasure of Zanzibar*, Catherine Palmer

- *A Victorian Christmas Quilt*, Catherine Palmer, Debra White Smith, Ginny Aiken, and Peggy Stoks
- *A Victorian Christmas Tea*, Catherine Palmer, Dianna Crawford, Peggy Stoks, and Katherine Chute
- *With This Ring*, Lori Copeland, Dianna Crawford, Ginny Aiken, and Catherine Palmer
- *Dream Vacation*, Ginny Aiken, Jeri Odell, and Elizabeth White—coming soon (February 2000)
- *The Rainbow Road*, Dianna Crawford—coming soon (February 2000)

Other Great Tyndale House Fiction

- *As Sure As the Dawn*, Francine Rivers
- *The Atonement Child*, Francine Rivers
- *The Captive Voice*, B. J. Hoff
- *Cloth of Heaven*, B. J. Hoff
- *Dark River Legacy*, B. J. Hoff
- *An Echo in the Darkness*, Francine Rivers
- *The Embers of Hope*, Sally Laity and Dianna Crawford
- *The Fires of Freedom*, Sally Laity and Dianna Crawford
- *The Gathering Dawn*, Sally Laity and Dianna Crawford
- *Home Fires Burning*, Penelope J. Stokes
- *Jewels for a Crown*, Lawana Blackwell
- *Journey to the Crimson Sea*, Jim and Terri Kraus
- *The Last Sin Eater*, Francine Rivers
- *Leota's Garden*, Francine Rivers
- *Like a River Glorious*, Lawana Blackwell

- *Measures of Grace*, Lawana Blackwell
- *Passages of Gold*, Jim and Terri Kraus
- *Pirates of the Heart*, Jim and Terri Kraus
- *Remembering You*, Penelope J. Stokes
- *Song of a Soul*, Lawana Blackwell
- *Storm at Daybreak*, B. J. Hoff
- *The Scarlet Thread*, Francine Rivers
- *The Tangled Web*, B. J. Hoff
- *The Tempering Blaze*, Sally Laity and Dianna Crawford
- *Till We Meet Again*, Penelope J. Stokes
- *The Torch of Triumph*, Sally Laity and Dianna Crawford
- *A Voice in The Wind*, Francine Rivers
- *Vow of Silence*, B. J. Hoff

HeartQuest Books by Catherine Palmer

Finders Keepers—Home, family, security . . . three things that lovely, independent antiques dealer Elizabeth Hayes is determined to provide for her adopted son, Nikolai. And Ambleside, Missouri, is just the place to do it. The beautiful Victorian mansion next door is an ever-present reminder of the stable heritage and gracious, old-fashioned ways Ambleside represents. Zachary Chalmers is shocked to receive an inheritance from an aunt he barely remembers—even if it is just a decrepit old mansion. Once cleared, the site will be perfect for the architectural firm he's designing. Out with the old, in with the new. That's Zachary's motto. Even as they clash over the fate of Chalmers House, Elizabeth and Zachary begin to discover dreams of a shared future—an idea vigorously supported by the irrepressible Nick! But are they willing to surrender to God's plan, which is greater than their own? Then a suprising revelation makes them wonder whether even a wrecking ball can put to rest the shadows of the past.

Prairie Storm—Can one tiny baby calm the brewing storm between Lily's past and Elijah's future? Evangelist Elijah Book is a fearless warrior for God—or so he believes. When a helpless infant is entrusted to his care, his zeal becomes sidetracked, as the fate of an innocent child rests with a woman Eli must trust in spite of himself. Storms of hurt and bitterness threaten to overwhelm Lily Nolan after the death of her husband and child. If there is a God, how could he abandon her so completely? Can she risk opening her heart to the orphaned Samuel? United in their concern for the baby, Eli and Lily are forced to set aside their differences and learn to trust God's plan to see them through the storms of life.

Prairie Rose—Kansas held their future, but only faith could mend their past. Hope and love blossom on the untamed prairie as a young woman, searching for a place to call home, happens upon a Kansas homestead during the 1860s.

Prairie Fire—Will a burning secret extinguish the spark of love between Jack and Caitrin? The town of Hope discovers the importance of forgiveness, overcoming prejudice, and the dangers of keeping unhealthy family secrets.

A Victorian Christmas Cottage—Continuing the popular Victorian Christmas anthology series, this collection of four original Christmas stories once again leads off with a heartwarming novella by Catherine Palmer. In "Under His Wings," a young widow leaves her home in Wales to settle with her beloved mother-in-law in a small cottage in England's Lake District. Finding work in the kitchen of the dashing earl of Beaumontfort, Gwyneth soon attracts his attention. He is charmed by her wit, her love for her mother-in-law, and her devotion to Christ. But unexpected developments at the lavish annual Christmas gathering threaten their growing love.

A Victorian Christmas Tea—Four novellas about life and love at Christmastime. Stories by Catherine Palmer, Dianna Crawford, Peggy Stoks, and Katherine Chute.

A Victorian Christmas Quilt—A patchwork of four novellas about love and joy at Christmastime. Stories by Catherine Palmer, Ginny Aiken, Peggy Stoks, and Debra White Smith.

The Treasure of Timbuktu—Abducted by a treasure hunter, Tillie Thorton becomes a pawn in a dangerous game. Desperate and on the run from a fierce nomadic tribe looking to kidnap her, Tillie finds herself in an uneasy partnership with a daring adventurer.

The Treasure of Zanzibar—An ancient house filled with secrets . . . a sunken treasure . . . an unknown enemy . . . a lost love. They all await Jessica Thorton on Zanzibar. Jessica returns to Africa with her son to claim her inheritance on the island of Zanzibar. Upon her arrival, she is reunited with her estranged husband.

Heartwarming Anthologies from HeartQuest

A Bouquet of Love—An arrangement of four beautiful novellas about friendship and love. Stories by Ginny Aiken, Ranee McCollum, Jeri Odell, and Debra White Smith.

A Victorian Christmas Cottage—Four novellas centering around hearth and home at Christmastime. Stories by Catherine Palmer, Jeri Odell, Debra White Smith, and Peggy Stoks.

A Victorian Christmas Tea—Four novellas about life and love at Christmastime. Stories by Catherine Palmer, Dianna Crawford, Peggy Stoks, and Katherine Chute.

A Victorian Christmas Quilt—A patchwork of four novellas about love and joy at Christmastime. Stories by Catherine Palmer, Ginny Aiken, Peggy Stoks, and Debra White Smith.

Reunited—Four stories about reuniting friends, old memories, and new romance. Includes favorite recipes from the authors. Stories by Judy Baer, Jan Duffy, Jeri Odell, and Peggy Stoks.

With This Ring—A quartet of charming stories about four very special weddings. Stories by Lori Copeland, Dianna Crawford, Ginny Aiken, and Catherine Palmer.